kiss CHASE

SCARLETT FINN

Also by Scarlett Finn

GO NOVELS
GO WITH IT
GO IT ALONE
GO ALL OUT
GO ALL IN
GO FULL CIRCLE

EXILE
HIDE & SEEK
KISS CHASE

WRECK & RUIN
RUIN ME
RUIN HIM

**THE BRANDED
SERIES**
BRANDED
SCARRED
MARKED

**FORBIDDEN
PREQUEL DUET**
ALL. ONLY.
ONLY YOURS

TO DIE FOR...
TO DIE FOR TRUTH
TO DIE FOR HONOR
TO DIE FOR VIRTUE
TO DIE FOR DUTY
TO DIE FOR LOVE

**LOVE AGAINST THE ODDS
STANDALONE COLLECTION**
SWEET SEAS
HEIR'S AFFAIR
RESCUED
MAESTRO'S MUSE
GETTING TRICKY
THIRTEEN
REMEMBER WHEN...
RELUCTANT SUSPICION
XY FACTOR

NOTHING TO...
NOTHING TO HIDE
NOTHING TO LOSE
NOTHING TO DECLARE
NOTHING TO US
NOTHING TO SAY
NOTHING TO GAIN
NOTHING TO YOU
NOTHING TO THIS

THE FORBIDDEN NOVELS
FORBIDDEN DESIRE
FORBIDDEN WANT
FORBIDDEN WISH
FORBIDDEN NEED

KINDRED SERIES
RAVEN
SWALLOW
CUCKOO
SWIFT
FALCON
FINCH

THE EXPLICIT SERIES
EXPLICIT INSTRUCTION
EXPLICIT DETAIL
EXPLICIT MEMORY

MISTAKE DUET
MISTAKE ME NOT
SLEIGHT MISTAKE

**RISQUÉ & HARROW
INTERTWINED**
TAKE A RISK
FIGHTING FATE
RISK IT ALL
FIGHTING BACK
GAME OF RISK

LOST & FOUND
LOST
FOUND

ONE

"AND THEY ALL lived happily ever after."

Her eyes were closed, her head drooped between her arms held in the stocks fastened to the exposed-brick wall behind her, but Aurora Maguire heard Bella finish the story and close the book; she hadn't slipped into delirium yet.

Rora had been here so long that the chains around her ankles had become an extension of her being. But becoming accustomed to her captivity didn't save her legs from feeling the cold or the exhaustion that came from constantly supporting her own weight.

Bella didn't suffer during her regular visits to her captive; she afforded herself luxury. There was something especially cruel about Bella's choice to leave a sumptuous armchair a few feet away from Rora's position. In view, but not in reach.

Fastened to the wall in this dark, cold, damp space, sleep was difficult to get. Whenever Rora did doze off, she woke up to pain screaming in her limbs and the crashing reality that she was at the mercy of a madwoman without any prospect of ever being freed. Being forced to stare constantly at the plush furniture only heightened her torture.

Bella had brought the chair into the room so she had somewhere to nestle in comfort while she read bedtime stories to Rora who'd been caught murmuring fairytales to herself in her first days here. Reciting the familiar tales was her subconscious' attempt to comfort her; it was a distraction technique. One that she didn't think she'd ever use again after listening to Bella read the stories over and over.

"Are you asleep, duckie?" Bella asked.

Rora didn't even flinch when Bella touched her anymore. The Black Jewel, as Bella was also known, had gotten tired of Rora's hair covering her face, obstructing her view, so she'd styled it in two plaited pigtails that started at the base of Rora's skull and draped forward over her shoulders.

The hairstyle didn't stop Bella from digging her nails into Rora's scalp when she wanted attention. In those moments, her jailor would grab handfuls of her hair to pull her head around. Rora doubted she'd get the knots out of her locks, not that she cared. It was difficult to care about anything when life was so downright hopeless.

Grabbing Rora's chin, Bella forced her prisoner's head back and slapped her face a few times. "I want to talk," Bella said. "Wake up! I want to talk to you."

"I don't want to talk," Rora mumbled.

The fairytales were hard enough to hear. Rora hated the sound of Bella's smooth, innocent voice. No one would know what depravity the woman was capable of just by looking at her or listening to her sweet lilt.

"Do you think of him? At night… do you think of him?"

"Who?" Rora asked, knowing exactly who Bella was referring to.

"Oh, you know who," Bella said, prodding Rora in the ribs. "Lift up your head… look at me."

Rora was given little choice. Bella grabbed the hair on Rora's head and pulled it up. The weight of her eyelids was difficult to fight, but she held them open just enough to satisfy Bella. "Who?"

"Exile," Bella said, smiling at her. "Do you think about him?"

Every minute of the day. Yes. Not thinking about him was impossible. There was nothing to do except think about the man who'd made her believe he was in love and then broken her heart.

"What do you want to hear, Bella?" she asked. Her throat was still hoarse from the screaming she'd done in the first couple of days, but she'd long given up hope that there was anyone around who'd hear her or come to her aid. "Just ask me what you want to know."

Delight and excited hope danced in the woman's eyes. "Tell me you love him."

"I love him," she muttered.

Bella scowled and let go of her captive to put a hand on her own hip. Rora's neck cracked when her head fell forward, but she let it loll there and didn't cry out, she was numb to the hurt. "Now I don't know if you mean that, do you mean that?"

How she wished she didn't. His betrayal was more painful than anything Bella could do to her. He'd had a choice, world domination or their love… He'd chosen the former. It might sound like a difficult choice, but to Rora, it had been a no-brainer.

The saddest part was, although he'd doubted his own integrity, Rora hadn't. She'd really believed that he would choose her.

Except Exile hadn't known when he'd made his choice that the device he thought held the Point was actually worthless. It didn't hold the computer program meant to facilitate his rise to infinity as he thought it did. All it held was a collection of stock images, landscapes from around the world. Beautiful, but useless.

Yes, she'd tricked him. But he'd never have known it if he'd only chosen her.

Rora had intended to go to the Point, alone, to destroy it somehow. Circumstances changed when Exile had decided to tag along on her trip. His choice forced her to make a split-second decision. Did she take him to the worthless device or to the real Point?

Exile, also known as Strike, had once stated that he feared giving in to temptation and slighting her in favor of the Point. Rora had told herself he wouldn't ever betray her, but there must have been some part of her that doubted her certainty because she'd chosen to take him to the decoy device.

Bella leaned in to whisper in Rora's ear. "I think he's looking for me." Bella giggled like a woman sharing a salacious secret with a willing girlfriend. "He just doesn't *know* he's looking for me."

Rora had given up trying to figure this woman out. It was tough enough to stay conscious. Deciphering insanity was beyond her.

Bounding back, Bella began to stroll around the dank space, her hand raised in a variety of gestures, complementing what she was saying. "I can't wait for the big reveal… when he finds out I'm still alive…" She squealed. "Oh, he'll be so overjoyed!" For a moment, the jailor reveled in the mental picture she was building about that reunion. Suddenly, her face fell to a scowl and she punched her fists to her hips. "His punishment will have to be particularly special…" Bella turned her eyes to Rora. "He shot me!"

"I was there," Rora said, clearing her throat and wishing Strike had aimed a bit lower.

"We were going to share you," Bella said. "If you hadn't been so naughty, we'd have been the perfect foursome. And beautiful Benjamin… he died for you… But you… you didn't follow him… Do you love him?"

This woman was obsessed with everything love and sex related. Didn't matter if it was male or female, or if there was decency involved, Bella saw people as toys to be shared much like children would be expected to share their plastic cars and dolls.

Rora's friend and mentor, Benjamin, was gone. Dead by his own hand. He'd committed suicide to prevent the secret they shared getting out into the world. Rora would've gone after him if Exile hadn't stepped in and convinced her not to pull the trigger.

Standing here, suspended against this wall, Rora wished she'd pulled the trigger. Strike had convinced her that she had something to live for: him. Then she'd shared the secret and he'd stolen it, choosing it over her.

Rora doubted there was a real choice from his point of view. It was clear now that he didn't love her. He never had. But she'd really believed his manipulations, even after he repeatedly told her not to.

Bella appeared in front of her, ducked down, peeking up with excitement glittering in her gaze. "Who are you thinking about? Is it Benjamin… or Exile? Who do you love the most?" When Rora didn't immediately answer, Bella huffed. "If you won't be honest and share like I do, then I'll just have to leave you here to think more about what you want to say to me."

Spinning around, Bella flounced off.

In the initial days, she'd been desperate for Bella to stay just so she could try to convince the nut to free her. Now Rora preferred to be alone. For Bella, this wasn't about getting answers or satisfying a cause. There was no getting out of here. Rora had figured it out quickly. Bella had brought her here for fun. Because she wanted to play with her.

There was nothing that Rora could say to get herself out of here, nothing she could give that would guarantee her freedom. Bella just wanted to torment her, and Rora would be here until the woman got bored and killed her.

Strike had always told her not to dwell in the past, but what else was she supposed to do when the best she could hope to get from the future was a quick death?

***

WITHOUT ANY WAY to measure time, Rora filled the seconds that dragged like days by fighting against the memories that plagued her.

She'd thought losing her family was the most devastating thing that could ever happen. But at least their abandonment had been involuntary. Her brother, Kyan, had slaughtered their parents and sibling, but he'd spared her.

Strike hadn't been so kind. Rora had given her heart to him, and he'd chosen to turn his back on her. He'd *chosen* to do it.

Squeezing her eyelids tighter together, she cursed herself for letting her former lover dominate her thoughts. He'd broken her heart for the final time just minutes before Bella had abducted her. But that grief didn't earn Strike the right to infect her mind.

Time. Nothing but time. Time to remember. The way his mouth had felt, the way his body had moved over hers. That brooding scowl. His knowing smirk… Rora had fallen in love. Damn her. But she had. She'd fallen in love with a man who couldn't love her back.

So caught up in her hatred of her own emotions, Rora didn't hear the door opening. Usually it clicked and clunked, forcing her to face the pending intrusion. But this time an unfamiliar hand slid onto her face before she'd even known the door was open. The rough texture of the skin and the width of the digits creeping up her cheek made Rora withdraw on a sharp inhale.

Someone ducked down in front of her; a man… one she didn't recognize. Who was he?

No one except Bella had been this close to her since she got here. It was startling to be touched by another person. For a moment, she got lost in the concern of his eyes; there was real empathy there. Was this another con?

"Aurora Maguire?" The voice came from him. He was talking to her. He sounded… worried. "Aurora, can you hear me? Are you conscious?"

"Who…" Her throat was so dry it hurt. "Who are you?"

After a breath of relief, he answered. "A friend. I'm here to help you," he said. "Let's get you out of here."

Dropping to a crouch, he did something to loosen the chains from her legs. Rora was confused, dizzy, tired, sore… she couldn't follow what was going on. He stood to reach over her head. She'd barely registered the metallic sounds above her before her arms were free and she collapsed forward, unable to steady herself.

"I got ya," he said, capturing her over his shoulder. "I've got you, let's go."

Rora hadn't eaten for days. She'd had morsels of food fed to her by Bella who enjoyed teasing her with it. Letting her have just a taste and then taking the sustenance away. Water was dripped into her mouth as Bella saw fit. But the Black Jewel had a habit of letting the liquid run down over her captive's body so she could lick it from Rora's chin or wherever else it ran to.

Rora was too out of it to even register pain or where they were going. There was darkness and movement, a floor, stairs, then she was getting wet. Opening her eyes, she tried to lift her head. She saw grass beneath her, felt a breeze on the back of her legs. The wetness falling on her… it was rain. But if it was raining and there was grass that meant… they were outside!

Tensing, she tried to kick. Where was she? What was going on?

Breathing in, she was about to scream when she was pulled down from the shoulder of the man carrying her and balanced on her tiptoes. Someone, this stranger, was holding her up. His body was against hers, and there was something cold behind her… What was that?

Lost, dazed, her head was spinning so fast that she retched.

Then suddenly she was dipped down and put on her ass, onto something soft… Blinking and disoriented, Rora tried to sit up. A vehicle door opened, a rush of cold air hit her. Wait… her mind caught up with her surroundings, she was in a truck… in the front seat of a truck.

Something soft hit her body, blinding her. Fighting with what she realized was fabric covering her face, she pulled it down as she sat up. A rumble vibrated from beneath her and it took a second for her to figure out that the vehicle was moving.

"Who are you?" she asked. Her voice was weak, but it was stronger than the rest of her. "Where are we going?"

"Just rest, Aurora, close your eyes and get some sleep. I'll explain everything later."

Her brain told her to argue, to kick and fight, but her body was trembling with shock and any remnant of adrenaline it could muster. Her eyes got heavy and she knew she was done. Whatever was going to happen, whatever this guy wanted, her fate was sealed.

Curling her legs up to her chest, Rora hooked the blanket over her head and let her body succumb to exhaustion.

TWO

"FLAME."

The word was a faint whisper on her lips before Rora opened her eyes. Once the sound traveled to her ears, she peeled her eyelids apart, only to find herself in darkness again. It wasn't absolute like it had been before, there was definite ambient light that her eyes could adjust to, so maybe she could pick out some features when they did.

Finding that she was lying down, she wriggled enough to figure out that she wasn't attached to that damned wall anymore. Her body was warm, and the air smelled… clean.

Yes, she wasn't in the basement anymore, she was loose. This could be her chance to be free.

A shot of pain fired through her skull when she tried to sit up.

"Oh, hey, don't sit up too fast."

That was a male voice, one she didn't know, and couldn't locate because her eyes were still adjusting. Rolling onto her back, she breathed until she could get her bearings. She was on a bed in, what she'd guess, was a motel room. Having spent so much time in rooms not unlike this one, Rora recognized the stained ceiling, the old-style TV, and the cheap print screwed to the wall. Yep, it was a motel room alright.

Blinking, she shifted her head to see the man was coming toward her. Tall, dark hair, straight nose, warm smile, and somehow vaguely familiar. "You… you're—"

"A friend," he said and sat on the edge of the bed. Rora tried to scoot away. He must have sensed her misgivings because he raised his hands in surrender and stood up again. "I'm not a threat to you. What do you remember?"

What did she remember? So much and so little. Picking her hand out from beneath the blanket, she was about to touch her forehead when she noticed the bandages on her wrists.

"I treated your wounds," he said. "You had cuts and bruising on your wrists and some chafing on your ankles… The marks on your back are fierce, but not infected as far as I can tell… I think after a couple of hot meals and a few decent nights of sleep, you'll be ok… The Black Jewel was kinder to you than she has been to others."

"The Black Jewel," she said and tried to sit up. The shot of pain hit her skull again, making her grab for it. "Damnit."

"You're ok, Aurora," this friend said, moving backward to sit at the bottom corner of the bed, facing her. "I promise, you're safe now."

Something in his next expression piqued her memory. "Wait," she said, shifting higher on her pillows. "I know you."

He cleared his throat and rubbed his palms on his thighs. Was that a sign of nerves? What did he have to be nervous about? She was half his size. Even at her best, she was no fancy fighter, and right now she wasn't even close to her best.

"Yeah, we've met."

"But I don't know who…" Inhaling, she got a flash of his face in another place. "You were… the guy at the bus station. The death or heartbreak guy!"

"That's not a great nickname," he said.

Feelings of disgust and violation poisoned her throat. "You're following me?"

"Looking out for you," he said. "I had to make contact. I didn't know that… The Black Jewel got to you so fast… I couldn't believe it when you went missing."

No, she refused to accept this. She didn't want this to be a part of her life anymore. The Black Jewel, Strike, this guy, it didn't matter, Rora just wanted to go back to her normal life. It might not be possible to go back in time, but she could decide what she would and wouldn't accept as her present, and this death or heartbreak guy wasn't going to be a part of it.

"Ok," she said and tossed back the blanket to see she was wearing a man's tee-shirt. Even though it wasn't hers, she'd take wearing it over being naked. Pre-empting the pain in her head, she knew to brace and breathe through it, so succeeded in sitting up this time. "Where are we?"

"In a motel."

The city didn't matter, the state didn't matter either. What mattered was Bella's anger over losing her captive and Strike who would've figured out her deception by now. Both of those things meant one grave thing to Rora: she wasn't safe.

"I appreciate you getting me out of there," Rora said, forcing herself onto her feet.

A rush of adrenaline helped her to go toward the door.

"Whoa, wait, where are you going?" he asked and was suddenly in front of her, blocking her path to the door. "I can't let you leave."

So the truth was coming out, he wasn't being altruistic after all. This guy had his own agenda. "One prison for another?" she asked and tried to side-step. "No thanks."

"I need your help, Aurora."

Funny that she'd once been the one in need of another's help. Maybe if she'd listened to Strike's refusal, none of them would be where they were now.

"I don't care," she said, trying to go the other way, but he was quicker than her. His persistence at blocking her made her growl. "Kill me or get the hell out of my way. This isn't a game."

The desperation in his eyes did little to sway her, though Rora did wonder if she'd worn that same look when she begged for Strike's help in Last Resort.

"You don't understand," he said. "I don't mean you any harm. I'll protect you."

Oh, that was enough to break through some of her cynicism, though not in a way that worked in his favor. Rora smiled and actually whispered out a laugh. "I guess you're a comedian? Rescue and protect is a bit outside your wheelhouse then, isn't it?"

Again, when she tried to swoop around him, he got in her way. There was nowhere else for them to go now his back was against the door. "I got you out of there. You should hear me out."

Maybe if he'd told her there would be a price for her rescue, she'd have had a chance to tell him to go to hell. Rora tried her best to hold onto her patience, but it was slipping fast.

"You don't understand what you've got yourself involved in," she said, recalling how her old friend, Buddy, once said something similar to her. "I don't know who you are. But I know you have no idea what I've been through or what's coming for me. The Black Jewel? She's the least of my worries. I screwed over a guy who won't rest until he's drained every drop of blood from my body. A man who won't stop. A man who has nothing to lose. A man who doesn't take kindly to being double-crossed."

"Exile."

Taken aback, some of the gusto left her sails and she blinked at him. "Oh my God," she whispered, trying to re-sort what she thought she knew. "Did he send you?"

Shaking his head, a proud smile crept to his lips. "No. *I* came for you, Aurora."

If he wanted a pat on the head, he'd be waiting some time. Rora couldn't shake her suspicion. "But… why?"

"Want a gym membership? Fresh supply of Viagra? Vitamin supplements? Free slots?"

What was he… It only took a moment for her confusion to clear. Shock took its place. He hadn't lost his mind, he was identifying himself. She did know him, and it wasn't only from the bus station, she'd been in communication with this guy for months.

Her lips parted, and she took a step backward. "Junker," she exhaled.

His smile widened. "Hey."

Until now, this guy had been nothing more than a digital pen pal; a man who she'd exchanged emails with a few times a week. Strike had once said she never got anything but Junk, except he didn't know the innocuous subject lines of her emails with Junker were an inside joke.

This man was her friend. Her suspicion dwindled, though she was proud of herself for recognizing there was more to who he was than a kindly stranger.

"Oh my God," she said, swatting his chest. "What the hell are you doing here? How are you involved in this? Why didn't you tell me—"

"I wasn't involved in it. I kept my distance until you went missing," he said, taking her hand and pulling her to the couch under the window. "Benjamin told me if something happened to him that I should be around to help you."

And he had. After Benjamin messaged her from his captivity to tell her he needed Exile, Junker had been the online contact who'd helped locate him. "You told me where to find Exile," she said, needing to know if he was aware of what they were facing. "Have you met him?"

"No," he said. "Even my sources weren't sure you'd find him in that bar. But I guess you did. Why does he want to hurt you?"

"It's a long story."

Driving her fingers into her matted hair, Rora winced when they got caught. But it wasn't memories of Bella's basement that smacked into her, she was assaulted by the memory of the first morning she'd awoken in Strike's bed. Starting to feel sick, she probably swayed.

Junker grabbed her. "Aurora!"

Shaken from her daze, she focused on him. Mouthing no words for a few seconds, she tried to catch up. "I... How did you find me?"

"I was lucky enough to get an anonymous tip," he said. "You were off my radar for a while after I told you about Last Resort. Finding you at the bus station was a fluke. I did my best to track you, but I guess I fell behind after you found Exile."

Yeah, because Strike knew when he was being followed whether he told her or not. Habit made him take evasive routes and his tech prevented him from being captured on cameras or tracked, so for a while, she'd have been under that protection… Except now she was figuring out that maybe he'd been shielding her from the good guys while tempting her to the dark side.

"Guess you did," she whispered.

"I got an anonymous tip that the Black Jewel had you. The message told me to retrieve you at a specific time and place… so I did." He'd saved her life. She couldn't deny that. But an anonymous tip suggested she had a benefactor, maybe one of Bella's posse wasn't so scared after all. "Aurora? Do you need to get more sleep?"

Why? Because she was sitting here going into these mini dazes every few seconds? "No," she said, drawing her legs up inside the tee-shirt. Hugging her knees to her chest, she dipped to rub her forehead against them. "It was about… what? Nine months ago you first contacted me?"

Finding the spam message in her junk folder that wasn't actually spam was accidental. For a while their communications were nothing more than small talk, jokes and flirtation. She'd taken it as kind of striking up a conversation with someone who dialed the wrong number by mistake… except in email.

She'd had no idea that Junker was in the same line of work as Benjamin or that the two men knew each other, not until after Benjamin disappeared and Junker's questions got more invasive. That's when he'd admitted knowing Benjamin and worrying for his safety.

Rora had been too busy following the police investigation to think about giving him specifics, and then Benjamin had sent his clandestine message to tell her that

Exile was their only hope and she'd started her own investigation.

She hadn't immediately thought to ask Junker for his help. Even when she did, he didn't have an answer for her right away. It had taken him some time to come up with anything, and he'd led her down a few dead ends before they got it right.

Never in a million years had Rora expected to meet him in the flesh or to have him come and save her from Bella.

"Benjamin and I hadn't known each other long when he asked me to look out for you. I guess he knew he was into something that might turn bad. I thought I was placating him when he told me to help you if something happened to him… I didn't know it would turn into… this."

"What changed? You got me away from the Black Jewel, great, thanks. But… why aren't we just going our separate ways? Why do you need my help?"

Sitting straighter, his shoulders squared. "While I was trying to track you, I learned that there's a piece of tech in play. It's… top secret beyond top secret." Squirming, Rora got a nasty taste in her mouth when the word DARPA crept into her mind. "What?" he asked, reaching over to touch her arm. "Do you know what it is? Where I can find it?"

With her teeth together, her eyes rose to his and she paused before responding. "No… no, I don't know what it is."

"I decided that I have to locate and retrieve it. To be honest," he said, rising to pace away. "I'm still catching up with it all myself, it's a bit… high octane for me."

"High octane?"

Turning to face her, he opened one hand and then the other. "There's something else… I don't know if you know, but Benjamin was worked up about some project of his getting out," he said. "He didn't give me specifics, but I heard on the grapevine that it might be out there. With this device in the open and Benjamin's program… Now that the two of them are loose, the shit is on… And word is… Exile has them both."

So that was it? Junker had some self-appointed mission to save the world from Exile who he believed had the DARPA device and the Point. Except, Rora knew the Point wasn't out.

Strike might have thought it was for a while, but he'd know different by now. Though he probably wouldn't be advertising that his once-upon-a-time lover had conned him.

Chewing on her lower lip, Rora wondered if she looked as guilty as she felt. She not only knew about the device and the project, but she might have been the one responsible for handing the device and the apparent project over to her former lover.

"Sounds like you have a lot on your plate," she said and got up, pulling the tee-shirt down. "You don't need me slowing you down."

Rushing to her, Junker put both hands on her shoulders. "You're the key to this," he said. "I don't understand all of it, but there's chatter about you. Maybe the Black Jewel didn't know it or maybe she didn't care, but she's done you a favor keeping you off the radar for the last ten days."

Shoving his hands from her shoulders, she felt a rush of anger. "I wouldn't call what I just went through a 'favor' of any kind."

"I know, I'm sorry," he said. "I am. I just… this is serious, Aurora. I need you to help me figure it out."

There was so much he didn't know about her involvement. But given the culpability she had, Rora couldn't deny that it was sort of her responsibility to help put this back in the box. Except, it wasn't as simple as that.

"Exile will kill me if he sees me."

"Then we'll make sure he doesn't," Junker said and smiled.

But there was nothing in this scenario to smile about. "You don't understand him. You don't know what he's like… You don't know what he's capable of."

Curiosity replaced his optimism. "But you do," he said. "What do you know? You did meet him, right?"

And then some. "I know that saying we'll stay off his radar is easier than it sounds. He sees you everywhere."

Saying the words made her realize how complacent she'd been. Looking left and right, Rora assessed the space. The first thing she did was rush over to close the curtains, keeping her face turned down as she did.

"What is it? What's wrong?" Junker asked.

"Do you have a phone?"

"A phone? Yes, I—"

"Turn it off," she said. He just gaped at her. Searching the room, she saw a matchbook on the table by the TV and went to retrieve it. "Give me your phone and your wallet."

Snatching them from him the moment they were free of his pocket, Rora hurried into the bathroom. Sealing the bath with its metal plug, she removed the cash from his wallet and tossed it to the vanity, knowing the bills could be useful. After wrapping the wallet and phone in towels and tissues, she threw the bundle into the tub and struck a match to set her parcel alight.

She opened the window just above to let the smoke out and watched the pile burn.

"What the hell is that smell?" Junker asked, coming into the room behind her. "Oh my god, what are you doing? Aurora!"

He tried to get by, but she sidestepped to block him. Only when she was satisfied that everything was beyond salvation did she turn on the water to kill the fire.

"No more cards," she said. "Everything has to be cash."

"Cash? Where will—"

"I'll get us cash," she said, forced confidence bolstered her. "Don't ever carry ID. If we get arrested, either of us, for anything, do not give your name or address. Don't give your date of birth, place of birth, nothing. Definitely not your social security number. Have you been arrested before?" He shook his head. "Good. Do you have family?"

"A sister."

"Ask her to liquidate her assets into cash and remove it from any financial institution. As for your assets? Well, if you've been on my trail or his, chances are, he's already siphoning from you."

"You… Exile? No, Exile doesn't know anything about me."

It was sweet that he thought so and she smiled. "First thing, I need a change of clothes… Do you have a plan?"

"Uh, yeah, kinda," he said. "But it doesn't involve being penniless."

Yeah, she maybe should've explained her actions before destroying his phone and wallet, but there was no time to be nice. They were already behind the curve.

Rora wasn't sure how long she'd been away from Bella's clutches, but there was every chance that the Black Jewel had been in touch with her prince when she found her prisoner gone.

If Strike knew she was free, he'd be mobilizing, meaning he had a head start. "We need money?" she asked. He nodded. "Ok, I'll get it. Do you have a car?"

"Yes, my truck."

Not ideal if it was registered to him, but their options were limited until they had funds because Rora didn't have Strike's ad-hocing skills. "It'll do for the ride back, then we'll need to ditch it," she said and tried to pass him, but he snagged her arm.

"Ride back? What are you—"

"We need money," she said. "When I need money, I get it from one person."

"Who?"

Widening her smile, her eyes drifted toward the mirror. "My banker."

THREE

"ARE YOU SURE you're strong enough for this?" Junker asked her.

There were so many ways that she could answer that question. Physically, Rora wasn't at her best. Emotionally, she was a mess. But there was no time to fall apart. It irked her that Strike's advice was echoing in her head. *Never let them see fear*, that's what he'd told her.

Her chin rose.

Junker had gone out to get clothes for her while she used his comb and the motel conditioner to tug the knots from her hair.

Once she was done, Junker had asked her to eat and rest, proving how little he understood the disadvantage they were at. There was no time for weakness; they had to get in the game. The chase was on, except she wasn't sure if she was the pursuer or the pursued… it was probably both.

They'd reached a compromise that balanced Junker's concern for her welfare and her need to get moving: they'd stopped at a fast-food place. Junker was insistent that she should eat, but all she wanted to do was get to where they were going. Eventually, she'd given in and agreed to the junk food.

Rora hadn't let him use the drive thru. Instead, she'd insisted that he park far away and walk in with his ball cap on and hood up. Cameras were everywhere, and unlike Strike, Junker didn't travel with his laptop, so he couldn't erase or corrupt images. He'd told her he'd stashed his computer in a safe place before coming to get her, just in case anything went wrong. Smart.

In truth, Rora wasn't sure she was wild about the idea of him having a computer at all. It didn't matter how much he insisted his system was secure, she was dubious about his ability to protect it from Strike's intrusion. And her ex would intrude every chance he got if it gave him an advantage, no doubt about that.

But she took some solace that they were finally on the road, making progress, even if it was slow.

"What's your plan?" she asked.

"Are you just ignoring my question?"

Yes, because it was a stupid one given how hard she'd fought to get on the road. Rora was hardly going to change her mind now and insist that he took her somewhere for a little R&R.

"Am I strong enough for a road trip?" she asked. "You said we're only a couple of hours from where we need to be. I've been on longer trips recently, trust me."

At least Junker had a truck instead of a bike. She'd probably vomit if she had to get on a motorcycle, simply because it would remind her of the time she'd spent with Strike.

"Yeah, but... with everything you've been through..."

Eating a fry, Rora tried to pace herself. Her stomach just wasn't strong enough to take too much right now. "A good night's sleep and a meal, that's what you said I needed. I'm eating right now, and I can sleep in the back if I have to."

"I said a few of both," he said. "And you're being vague, I... I don't like vague."

A faint smile touched her lips, vague was kind of like implication... The memory of Strike telling her how he didn't imply faded into her mind, and it made her feel ill enough to toss her fry back into the paper food sack. Her appetite wasn't up to thinking of him fondly.

"You said we needed money, didn't you?"

Junker was concentrating on the road. "Yeah and you seem damn sure you can get it from somewhere."

"I am," she said and then muttered, "if I don't get a knife between my shoulder blades first."

With his hands tight on the wheel, he glanced at her and then the road. "Are you kidding? You're not going to rob a bank, are you?"

In a bank robbery she'd more likely be shot than stabbed, but now wasn't the time to be pedantic. "A bank? Talk about security camera central. No, no banks. No way."

Though if it came to a choice, she'd take being arrested over coming face-to-face with Strike.

"You're paranoid," Junker said. "I never picked that up about you when we exchanged emails."

Rora couldn't even remember what her awareness level had been like back in what felt like another lifetime. It certainly hadn't been as high as it was now, post-Strike. "A lot has happened to me recently," she said. "And I prefer to think of myself as smarter for it, not paranoid."

Scrunching the top of the bag, she put the rest of the food on the floor. "You should eat more."

"I will, just pacing myself," she said, which wasn't the full truth.

The highway was long and glistening wet in front of them, reflecting the artificial lights above. They drove for a while saying nothing to each other.

"What's he like?"

Rora hadn't expected to hear any voice, she'd been too lost in her thoughts… Though she had no idea what had been in her mind, it had just been drifting. "Who?"

"Exile."

Like she needed to hear that word again.

Gritting her teeth, Rora pulled her legs up to hug them to her chest and rolled her eyes upward trying to think of something non-committal to say. "Vague."

"Is that your way of telling me that I won't like him?"

Junker's curiosity made sense, but Rora had no interest in satisfying it. "I thought we were staying out of his way," she said, not acknowledging to herself how much of a hypocrite she was being. Rora had been curious about Strike too, and if Junker did find himself meeting the man, he should be prepared. "To make that judgment you'd have to meet him. Besides, weren't you the one who declared he'd just become the world's most dangerous man? If he has what you say he has, then God help us all."

"I'm still hoping he'll be reasonable," Junker said. She scoffed. "Come on, we don't know exactly what he has, or what it's capable of. Until we find that out we can't make any assumptions."

Evicting Strike from her thoughts was proving impossible. "We have to think fast and work on assumptions," she muttered.

"Why?" he asked. "Why not take our time and—"

"Because that's what he does," she said, frustrated. "We're running behind right now. You don't know what he's like."

"But you do. You do know what he's like."

This guy was nothing if not persistent, her patience snapped. "Look," she said, twisting toward him. "I don't know your full story, you don't know mine. Let's just guess that for the time being neither of us is lying. You're here to help me and I'm here to fix this."

"I thought it was the other way around," he said, frowning at her. "This is only going to work if we trust each other. It's going to get difficult and it could get messy. Exile's not going to just hand over whatever he has."

If it was Junker's plan to ask and expect to receive, then he was in serious trouble, and it was her responsibility to warn him. "There's one thing you need to know about Exile. Something you have to remember every single minute. Every. Single. Minute. You can never forget it."

"What?" he asked. "What is it?"

"You can't trust him."

He paused for half a second. "You're sure about that? You don't think there's any chance we can appeal to—"

"No," she said. "There's no part of him we can appeal to. He has an agenda and once he's made up his mind, there's no changing it."

Junker considered that for a few seconds. "If you're right, we'll have to take drastic action."

Letting that statement hang in the air, Junker kept driving.

Rora's drifting mind stuck on an alarming thought, if Strike was so mad at her that he was willing to end her life, was she willing to do the same in return? Could she stand aside and let Junker pull the trigger? Could she pull it herself?

"I held a gun to his head once," she admitted, the words slipping from her lips at the same time numbness seeped back in. "I couldn't pull the trigger."

"You… why?"

She couldn't pull it because she loved him, but she wasn't ready to confess that particular shame to Junker yet.

"Let's just get there and get this over with," she said. "I need to pick something up on the way."

***

COMING BACK HERE was a major risk, but what choice did she have? Rora needed money. No, it was more than that. She needed cash, physical bills, and there was only one place she knew to get them that didn't involve stepping in front of a camera or using ID.

After giving him directions and telling Junker where to park, she took off her seatbelt. "Stay here."

"Wait," he said, grabbing her hand before she could get out of the truck.

But when she turned, her companion wasn't looking at her face, he was looking at his hand holding hers. She didn't like his expression, so tugged hers free.

"What?"

He shifted. "I have to come with you."

That was the last thing she needed him to do. If he pushed the issue, she'd give up on her plan before she gave in to him. Except if she aborted, they'd be screwed. Rora had no plan B. She was still new to this world and her teacher had screwed her over, so she was winging it.

"I'm not going to run off," she said, because that would be her concern if she was in his position. "I'll come back."

"Then why can't I—"

"Because we have to work on the assumption that Exile doesn't know you're involved, or at least that he doesn't know you're with me," she said. "We can't take any risk that he'll see us together."

Until now, she hadn't confessed that Exile was related to this part of her plan. "How would he do that?" he asked and nodded at the cupcake in her hand. "And what's that for?"

Having been the one to say they needed to trust each other, it seemed sort of wrong that she was lying, but Rora didn't see that she had any choice. "I'm hungry," she said, doubting he bought the excuse, but she stuck with it. "I'll finish it while I walk."

Junker scanned the street. "Walk? Where are you going? Shouldn't I at least know that? You said Exile wanted to kill you. This is a rough part of town and it's the middle of the night. Why don't we wait until morning, when it's light out and visibility is better?"

Waiting until morning wouldn't make them any safer. This was the city she'd first met Exile in, and she knew the area because she'd been here before… Exile had brought her here… to make love to her for the first time.

Rora cursed herself for letting another positive memory of him interrupt her rhythm. "Because if he is in town, I know where he'll be right now," she said, "and it's not here."

She didn't blame the flash of confusion on his face. Though if he thought about it for long enough he'd realize that this was the same city he'd told her to find Exile in. "I don't…"

Twisting to face Junker, she laid an arm on the back of the seat. "I know where Ex keeps his stash. We have to take this risk. If he's there or he's cleared out, then it's over. But

I'm betting that he'll assume I won't have the balls to come here."

"Wait," he said, his brow creasing. "You're planning to steal… from Exile?"

She smiled and shrugged. "He stole from me first."

This time, Rora kept her hands out of Junker's reach when she leaped out of the car.

Choosing to do this was beyond risky, it was insane. But she was used to people calling her crazy, and Rora was starting to get used to the notion that she wasn't normal.

Going to the end of the block, she turned the corner out of Junker's sight. Pulling her hood up over her face, she hoped Strike wouldn't see her approach. There weren't any traffic cameras in this area, but he had access to everything. Everywhere. Even those cameras in the heavens that mortals like her couldn't see.

Rora wasn't naïve enough to think that she would get away with this. For one thing, Strike had told her that Opal would alert him to anyone triggering the thermal sensors scattered around the loft. As soon as she went inside, he'd know she was there, so she'd have to get in and out fast.

There was a high chance that he'd gone; she doubted he was anywhere near this city anymore. But she had to take a chance, and what she'd said to Junker was true. Rora was sure that Strike would be arrogant enough to think she'd be running scared… which was exactly what she should be.

Darting across the street, she ran down a block, cut across an alley, and then went up another block. She wasn't taking any risk that Junker would be able to follow her either on foot or in the car. So she chose a route that a car couldn't travel and one that was quiet enough that she'd notice a person behind her.

She didn't trust Junker yet, so it was fair that he didn't trust her, despite what she'd said. Earning Junker's trust was low on her agenda. It wasn't like she could trust herself to judge anyone's character anymore anyway. She'd really believed that Strike loved her. She really had. Being wrong had cost her and she didn't want to pay it again.

Rora was so determined to get in and out fast that she didn't even pause when it came to crossing the threshold of the building. Running up the stairs, she knew Opal would be notifying Strike of her intrusion at this very second. He'd probably be bringing up images. Maybe he'd recognize her, or maybe if it was just a rainbow image, he wouldn't.

Didn't matter.

She got to the top floor and exhaled her relief when she saw that his things were still here. Dashing across the room, she intended to go straight to the chest. Rora made the mistake of breathing in.

She stopped dead.

Damnit.

Over the dank smell coming from the damp walls and the scent of fresh rain seeping into the moss that bled through the cracks in the window, she could smell… him.

Her mouth opened in a silent sob and she slapped a hand over it.

She'd been afraid to come back here in case he was here, or he'd taken his things.

It hadn't occurred to her that she'd have to look at the bed… that bed. The bed they'd first made love in.

Her lip wobbled, so she pulled it into her mouth with her teeth, holding it tight and ignoring the stinging pain of her own bite. A dribble of a tear seeped from the corner of her eye.

Angry at her body's rebellious reaction to being in this place, she balled one fist at her side and marched across the room. There was nothing to cry about. Nothing to reminisce about. Strike wasn't a lover lost to death or another tragedy. He wasn't torn from her against their will. Their relationship didn't deserve to be mourned.

Wherever he was right now, he was laughing at her. Probably sneering at the image of her crossing to his chest. He'd always told her she didn't belong in his world and he'd only mock her attempt to fight back, but that didn't mean she was going to give up.

Damnit. The chest was fastened shut with a combination padlock.

Thanking adrenaline and necessity, she grabbed the flashlight from beside the mattress and took it to smash the padlock from the chest. A rush of gratification for the spurned woman within her was happy to see his property broken on the floor. It was only a padlock. He'd replace it for a couple of bucks, but it was symbolic.

But she didn't have time to revel in the hollow triumph. Pulling open the lid, she let it fall back and shoved aside the clothes, towels, and other personal effects. At the bottom of the chest were several rolls of money. She didn't take them all, but she took a few, because she didn't know how much they would need and she didn't want to come back here.

Rora felt no guilt about taking the money, like she would if she was stealing from someone else. Strike had emptied her accounts; he had full access to all her money. If he was that pissed, he could just take money out of the trust he said hers was sitting in. Not that it would be sitting there anymore.

Just as she was about to reach for the lid, she noticed something under the corner of a tee-shirt. Tilting her head to get a closer look, she was shocked to discover what it was. Pushing the tee-shirt away, she picked up the small rectangle. It was the picture from her driving license, no license, just the picture. When the hell had he gotten that?

What was he planning to do with it? Probably plant it somewhere as evidence or use it to create an ID he could plant on her if he ever got the chance.

Stuffing it into her pocket with the money, she grabbed the lid to close it. Then with a smile on her face, she took a bite from the cupcake and placed the rest on top of the chest, right in the middle.

Screw him.

Striding out of the loft, she left the building and started her journey back to Junker. If Strike hadn't known she was still alive before, he'd know it after tonight.

Sliding into the car, Rora breathed out.

"Are you ok?" Junker asked.

"Just drive," she said, sucking her lip and trying to be discreet about wiping the moisture from the corners of her eyes.

During her time at Bella's mercy, Rora hadn't been able to stop thinking about her ex, yet one of the first things she'd done with her freedom was to return to his sanctuary.

"Did you get it?"

"I got it," she said, taking off her shoes and climbing into the back seat. "I need to sleep."

Adopting a fetal position, she pulled the blanket up over her head as she had the last time she'd slept in this truck. Only this time she wasn't blocking out her ordeal, she was hiding the shame of her grief.

Strike was some kind of bastard for doing this to her, and as soon as she got the chance, she'd make him pay… somehow.

FOUR

"FLAME," Rora called out, sitting bolt upright.

Taking her time to absorb her surroundings, she found she was in the backseat of a vehicle, warmed by the sun that was brightening the road around them.

Junker was trying to catch glimpses of her from his place in the driving seat. "Are you ok?"

"I'm fine," she grumbled, rubbing her face and pushing the blanket from her body. "Where are we?"

The question came out on instinct, but it didn't really matter where they were, only how far they were from wherever they were going. Junker seemed to be on a mission, and she could respect that, as long as it didn't get in the way of hers.

"Remember I told you I stashed my kit in a secure location in case things went south?" Junker asked. "I need to go pick everything up."

Yes, she remembered, he'd told her the previous day. Retrieving his possessions made sense, but she was a little disgruntled that it meant a detour. "There are ways to protect your technology that don't involve hiding it," she mumbled, climbing into the front of the car. "How long until we get there? Can we stop for coffee?"

"By email, I got the impression that you were an optimistic person, you seemed… fun."

Yawning and picking sleep from her eye, Rora pulled down the visor and used the mirror to check her appearance. "And?"

"So far, I'm not getting that from you."

She couldn't bring herself to crack a smile or even care that she was disappointing his expectation. "I'm fun," she muttered, pulling her feet onto the seat. "Where are we on the coffee?"

"We're only a half hour away from our destination," he said, glancing her way once, then twice.

Her jaw slid to the side. "Quit eyeballing me."

"What's flame? You say it every time you wake up."

Breathing out, she wondered if this was how Strike had felt when she kept questioning him. "You know, by email, I got the impression that you were relaxed," she sneered, sort of mocking him and hoping that he'd pick up on her displeasure. "So far I'm not getting that from you."

"I guess neither of us is at our best," he said. "Hard to just chill when we know the fate of the world is in our hands."

If he felt the weight of the world on his shoulders, she should be working to take some of the burden. After all, a lot of this was her fault. It seemed like her mood was permanently sour these days, and she had to work to remind herself that Junker was new to this and trying his best.

"Don't worry so much. We're not the only ones interested," she said. "There are… contingencies."

Infused with new energy, Junker leaped on her statement. "What does that mean? If we fail, you think that someone else will stop him?"

Stop him from doing what? That was the question. Rora wasn't as worried as Junker, but that was because she knew something that he didn't. The Point wasn't really in play.

"I know that the world is safe… for now. But if, for whatever reason, it gets unsafe, there are people we might be able to appeal to for help."

"Who?"

During her liaison with Strike, she'd learned a lot. Part of that education included meeting people who might be interested in saving the world if it came to it. Like Shula's X… and the NSA. But at the moment, Rora wasn't going to show her full hand. Not until she knew more about Junker.

It didn't usually take her this long to judge a person's character, and she did have history with Junker, who also had Benjamin's endorsement. But still sluggish after her stay with Bella, Rora was also reeling from being stung by her former lover, making her question her own ability to judge someone's virtue.

"I'm not ready to answer that," she said.

"You don't trust me."

"No, not really," she said, figuring that was at least some kind of honesty, whether he liked it or not. "Do you trust me?"

"Yes," he said immediately.

Turning to him, some of her aggravation faded. It was impossible to be wary of a person so obviously naïve. "Really?"

"Why shouldn't I trust you?"

She tried to restrain her scoff. "Why shouldn't you? Because you don't know me. Because emailing someone for a few months doesn't give true insight into what they'll do in a life or death situation. Often, we don't know what those closest to us are thinking or how they'll act on a daily basis. How can we expect to know each other when we're practically strangers?"

He thought about this for a minute. "Benjamin talked about you. A lot… You guys had a thing, didn't you?"

"Back in the day, yes," she said. The glimmer of her good humor faded. "But not recently. I don't want to talk about me and Benjamin."

He gazed out the windshield. "We have to find him. If he's out there somewhere… after all this time. Do you think he's alive?"

It didn't even occur to her that Junker wouldn't know Benjamin's fate, but she didn't appreciate being reminded of it. "What did I just say?" she snapped, startling him.

"Sorry."

Rora had never been a bitch, not like she'd just been to Junker. She could hold her own if she had to, but she couldn't attack an innocent person for asking a question. "Junker... I cared a lot about Benjamin and it's been a tough few months. I'm sorry. I didn't mean to snap."

"I'm asking a lot of questions," he said. "I'm sorry, I shouldn't push. You have been through a lot. Just... if you want to talk, I'm here. You're not alone anymore."

Like he'd read her mind, he touched on her biggest vulnerability. Glancing at him, they held eye contact for a score of seconds.

Rora kept looking at him after he faced the road again. "What's your plan?" she asked. "You said you had one."

"Exile's the key to this, sure, but he's not easy to track down. Do you remember how long it took us to find him the last time?" She nodded. "We don't have the time to go through that again... One thing you said last night intrigued me... You said if he was in the city, you'd have known where he was. The way you said it... you were confident." Again, she nodded. "Do you think you could find him again?"

She sighed. "If I knew what city he was in, sure. But I think he's on the move."

"Why?"

Revealing her logic wasn't betraying any big secret. "I think if this device and Benjamin's work are drawing interest, he'll want to make himself a difficult guy to pin down. Best way to do that is keep moving."

That and she'd noticed the chest she'd raided in the loft was light on apparel and tech.

He bobbed his head. "I have to say, I thought the same thing. If we could find out what city he was in, could you track him?"

"Is that why you asked me to help?" she asked, twisting her body toward him. "I'm not a sniffer dog." Although she had once referred to herself as a cadaver dog after Strike called her a homing pigeon. "I can't hunt him down."

"That's ok," he said, reaching over to put a hand over hers on her knee. "I've put the feelers out. Once I get to my computer, I'm hoping we'll have something."

Confronting the truth that she'd have to see Strike again, she slid her hand out from under Junker's, though that left his palm on her knee. "The device, the top-secret tech you mentioned, what is it?"

She'd seen it, held it in her hands, but she still didn't know what it was designed to do.

"I don't know exactly," Junker said. "But I know he got it from someone in government, someone at the highest level."

That wasn't exactly true. He'd picked it up from the carpet after leaving her boneless and aroused on a motel room floor.

Rora cleared her throat. "Why would they hand over something like that?"

He shrugged. "I don't know. They're sympathetic to his cause? He has something on them? I can guess, but I don't have any evidence of their motive."

Rora didn't want to be bitter, but she was definitely sliding toward it. "He doesn't have a cause," she muttered, her negative mood returning. "He has a hard head."

Junker was innocent in his confusion. "I... don't know what that means. You mean he's logical?"

"No, I mean he's stubborn," she said. "Imagine the worst-case scenario and assume that's how he got hold of it."

Junker sucked in a breath. "Then I'd guess he got someone else to get it for him. That he somehow conned them into it... Maybe they didn't even know what they were getting. Then he could honestly say he didn't receive the tech from a government agent; that it was given to him by the innocent party. Less of a crime to get it from a willing civilian than to blackmail or bribe a government official."

To distract herself, Rora popped open the glove box. "Willing," she muttered.

Junker watched her investigate and pick out a candy. "He's a smart guy," he said. "No denying that he knows what he's been doing."

"He's been doing it a long time," she said, sucking on the candy and fashioning its paper into a triangle in a series of folds and tucks.

"Did you… spend time getting to know his history?" Everything he was comfortable with sharing. "You never told me why you and he fell out. Seems like you were friends at one time."

She shook her head and sucked hard. "Not friends. Exile isn't interested in making friends. I can make my own assumptions. No one gets a reputation like his unless they know what they're doing."

"Have you heard what people say about him?"

Narrowing an eye, she let her focus creep around to him. "That better not be hero worship I hear in your voice," she said and was taken aback by his open smile. It had been a while since she'd seen a man smile.

"I keep my hero worship in my other pants," he said. "But I have heard about some of the jobs he's done. I wouldn't mind asking him a few questions. I'm capable, but sometimes he shows ingenuity that's… unparalleled. He thinks of contingencies that the rest of us wouldn't even imagine planning for."

"That's how you stay out of jail," she said. "Those of you who do this for research and ethical purposes don't have to worry about going to prison for life. He does."

It was obvious that Junker was intrigued, and it was interesting to see Strike from an innocent person's perspective. "Do you think that's why he flies so low under the radar? Prison? Must get lonely, don't you think?"

She resisted the urge to laugh in his face, but it was difficult. "He doesn't like people."

"Might make him difficult to tail," he said.

"Is that your plan?"

"The plan is to find out what he has, what he plans to do with it, and how to take it from him."

And Junker thought Exile would reveal that through his actions? Rora didn't need to waste her time. "Let me save you some time," she said. "You said he has this top-secret tech? I'd guess he plans to use it to his benefit. And if you want to take it, you better be willing to put a bullet in him. Exile won't give up his computer for anything."

That got his attention. "You think it's in his computer?"

She knew it was in his computer because she'd seen Strike sitting in Buddy's living room installing the device in Opal. But she couldn't give Junker those details. "If that's what it's for, why wouldn't he put hardware in his computer?"

There was suspicion in his eyes when they next met hers. Oops, she hadn't meant to put herself in the spotlight. "I don't know what it looks like, its size, or if it needs to be integrated to work. It might have an independent power source and operating system."

Time to backtrack and downplay her knowledge. "True. So, you have to find out. But, I don't have a clue how you're going to find him."

"I've got people looking," he said, and she folded her arms, unconvinced. "Oh, ye of little faith."

Her dubiousness wasn't doubt of Junker's skills. Though she knew Strike could avoid detection and that even if they did locate him he could shake a tail. But the truth was, she didn't know if she wanted Junker to find him.

No, even that was a lie. She *knew* that she didn't want Junker to find Strike. If the men came face-to-face, one of them was going to have to blink first, and she doubted that it would be the one determined to kill her.

FIVE

FOR FOUR DAYS, they were on the road.

Rora was getting used to living life on the move, but it wasn't any rooted attachment to the lifestyle that caused her to be unhappy when they finally stopped to make camp in a hotel room nicer than any she'd stayed in since this ordeal started.

Hugging her pillow with one arm, Rora held open the hotel room door for Junker. "I am so glad you like this plan," Rora muttered when he passed her carrying two heavy backpacks full of supplies.

On the road, she'd had time to get to learn more about the man she'd only known through email until this. While she didn't understand much when he talked about his work, she found it refreshing to hear the joy in his voice whenever his sister came up. Rora envied his fervor; she barely remembered what it was like to have a family, let alone to be proud of them.

Closing and locking the door, she examined the space. The room was spacious and cleaner than most of the motels she'd stayed in with either Junker or Strike, though she'd discovered that the former had a better appreciation for comfort.

After picking up Junker's supplies, they'd set up in a motel to give him time to check his sources. The whole time he'd been connected to the internet, she'd been jumpy. Rora hadn't been able to sit down and relax; she was up, poised, pacing, listening for every sound outside and wringing her hands.

As she'd expected, none of Junker's contacts had a line on Exile. But they did have a rumor for him to follow up. Rumor, the internet seemed to be full of those.

Unfortunately for her, the rumor Junker wanted to follow up involved the Black Jewel, who, it turned out, was looking for Exile too. Junker thought nothing of telling Rora that the Black Jewel was easier to trace and to follow, like he'd forgotten what she'd just been through with the woman.

Junker had tried to insist that he wouldn't let her be hurt, but his naivety and compassion had made her so uncomfortable that she'd stuttered some excuse about needing to soak in the tub to help her relax. The only reason she'd said it was to buy herself some time alone. The trouble was, she hated taking baths, hated it. From the minute she'd sat down in the water, she was bored. As much as she'd wanted an escape from Junker, she couldn't find any escape from her thoughts. Damnit.

After killing some time in the tub, Rora had got out to have Junker declare that the Black Jewel was on the move and had an open-ended reservation that they had to chase down. Determined not to show Junker that she was reluctant to sneak up on the Black Jewel, Rora didn't flinch. She'd told him to pack up and get the truck.

Since then, they'd been on the road, resolute that they'd get to this city before the Black Jewel, and they'd succeeded. They were here and Bella, was due to arrive tomorrow at a hotel a block over.

The Black Jewel's reservation was flexible, suggesting she could be planning to stay in town for a while. They had no word on whether Exile was coming into town with the Black Jewel, or if Bella's plan was simply to sit still and wait for Strike to come to her. Probably the latter.

Without knowing what to expect or how long they'd be stuck here, she and Junker had stopped to get supplies of anything they might need on the way. Given Junker's understanding of comfort, and Rora's willingness to spend Strike's money, they'd spared no expense.

Finally, Rora had enough clothes that she could spend some time choosing an outfit. They had bought snacks and playing cards to keep them occupied, and Junker had a ton of tech that he planned to use to help them achieve their goal.

All they had to do now was settle into their hotel room and wait.

Since she'd left Bella's dungeon, Rora's neck had been stiff, something the various motel room pillows didn't help soothe. After one of his solo shopping trips, Junker had surprised her with an orthopedic pillow. His generosity had overwhelmed her into silence. Sure, it made sense to have a pillow that would help her neck, but she hadn't expected him to think of her comfort.

Tossing her special pillow to the bed, Rora thought about a shower.

"Do you want a bath?" Junker asked. "I've got a bunch of stuff to setup."

Telling him that taking baths relaxed her had been a mistake. Junker suggested it every time they stopped somewhere new. But, to cover for that first night's lie, Rora had to maintain the pretense.

"Do you need help?" she asked, watching him lift both packs onto the end of the big bed.

There was a wall-mounted TV in this room above a nice oak dresser that had a matching coffee table in front of it and a couch and armchairs around it. Kicking off her shoes, she wiggled her toes in the pile of the carpet and delight coiled through her.

Junker must have noticed her smile because he stopped unpacking to smile back. "Happy?"

"This carpet is amazing," she said and scanned the clean walls and crisp coving. "The drapes look heavy too."

They were on the bottom floor, so their room opened onto a porch that faced the parking lot and then the street. Convenient for a quick getaway… another lesson she'd learned from Strike.

"Nicer than some of the dives we've been in, huh?"

Oh, he had no idea. Wandering around, Rora admired the picture on the wall and ran a finger along the dresser to find there wasn't a speck of dust in sight. Junker unpacked more tech, laying things out on the bed.

Rora went over and sat down to pick up something that looked like a tiny camera. "Where are you going to put this stuff?" she asked.

"Anywhere that will give us a view of the Black Jewel's movements. I'll go have a look around her hotel. This is why I was so determined to get here before her. I should be able to sneak into the hotel's system and figure out which room is hers and where it is in the building. I'll find outside locations to position the cameras to get footage of the inside of the room. Covering the lobby, the restaurants and bars is easy, but I won't be able to get into her room. The cameras are discreet and can be switched to night vision. When she arrives, we'll be able to see her… And if Exile shows up, we'll see him too…"

Parting her lips, Rora was about to speak, but stopped herself to draw a breath between her teeth. Junker was still unpacking and she hoped he hadn't noticed.

If Exile showed up, rather if Strike showed up, he wouldn't be visible on camera. Well he would be visible, but his image would be distorted. That meant if Bella was close enough to him, her image would be distorted too.

Her stomach churned. If Strike showed up for Bella, which Rora guessed he would at some point, she might have to watch footage of them… together. Whether his image was distorted or not, Rora really didn't want to watch that. If he was naked, he couldn't be carrying the tech that messed up his image and voice on recordings, meaning they'd see every detail.

"You ok? You look a little pale?" Junker asked. She swallowed her nausea, sure her expression was queasy. "I thought you were starting to feel better."

She was getting over the trauma of her imprisonment. Her appetite was back, but she wasn't sleeping great. The same nightmare kept waking her up, night after night. No matter how many times she fell asleep, whether it was in the truck or at night in a motel room, she had the same nightmare every time.

"I'm going to get in the tub."

Having a bath might not be her idea of great fun, but it gave her space and she appreciated the time away from Junker. If she wasn't in the room with him, she didn't have to lie to him, something she was appreciating less and less. Rora had embraced her new friendship with Junker and was beginning to believe that he was a good person.

But that was a bad thing. Bella and Strike were not good people and they would eat Junker for breakfast. He'd be blindsided by their laughter if he started to talk about morals and righteousness.

Rora feared for her new friend's safety. Junker had honor and would hesitate before taking someone's head off. Strike wouldn't.

Before she got to the bathroom, she spun around. "Junk," she said. He looked over his shoulder. "Exile shot Jewel once." His brow came down. "He was… trying to get out of a dangerous situation and Jewel was being unreasonable… So, he shot her shoulder."

"Harsh," he said, taking his focus from his tools to face her. "Do you think that she's looking for payback? If he's smart, he won't show… You didn't tell me this before. It might've changed our decision to go this route."

"I think he'll show," she said.

"I wouldn't show up to see the woman I shot… Do you think she wants to kill him or that he's coming to finish the job? Do you think he'd win?"

"Don't bet on it, Jewel usually travels with a posse," she said. But Junker had been in Bella's house, if he'd done any kind of recon he'd know that the beauty had men to do her dirty work for her. "But she won't kill Exile."

"How can you be sure?" he asked, his attention becoming keen.

"Two reasons. The first is she needs him to finish Benjamin's work. Exile's the only one who can optimize its potential."

"And? What's the second reason?"

This one was harder to say. "She's in love with him."

The surprise that struck him widened his eyes. "They're a couple?"

"Were… I don't know about now. I think they hook up when they get together. The violence, the hatred, it's all foreplay to them."

Squeezing his lips together, he seemed to be thinking about how this changed things. "We know they're dangerous. But you think she'll probably forgive him for shooting her since the wound clearly wasn't fatal."

Unfortunately, it hadn't been. Rora had never thought she could be the type of person to wish another dead, but if Strike had executed the Black Jewel in Wonderland, she'd have been saved from so much pain.

"She won't kill him, but Jewel will punish him," she said.

Junker took a step toward her. "Punish him, how?"

That was something Rora didn't want to imagine. As gruesome as it might be, it would also be intensely intimate for the couple. "I don't know, but it will probably be sexual… and violent."

As Rora's mind started to drift again, Junker's just seemed to be perplexed. "He's stronger than her, but he'd tolerate violence?"

Violence was a stable in Strike's life. "If Exile wants her… he'll let her do whatever she wants to him."

"Why?"

Resisting the urge to sigh, Rora knew it was impossible for someone as pure as Junker to understand. "Because it's what Exile believes he deserves, and he can take it," she said. "He can take the hits, the whip, the hatred; he gets off on it because it makes him hate her. He wants to hate her. Because as long as he hates her, he'll never love her… Except he does love her."

Junker stopped in front of her, wide stance, arms folded, and a frown on his face. "You're not making much sense, Aurora."

No, and she was starting to feel that churn of frustrated emotion. "He won't admit to himself that he needs any human connection."

His chin rose, and he peered down his nose. "Aurora," he said. "Did something—"

"I'm going to get in the tub," she said and spun to head for the bathroom.

Every time she edged into a conversation with Junker that hinted she might be ready to drop her guard, she made an excuse and ran away before it could go too far.

Rora wanted to trust him, she wanted to relax and let him in, but it was becoming more obvious with each passing day that it was unlikely she'd ever trust anyone again.

Nice as it would be to have someone to lean on who she could reveal any truth to and know they'd stick around to support her, she'd learned a hard truth with Strike. She'd thought her ex could be that person. He was unlike any other man she'd ever known. Rora had been willing to accept him, to stand with him through anything. It was just a shame he hadn't been interested in reciprocating.

While the water filled the tub, she stripped off and slapped her hands down on the vanity to lean in and glare at her reflection. "Stop thinking about him," she growled at herself. "Stop it."

Squeezing her eyes closed, she let her head drop. Her neck screamed in protest, but the physical pain was more welcome than the heartache and sorrow.

Drawing in a breath, she lifted her chin to look in the mirror again. Strike's reflection behind hers startled her. Gasping, she spun around, falling back against the vanity, but… he wasn't there. She was alone.

Rubbing her face, Rora wanted to slap herself. He wasn't here, of course he wasn't; there was no window in the room, and the door hadn't opened. He was in her head, all in her head, just like their love had been.

There were times in the past when she'd been sure she was losing her mind. But it hadn't been as potent as this. Her grip on reality was loosening and she didn't know what would happen when she finally gave up and let go.

SIX

THE BLACK JEWEL had shown up at the hotel on time.

For two days, Rora and Junker sat on the couch in their hotel room and watched Bella go about her life. Junker had set up the cameras so they could see their mark eating dinner in the restaurant, and breakfast in her room at the table in the window.

Their choice not to stay in the same hotel as Bella had been deliberate. It gave them options and discretion.

In order to keep an eye on Bella's suite, Junker had placed cameras outside the windows of the building opposite the hotel, which happened to be a department store. From those cameras, when the curtains were open, they got a partial view into Bella's bedroom and across the living room to the door.

"You're quite the tech genius," Rora said. "Every time I see this set up I'm impressed all over again."

"Do you want a drink?" Junker asked and leaped up to go to the fridge.

Yes, this room even had its own fridge. It wasn't stocked, but she was happy not to have to pay minibar prices. "A soda?"

"No," he said, turning to show one bottle of wine and one of whiskey. "Which do you like?"

Booze was an unusual choice for Junker, but he brought both bottles over to her on the couch. Although she might have preferred the stronger liquor, Rora selected the wine.

With the way her mood had been and her wish to erase her ex from her thoughts, she'd probably have kept on downing the whiskey until she passed out, which wouldn't be close to smart.

"Do we have a corkscrew? Where did you get this?"

"I got it when I was out earlier," he said, taking a Swiss Army knife from his pocket. "I thought we could use something to pass the time."

And she wasn't going to say no to the novelty of alcohol. "It's been an age since I had a drink," she said, watching him pull a corkscrew from his knife to open the bottle.

"You deserve one."

Trying to remember when she'd last had alcohol, Rora recalled Bella's date rape, making her glad she was witnessing Junker open the glass bottle. Be that as it may, when he offered the bottle to her first, she shook her head. "After you."

Though it seemed that he noted something behind her smile, he took a drink anyway. Rora was happy to accept the bottle next and after taking a long mouthful, she sat back on the couch and tucked her feet up, pulling her knees to her chest.

Twisting into the corner of the couch, he laid an arm along the back to look at her. "So, Aurora, now we've spent all these hours, all these days together, you have to be ready to tell me something about yourself... Do you trust me yet?"

She assessed him. "Trust is... it's difficult to give when you don't trust yourself."

"You don't trust yourself?" he asked. "You should. Benjamin trusts you, he wouldn't trust you if you weren't a good person. Give yourself some credit."

With her mouth around the bottle, she examined him as she drank the wine. He was attractive, clean-shaven tonight, she had seen him with stubble too, and either worked. His hair was neat, not too short, and he was happy in the blue jeans that matched his eyes. He had long lashes and a twinkle in his eye that made him approachable.

Lowering the bottle from her lips, she handed it to him, and waited until he'd had a drink. Once he'd removed the bottle from his lips, she took a tentative step toward trusting him.

"Benjamin is dead," she said. His ease vanished. "He shot himself to protect the secret."

"The secret?" he asked. "Oh my God, Aurora. I'm so sorry."

Putting the wine on the table, Junker didn't even glance at the screens set up on the coffee table and dresser. He pulled her into his arms like it was some sort of comfort, but Rora stayed rigid while he held her, stroking her hair.

This kind of affection was foreign to her. Benjamin would hold her, but she never felt protected in his embrace. Strike had made her feel protected, whether he held her or not, but there was little tenderness in his arms.

Somehow, Junker gave her both.

The man who'd read her emails, responded with sympathy, advice, and jokes, was here, holding her. For the first time in a long time, she felt both safe and cared for. But it made her uneasy. The moment she began to relax was the same one she pushed him away even in spite of her decision to trust him.

Still in his arms, she peeked up to see the same intensity in his eyes that she'd noticed at the bus station. Whenever their eyes met, there was something there, but she couldn't put her finger on what it was. Was she looking for something in him or was it the other way around? She felt needed. Respected…

Her thoughts were still swirling when he leaned in. His lips touched hers gently and held there in a brief breath of invitation and acceptance.

Pushing forward, he opened his mouth and kissed her harder, tipping his head to the side in a silent request for her to reciprocate. She didn't know what to do. Rora knew it was polite to respond when a handsome man kissed her.

It was a nice kiss; warm, comforting, and cleansing in an odd way. Her eyes were still open, again, not polite, but her rudeness ended up working out because from the corner of her eye, she spotted something on the nearest screen.

"Oh my god," she said, shoving Junker away to slide down onto the floor.

"I'm sorry, I—"

"No," she said, bumping her fist on the inside of his knee. "Look!"

He twisted to look at the screen she was pointing at, which meant she ended up between his shins, but she didn't care about that now. Shaking her finger at the image of the corner outside Bella's hotel, Rora was mesmerized by the blurred shape.

"It might be a fault," Junker said, putting his hand on her crown to stroke her hair.

Ignoring his physical affection, she was too transfixed to object or move his hand away. "That's no glitch," she said, her finger almost making contact with the screen. "That's Exile."

Even though it wasn't the one she knew him by, just saying the name made a tremor go through her and stop in her throat.

He was here. Just a couple of blocks away.

"Are you sure?" Junker asked, excitement making his fingers scrunch her hair. "How do you know?"

"Because he has tech that distorts his image," she said. "And there's a service alley down there. He's probably been inside the building already, but he'll want to make a quick escape if he has to, so he won't trap himself inside. And if the Jewel is…"

Just at that, Bella walked onto the other side of the screen toward the blurred guy who then went into the alley. "The Black Jewel," Junker said. "We have to wait and see if she talks to—"

"That's him," she said.

It was odd, Rora's instincts could feel him. A thrumming in her belly betrayed her awareness, but she couldn't figure out if the root of it was excitement or fear. She didn't need to see her ex's face, she recognized his boots, his jeans, the way he stood, the way he walked. That was Exile. Without a doubt.

Her eyes closed. This was on. It was real. It was happening.

Junker ruffled her hair and used her head to boost himself onto his feet. It took her a minute to realize that he was moving around the room.

Dragging her eyes from the screen just as Bella disappeared into the alley, Rora grabbed the seat of the couch and pulled herself onto her knees. "What are you doing?"

"I have to get close if I want to listen in," he said, pulling on his jacket.

Panic hit her hard. "No, no, no," she said, clambering onto the couch to lunge over it and grab his jacket as he passed. "You can't. You won't be able to listen in. He won't let you."

"I have tech of my own. If I have to get close—"

"Then he'll kill you," she said.

Curling his fingers around hers, Junker peeled them from his jacket and went to the nightstand drawer. Retrieving something, he showed her a gun and checked the clip. "I'll be ok with my little friend."

It was just a handgun, but his wide smile was endearing. Sighing, she sank down onto her heels, resting her hands on the back of the couch. Junker's confidence was misplaced, but he wasn't going to be talked out of his plan.

"Don't let him get near you. If he gets his hands on you, that'll be it. He'll break your arm, or he'll knock you out… and he carries a knife."

Tucking the gun into the back of his pants, Junker came over and put his hand on her head. "My little friend works from a long way away."

He bowed and kissed the top of her head. She grabbed his hand. "Just… only shoot if you absolutely have to, ok? And… aim for an arm or a leg…" His eyes narrowed. "I don't want to have to bail you out for murder."

He smiled again and nodded. "I'll be back soon."

Rolling her lips into her mouth, Rora could only sit there and watch him go. Long after he was gone, it occurred to her that she could've offered to join him. But she reassured herself that Junker was in shape, he had enough muscle that he could take care of himself… against anyone except maybe Strike.

Flopping onto the couch face first, she locked her hands at the back of her head. This was going to be a long night.

***

ALMOST AN HOUR later, a frustrated Junker returned to the hotel room.

Rora was sitting in the middle of the bed, watching the surveillance screens from across the room, when the door opened, and he came storming in.

"What happened?" she asked, leaping off the bed to run to him. Her eyes darted over his body, checking for any obvious injuries. "Did he break you?"

Snatching his fingers, she inspected one hand and then the other, flipping it over and bending all the digits.

"No," he said, curling his hand to link their fingers. "I didn't find him… or her."

Junker guided her to the couch and sat them down, moving the gun from his pants to put it on the table.

"They weren't in the alley?" she asked but wasn't really surprised.

He took off his jacket. "Anything happen here?" he asked, scanning the equipment. "Did you see him?"

"No," she said, because it was true.

Except in her desire not to see anything, Rora had chosen to sit on the bed, on the other side of the room, where she couldn't make out too many details on the various screens laid out. Seeing Strike messed with her head in a way she wasn't equipped to handle.

Part of her wanted to seek him out, to smack him in the chest and then kiss his face off. As sad as it may be, there was still a part of her that couldn't come to terms with not being his girl, even in the platonic sense… if they'd ever been platonic.

It was pathetic, but a section of her brain, a tiny one, was whispering to her, telling her to go to him, telling her that Strike would never hurt her. She needed his strength… missed him… the him she'd thought he was.

Her lip curled at the hatred she felt for herself.

Junker had never met Exile in the flesh. His only chance of finding him was by tracking Bella and hoping the Black Jewel led him to his man. Tonight, that hadn't happened, and her friend was disappointed, but Rora had known it was going to play out this way.

As they sat there looking at the camera feed, Bella came into view. She walked down the sidewalk, through the hotel lobby and returned to her room.

"Where the hell is he," Junker exhaled, scrutinizing the screens, hoping for a clue. "You were right; I should've listened to you. If we can't see his face or find him to hear his voice, how will we learn what he has? How will we know what he plans to do with it?"

"Are you giving up?"

"No," he said and spun to look at her, grabbing her hand. "Being covert isn't going to work. We have to be more direct… We should ask him."

She hadn't expected Junker to say that and didn't like the suggestion at all. "Uh, we should… what?"

Determined hope radiated from him. "We'll arrange a meet," he said. "Why shouldn't he meet me? He's not going to view me as a threat."

Worry made her shake her head fast. "I don't think that's a good idea. You can't confront him. If you end up in a fight…"

Raising her hand, he pressed it to his lips. "Not a confrontation, not a fight. We'll be professional and talk, man-to-man."

She was incredulous. "Reason with him? We talked about this, he can't—"

"How will I know that if I don't try?" he asked. "I have to put eyes on the guy, to let him know I'm around, I'm watching him. We can't stay in this holding pattern. What's the alternative? Every minute that passes is another minute this is out there. He could be doing anything with it."

Yeah, but not what he wanted to do, because Strike didn't have the Point. "I don't think it's a good idea to aggravate—"

"Ok, then let's get our ball and go home," he said though she knew he didn't mean it.

Home. Her gaze drifted toward the door. Strike was her home, that's what she'd told him. That might not be true anymore, even if it felt odd to think that way. But if she wasn't here, chasing this DARPA device down, doing the right thing, where was she going to run to?

Without a home, family, or friends left, there was nowhere else for her to go. It wasn't like she had to rush off for any important appointments.

This was going to happen whether she liked it or not, and so it was time to reveal her contingency.

Breathing out in a huff, Rora took her hand from Junker's and admitted a truth. "There's a bar, a dozen blocks east toward the river," she said. "It's called Apocalypse."

"How do you know that? You said you hadn't been here before."

"I haven't," she said. "But I thought it might come to this. I knew if you wanted to get anything from Exile that you'd have to talk to him. So I talked to a doorman, the young guy, and I asked him about it."

"Why would you—"

"I asked him about the crappiest, scariest hole in town. I wanted to know where the lowest of the low hung out. He told me about one place and I asked about the one on the rung below it. Turns out, Apocalypse is as bad as you'll get around here."

Junker wanted to understand, she could see how he was trying to be patient in figuring her out. "Why would you ask about—"

"You'll find Exile there. In the darkest corner. That's where he'll be."

Clarity made his chin rise. "Like Last Resort. The darkest corner. I remember. But…" Brushing his thumb across her cheek, he got closer. "You'll have to come with me, I… I don't know what he looks like."

And that suggestion was why she hadn't told Junker before. The last thing she wanted to do was come face-to-face with her ex-lover. "You'll find him," she said, but got up to retrieve her shoes. "I'm not coming inside, but I'll ride over with you."

Doing something was better than doing nothing. Traveling with Junker saved her from sitting here wondering if he was going to come back alive. Staying in this room another minute would give her cabin fever.

"Ride? You don't want to walk?"

Smirking at him over her shoulder, she pulled on her shoes and grabbed her jacket. "No. Always ensure you can make a quick escape… especially with… Exile." It still felt weird using Strike's alias. It was the name the criminal world knew him by, but it wasn't the one she'd used for him. "Get ready, we're leaving now."

Snatching his wrist as he grabbed his jacket, she pulled him across the room and out the door.

SEVEN

DRIVING ALONG THE riverside, they'd peeked up every alley until they'd found the right place. Even though they didn't know the area, it didn't take long to find it. The vertical sign painted on its black door stating its name was sort of a giveaway. Unlike the other black-doored bar Rora knew, this one actually had a handle, meaning it was more welcoming by default.

Asking Junker to park at the corner, so she could see down the alley and have a view of the door, Rora's adrenaline was simmering when he turned off the engine.

"Ok," Junker said, blowing out a breath. "You're sure he's in there?" She nodded, but couldn't take her focus from ·the door. "And that I'll know who he is?"

"You'll know. He'll be the only guy not drinking and the only one working on a computer… Oh, and he'll have a look on his face like just breathing pisses him off."

"His computer," he said, whipping around. "He'll have his computer? That's amazing, we can—"

"Don't touch his computer." Opal hadn't done anything to Junker and messing with her was going to set him on the wrong foot with Strike. "You said this was going to be civil and if you touch his laptop, it won't be. You're a computer guy. How do you feel when people touch your hardware without permission?"

"Got it," he said and took her hand to kiss her knuckles.

"And please, don't say my name to him." Any of her names.

"Ok, stay here. Don't move. If you get scared hit the horn, I'll come out."

She smiled and picked her legs up to cross them. "I won't get scared, Junk. Go on."

Seeing his smile turn away, she got a shiver. He was more than just attractive, he was a kind of hunk in his own way, more polished than Strike, but not too polished that anyone would challenge him for being in Apocalypse.

Junker got out and walked about thirty feet down the alley to the Apocalypse door. He glanced back in her direction just before going inside. Once he was out of sight, she exhaled; all she could do now was wait.

Chewing her lip, Rora counted the seconds and began to panic about what she'd do if he didn't come out again. She wasn't afraid to go into Apocalypse; it looked like a nicer place than Last Resort and she'd thrived there. On top of that, she'd lived with Buddy. Dealing with his poker pals and the heavy metal guys he brought around was equivalent to getting a PhD in Badass.

But she wouldn't be able to drag Junker out on her own if he started a brawl.

Funny that the dozens of big scary bikers didn't worry her, but one guy did. Her former lover. The idea of seeing him terrified the crap out of her. He'd be mad, so mad, and she wasn't going to beg his forgiveness for the Point bait and switch.

But a kind of peace settled over her when she realized that if anyone was going to take her out of this world, put her out of her misery, then Strike should be the one to do it. He'd told her not to put a bullet in her head. He'd prevented her from committing suicide and saved her life.

Every day she had from then on only happened because of him. Sure, he'd kept her alive to use her for information, but her choice not to pull the trigger was driven by him.

One minute passed and then another.

Convincing herself that the length of time was an indication the men were talking, Rora tried to ignore her anxiety. Less than a minute later, the door opened again, and Junker came out of the bar.

Pouncing to her knees, she braced a hand on the seat and one on the door. He seemed to be staggering, was he staggering? He took a hand to his jaw, then the other followed. His arms weren't broken, good. But yes, he definitely stumbled to the side.

Grabbing for the car door, thoughts of everything but getting to him went out the window. Rora leaped out and ran down the alley.

"Junk," she gasped, catching his body with hers. There was a daze in his eyes and redness on the jaw he was rubbing. "Oh my God, what happened? Did you find him? Did someone hurt you?"

"Exile's got one hell of a right hook… but I think his left is stronger."

Gritting her teeth, fury burned inside her. Junker had gone in to have a conversation, he was a nice guy, a kind guy, and that bastard in there thought he could throw his weight around just because he was him.

Rora didn't even realize she'd stormed right past Junker. She wasn't thinking about anything except her anger. Marching into the bar, she took about ten seconds to pick out exactly where Strike would be.

Setting him in her sights, she wound her way across the room, through patrons who were probably gawping at the raging, fuming woman with purpose in her step. But Rora didn't care, she kept her destination in sight and didn't flinch.

Shoving a hand onto the lid of his laptop, she slammed it shut and with her hand still on it, she bent toward the man seated in the corner.

"Who the hell do you think you are?"

Strike's eyes narrowed on her as he leaned back. "You always find your way home to me, Cupcake," he said, a smug slant to his lips.

Oh, he infuriated her. "I have not come home to you," she snapped. "You are a horrible, despicable, disgusting human being who wouldn't understand decency if it smacked him in the face!"

Rora's adrenaline was pumping hard, but Strike was almost serene in the way he considered her. She didn't expect him to surge to his feet and grab up Opal. With his other hand, he seized the back of her head, sinking his fingers into her hair and using that grip to turn her around.

Although Rora screamed and snatched for his fist that was lost in her locks, no one tried to help her.

Strike propelled her across the room toward the door. They were most of the way to the entrance before she saw Junker just inside.

"Hey!" Junker said, rushing over when he noticed them.

But Strike wasn't slowing down. "Get the fuck out, Square."

Rora eyed her newest friend. "Move! Stay out the way!"

Junker had no time to do anything. Strike forced her outside. As soon as they were in the alley, he thrust her forward, letting go of her hair.

Spinning around, Rora wasn't surprised to see fury in Strike's eyes; it was exactly what she'd expected. He shoved Opal onto the lid of a dumpster, freeing up both of his hands before stalking toward her. Rora swallowed hard, bracing when he grabbed her throat and rushed her back against the wall.

It was in that moment her thoughts caught up with her actions, and she realized the peril she'd inadvertently welcomed by putting herself in front of him again.

"You want to get physical with me, baby?" Strike growled.

"Hey! Let her go!"

Junker rushed up behind them and grabbed Strike's shoulder. As Junker pulled him back, Strike used the turn for extra leverage to hit Junker hard. Junker went down.

Rora screamed and punched the back of Strike's shoulder to little effect. Her ex whirled around and grabbed her fist, slamming it to the wall. Getting in her face, he seized her chin and pulled it up, making her neck ache.

"You move on fast, Kero, lightning fucking speed. Guess getting guys on the hook is your skill." Baring her teeth, Rora located her fury and brought her knee up, but he grabbed it before she could make contact with his groin and shoved it downward. His excuse for a laugh was little more than a groan. "You only get to use that one once." Looming closer, his mouth opened just a breath from hers. "And I'm not so sure you're done with those."

"Dream on, Exile."

The twitch in his eye was curious, but there was no time to think about it. Junker groaned, drawing Strike's attention from her. She tried to go to Junker, but Strike stole her arm and dragged her away from her new friend who was still laid out on the concrete.

With a tight grip on her upper arm, Strike hauled her across the asphalt and thrust her up a stair into a shadowy double-width doorway.

"I'm disappointed," he said, getting down into her face. "I've been watching you for days, waiting for you to visit. It's almost insulting that you'd send your bitch to me first. What did you think I'd do to him?"

When she pushed forward, he slammed her back to the metal door. "Junker isn't my bitch," she spat.

"He's your something. And if I find out he's touched you, I'll cut off his hands. It'll be a real surprise for him when he finds out he's been messing with my girl. He doesn't know about us, does he?"

"There is no us," she said, trying to wrestle her arm away. "Let me go."

But every time she tried to get away from the corner he'd put her in, he used his body to push her back into it. "How'd he find me?"

Sneering, she enjoyed telling him the truth. "*Your* bitch led him to you," Rora said, wearing a smirk.

But his frown deepened. "What the hell are you talking about?"

"Your beautiful Black Jewel," she said, mocking him with each word. "She's not as discreet as your woman should be."

Strike didn't check a woman out like any other man would, his gaze was always sinister. "Well you would know," he said, admiring her lips.

Rora gasped when he spun her around and thrust her chest-first into the door. Planting her hands on the door, he kicked her feet apart.

First thing he did was reach around to take both of her breasts into his hands, squeezing them tight.

"What the hell do you think you're doing?" she asked and tried to push back.

But he flattened his body on hers, pressing her into the door. Grabbing both her hands, he stretched them above her head, holding them tight by her wrists in one of his capable palms, rendering her immobile.

His lips moved through her hair to the top of her ear. "Checking for weapons," he said, running a hand down her waist and over her ass. "I'll be disappointed if I don't find any."

Pulling her skirt up, he exposed one ass cheek. She bit her lip when he gripped it, doing her best not to give him the satisfaction of any reaction. But when he pushed his hips against her and she felt the ridge of his erection through his jeans, she had to close her eyes.

"What's wrong, Cupcake? Not gonna fight me off?" Fighting would prove her hatred, but that was probably exactly what he wanted. "I could fuck you right here," he growled into her hair and tugged the elastic of her underwear. "Maybe that's what you want… you want me to fuck you, baby? You know you should hate me, but you want it."

His words were little more than a sinister growl, fogging her hair as he rubbed his face in it. Disgust rose within her, but it wasn't aimed at him, it was all for her. He wasn't wrong.

That first night in the Last Resort parking lot after Strike had broken a patron's arm, Rora had been aroused by him, and that same part of her was switched on now. She was feeling with her body, her hormones, not her mind or her good sense. It took every ounce of her willpower not to push her ass back into him and encourage his grinding.

Hating him. Loving him. Rora had thought she'd never be able to understand Bella and Strike's relationship, but she got it now. She got how the need for another person could eradicate all sense, even that of self-preservation. If going insane was as seductive as loving him, Rora was a lost cause.

His fingertips stayed beneath the narrow band of her thong and began to slide around her hip to her mound. They began to descend, going so far as to make contact with her Brazilian before she forced herself to lift her chin.

"Don't. Please, Strike," she gasped, wanting to sound angry, but coming off as pleading.

If he touched her, if he started to stimulate her, she couldn't trust her willpower to hold. If she gave in to him, she'd hate herself forever, though she doubted she'd regret it no matter how much she wanted to.

Just like Bella, Rora would find herself craving the object of her hatred and that internal conflict would destroy her.

His fingers stopped the moment she uttered the words. "You're nothing like her," he said as though he'd been able to read her mind. "You think that loving me and hating me at the same time will turn you into Bella… it won't."

The sound of understanding didn't ease her anxiety. It dampened her eyes and for a breath, she recalled sharing her secrets with this man and listening to his.

"Strike," she whispered.

He slid his palm from her wrists up over the back of her hands and instinct made her part her fingers to receive his between hers.

"I taught you to defend yourself or die," he said, something more tender about the way his mouth moved in her hair now. "Tell me you're armed, Cupcake. That's one disappointment I couldn't handle."

Tightening her fingers around his, her head moved, responding to the not-really-there caress of his lips on her scalp. "There's a switchblade in my cleavage."

He breathed out a long rush of quiet relief. "Next time, use it."

"Why do you care?" she asked.

He'd dumped her for a device, and that reminder made her tense. He could be soothing and relaxing her before wedging a blade in her ribs as payback for her betrayal.

"Haven't taken over the world yet, have I?" he said above her ear.

Probably not through lack of trying. She lifted a shoulder to push hair from her mouth. "Are you saying there's hope for you yet?"

"Hmm," he groaned. "Wouldn't go that far. And I warn you, I will bring Armageddon if I don't get my picture back…"

"Picture?"

"The picture you stole from the loft." Why did he want that? And if he'd known she stole the money, why wasn't he asking for that? He must have felt the shock vibrate through her. "I'm no more done with you than you are with me… Be bad, baby, you know what it does to me."

Hauling her around again, he thrust her back to the door, squashing her to it with his body, his forearm somehow coming to rest at the base of her skull as it had so many times when he'd kissed her. His eyes slid to hers, so close to hers, just as they had been at their most intimate moments.

Before she could think about his intention or where this may be going, Strike spun away suddenly, his fist raised, ready to lash out again. She jumped to action and grabbed his elbow to stop him from hitting the man he must have sensed barreling up behind them.

Leaping around Strike, Rora planted a hand on each man's chest, putting herself between them. "No! No fighting," she said, looking from one to the other. Strike was pushing harder, or maybe Junker was being gentler because she was in the way, it could be described either way. But she laid her focus on Strike who was glaring at Junker over her head. "Break my arm or holster your pistol, Exile."

It had to be her use of his alias that surprised him. Each time she said it, he looked at her like he didn't know who she was talking about.

"If you've got something to say, Square, say it," Strike spat.

Rora turned to Junker, hoping he'd calm down. It took a minute of just breathing before he spoke. "We want to meet," her new friend said.

"We?" Strike asked. She couldn't even look at him when he had that incredulity in his voice. "Meet about what? We're meeting right fucking here. What do you call this?"

"We… well—"

"We're not going to talk out here on the street," she said, taking over from Junker who was beginning to stutter. "We'll meet in Jewel's hotel tomorrow… ten PM."

"I was gonna get an early night tomorrow," Strike said.

She spun on him to glare. "You don't sleep," she said. "And you're a curious guy who isn't afraid of us. So, show up, or don't, but I think you'll want to hear us out."

Being ambiguous was a ploy. Rora hoped Strike would assume they were dangling the Point because that would bring him to the meeting. Other than that, he had no incentive to be there.

"You teasing me?" Strike asked.

"Stop fucking around," she said, smacking the middle of his chest with the heel of her hand.

But he wasn't done being facetious. "How will I know where? You're not dumb enough to come to the suite."

Rora turned her attention to Opal who was still on the dumpster further down the alley. "I'm sure you'll figure it out, Exile," she said and turned her back on him.

Taking Junker's hand, she pulled him away having learned for sure that these two guys couldn't get along.

"Do you think he'll come?" Junker asked when they got back into his truck.

Strike was glaring, still in the alley where they'd left him. She didn't take her eyes off him until Junker backed up, taking them from each other's view.

"He'll come," she said, putting on her seatbelt. "If he wasn't curious he'd have killed us both on the spot."

"Now we just have to figure out a way to convince him to do the right thing."

With skepticism, she scrutinized his profile. Even in spite of what he'd just seen, Junker thought there was wiggle room in Strike's conscience? "Let's come up with a contingency plan… just in case."

EIGHT

RORA GOT OUT of her morning shower and wrapped herself in a towel. When she turned to wipe the steam from the mirror, she froze at the sight of what was on the vanity waiting for her.

A cupcake.

Her lips parted to let more air enter her tightening lungs. She looked around the small room but was definitely alone. That bastard! He had no honor, no decency, no morals. She didn't know who she was madder at, him for invading her personal space or herself for not realizing he would.

Snatching the cupcake, she tore the sponge to pieces to toss it down the toilet, having no intentions of eating something that could be tainted. She flushed, happy to wave goodbye to her smug ex's intrusion.

Just as she was about to ball up the paper case, she noticed something drawn on the inside. Inspecting it more closely, she read a street name, a marker of where Apocalypse was, and an X marking a spot further down.

With the paper still in her hand, she left the bathroom, scrutinizing the map and wondering if Junker was back with breakfast yet. She didn't expect to find Strike sitting on the couch, watching the video feed of the streets around them, a take-out coffee cup perched on one knee, his palm flat on the other.

"Oh my God," she exclaimed and ran over to put herself in front of him. "Strike!"

"Brought you coffee," he said, holding up the cup and then leaning forward to perch it on the edge of the table. "You're snarky without it."

His palm slid to his thigh, and she noted the picture she'd taken from the loft was beneath his fingers. But she didn't have time to think about what that meant.

She grabbed his arm and pulled him to his feet. "You have to get up! You have to go! Junker will be back any second!"

Strike just blinked. "You think I'm afraid of him?" he asked, lifting his arm out of her grip and tucking the picture into his pocket.

She'd only managed to get him as far as the end of the couch, but it was enough to allow her to get behind him to start pushing him toward the door. "You might not be afraid, but you shouldn't be in our personal space looking at our stuff!"

He scoffed and turned away from her pushing hands to face her. "You're smart enough to know Opal and I have been monitoring your feeds. Do you think it's hard for me to miss a spike like this? Intercepting it is nothing. Your bitch doesn't know how to mask his signature, not enough to fool me anyway. Do you know the kind of power this pulls from the grid? The bandwidth he's using? His setup is so crude it's amateur. But maybe I should thank the square, he saved me a lot of legwork."

Surrendering to the fact he'd do nothing against his will, and that the damage was done, Rora exhaled. "Strike," she said, putting her hands to her hips. "What do you want? Why are you here?"

"We need to get our plan straight."

That was shocking enough to bring her up short. "We?" she asked, her eyes widening. "We? Are you high? There's no we!"

But as was typical of him, he ignored her objection. "You only have to remember three things," he said, carrying on like she hadn't just basically laughed in his face. "One, you need a gun."

He pulled something out of his pocket and she was surprised to see a pistol in a small ankle holster. "What is that? I don't want that!"

But he took her wrist and turned her hand over to slap the gun onto her palm. He kept his hand over the weapon, pressing it down. "You point this at my head, not yours. I don't want any repeat of Wonderland. Remember, you had your one."

Rora tried to tug her hand away, but he kept hold of her for a second before lifting both of his hands, leaving her with the weapon. "Strike!" He was so frustrating. "What makes you think if I get a chance to point this at your head I won't pull the trigger?"

Why wasn't he mad at her? Why wasn't he trying to kill her? Was this a case of mutual destruction or was he expecting her to give up the real Point? It could be more manipulation. Maybe he'd got past anger and decided to manipulate her feelings for him to get what he wanted, just like he'd done the first time they were together.

"You had your chance to do that once, you didn't take it."

She gritted her teeth, filled with frustration and anger. "I was in love with you," she hissed. His hand rose like he intended to touch her face, but she stepped back. "I got over that."

A second of… something, passed between them, but he let it go to continue. "Two, take Opal." Fresh shock made her forget what had come before. "Hold the gun to my head, and take Opal… Try not to shoot Bella; I'll take care of her."

Rora knew how infuriating this man could be. She'd been dismissed by him in the past; he was used to being in control. But his attitude still aggravated her. "You can't be serious."

"Let your bitch say whatever he has to say, pull the gun, take Opal. The last thing's the most important, follow the map, meet me at midnight."

"Midnight?" she said, confused. "Strike, what game are we playing?"

Stepping in close, he trailed a fingertip along the top edge of her towel over her breast. "Kiss chase and I get to pick where I want your mouth when I win."

Rora slapped his hand from her body. "You're touching me."

"Get used to it," he said and winked. "Get dressed before your bitch comes back. I don't want him seeing you like this."

Strike started for the door. "He won't care about seeing me in a towel when he's already seen me naked."

It was probably petty of her to state that just to get a reaction, but she enjoyed seeing him tense up. Strike paused at the door and met her eye, his gaze cooled to a spiteful anger until his jaw ticked. When she saw that, she grinned and folded her arms, daring him to start a fight with her.

But he didn't say anything else, his chin just moved like he was grinding his teeth, then he turned and walked out, leaving her with a gun she'd have to hide from Junker and a map she didn't know if she'd follow.

"You're ready for this?" Rora said, peeking up at Junker. "Right?"

They'd reserved a private conference room at Bella's hotel and chosen to arrive early. Ascending the stairs that led from the lobby to the mezzanine floor above, they sought the room marked 'three.'

Junker seemed relaxed. His ease was making her kind of edgy because she was anything but calm.

"I'm ready, Aurora," he said and smiled at her. "Are you ready?"

To be in a room with the woman who'd held her captive and tortured her? To sit at the same table with the man who'd shattered her heart and now seemed to be playing with her?

Junker put a hand on room three's door handle and the other on her hip to direct her in front of him.

"Not even slightly," she murmured, but put her hand on his to push the handle down.

On entering the room, she did her best to project confidence. The small space contained an oval walnut table, surrounded by six chairs, three on each side. That was it, other than a fake plant in the corner and a Monet print on the wall. No cameras, no windows, no escape.

She and Junker weren't the only ones who'd decided to arrive early. Strike and Bella were already seated at the table, side-by-side.

Both of them stood up when Rora and Junker came to a stop just inside the closed door.

"Duckie!" Bella exclaimed and opened her arms.

But when Bella started around the table toward them, Junker put himself in front of Rora. "Keep your distance."

"Aww, he's possessive," Bella said, sounding like her lip was out in a pout. "We're all friends, everyone has to share… We will be the closest of friends. My Arousing Aurora is not afraid; there is nothing to be afraid of."

"She's afraid of imprisonment and torture," Junker said.

"Unfortunately, our wonderful prince has forbidden me from restraining or intoxicating my duckie tonight. But there are other forms of play. We three have a special affinity that cannot be restrained or denied. You may be allowed to join us, if our prince agrees to share us with you. But you cannot keep us apart."

"I promised to keep her safe."

Rora was afraid to look at Strike for fear he might choose to challenge the other male near Bella, who he considered his turf. She'd never heard Junker this tense before, and knew she'd have to diffuse this strain fast.

Sliding a hand down his arm, Rora got his attention. "It's ok," she murmured. "I'm ok."

Taking his hand, she led him over to their side of the table and all four of them sat down at the same time. Opal was at the head of the table, and after glancing at the laptop, she lifted her attention to Strike to find his on her. That mind, whatever was in it, he was keeping it to himself.

"We thank you both for coming," Junker said. Bella grinned, and Strike nodded once. "I'm sure you know why we're here."

"This is a waste of time," Strike muttered.

Bella laid her hands on the table. "Meeting down here is silly, we should go upstairs. I have a huge suite… and a beautiful bed."

Rora could only feel bad for Junker who didn't follow why Bella would make such a random statement. He didn't understand the woman, not that many could claim to. It wasn't so long ago that Rora had been the one in Junker's oblivious position.

"I… uh—"

Bella's sultry attention drifted to her. "Did you miss me, duckie? Shall I read you a story?"

Struggling to restrain her anger, Rora didn't feel fear; it was rage that made her insides quake. "How about I hold the whip this time?" she hissed.

Bella circled her lips and put a hand on Strike's shoulder, letting it slide across his chest to the opposite one so she was draped on him. "We could share his torment."

Blinking her attention to Strike's cool gaze, Rora thought about inflicting pain on the man who'd betrayed her, and smiled, keeping her lips tight. "I'm not averse to that idea. Strip him and string him up."

Squealing, Bella surged to her feet. But Strike seized her wrist and yanked her back into her seat. "You didn't come here to fuck around with games," Strike said, focusing on Junker. "What do you want, Square? The Jewel? You can have her. I don't give a fuck about that one."

Rora didn't read anything into the brief look Strike cast in her direction and turned her own attention to Junker. Letting Strike play any more with her already messed up head would be a recipe for disaster.

"If he wanted the Jewel, all he'd have had to do was show up," Rora said. "It's not like she knows how to keep her legs closed."

"Something you learned from her I guess," Strike said to her horror. "This one seems so nice and… suburban, Kero… Just your type… like Gallagher."

"Don't talk about Benjamin," she growled, infused with a fresh surge of fury.

"Suburban isn't my typical type," Bella said, probably not seeing the venom spitting between Rora and Strike. "But I like trying new things. Is that why we're here? To try each other?"

"We're here because," Junker started and stopped to clear his throat. "Because I want to appeal to your decency."

After a second of silence, Strike and Bella looked at each other. Strike slapped a hand on the table as Bella tossed her head back in a hearty laugh. Deflated, Rora didn't like their mocking, but she'd expected it.

"Decency?" Bella asked. "What's that?"

Strike nodded at Rora. "I bartered mine to her."

Ignoring him, Rora leaned toward Junker. "I told you. This is a lost cause."

"I don't believe in those," Junker said, giving her no choice but to flop back in her chair. "What you're planning, Exile, whatever it is, you have to understand what it could do to the world."

"I understand just fine," Strike said, locking his fingers together on the table.

"And you're… you'll sacrifice every other person in the world for your own benefit?" Junker asked.

It was sweet that Junker seemed unable to fathom Strike's position. Putting a hand on his forearm, Rora wanted to comfort him.

"Might spare one or two people… maybe," Strike said.

"I can't let you do it," Junker said. "Whatever you're planning, I'll figure it out and stop it."

"Figure it out?" Strike asked, his eyes drifted to her and he raised his brows. "Finally learning how to play the game, Ro?" This time, his gaze was more intense. She sucked her lip into her mouth, chewing on it hard. "Don't be nervous, just do it."

"Do it?" Junker asked, confused. "Do what?"

Confident, Strike didn't flinch. "If there was one thing I taught her, it was the power of contingencies. Whatever you've got going on Redd, it's not working," Strike said, leaning a fraction closer to her. "It's down to you. Are you gonna make me proud, Kero?"

Sucking a breath through her nose, she didn't want to be his pawn, but couldn't deny that separating him from Opal would give her side an advantage. Raising her knee beneath the table, she reached down to slide the gun from her ankle holster.

Pouncing to her feet, Rora pointed the gun at him. "Don't move," she said.

Strike just sank back in his chair, his back straight. He played his part well, appearing unimpressed, though unruffled.

"Oooh, a twist," Bella purred. "Do it, shoot him, duckie... We'll play with him as he bleeds."

Tempted as she was, Rora wasn't intending to shoot Strike, not as long as he stayed there on his side of the table.

"Get up, Junker, go," she said to him, grabbing at his jacket to urge him from his seat.

"What are you doing?" he asked, leaping up.

Rora pushed him toward the door. "What needs to be done."

But instead of following, she moved up the table and bent over to snag Opal. Still playing his part, Strike chose that moment to lose his ease. Even though they'd both known this was his plan, Rora still got a weird sense of satisfaction when Strike sat upright and laid both open hands on the table like he was pissed and caught off-guard.

"There's nowhere you can hide from me," her ex hissed. "I'll always be hiding somewhere close by, ready to pounce."

"Peek-a-boo," Bella said and laughed, but lounged against the rigid Strike. "She is so sexy when she's threatening you, prince. I want to watch you hurt her. Can I? Can I watch?"

Edging toward the door, Rora kept the gun trained on Strike, believing him to be the greatest threat. Besides, if she pointed the gun at Bella, Rora didn't trust herself not to shoot. One side step, another, and then she was almost at the door. Junker opened it and gestured her out.

"You bitch," Strike growled.

"Guess this bad is beyond even you," Rora said, lifting the gun and running out.

Hiding the weapon behind the computer she clutched to her chest, Rora only cast her eyes upward once they were halfway across the lobby. Strike stood on the mezzanine, glaring down at her with Bella at his side.

Junker put an arm around her. "We've got to get out of here."

The lobby was crowded, so Junker probably thought it gave them cover to get out, thinking Strike wouldn't hurt them in view of this many witnesses. But this was Strike's plan, though she didn't understand it yet, he wasn't coming after them.

All the way back to their hotel, Junker was looking over their shoulder. But she knew better. Strike didn't want to follow them, he knew where they were sleeping. He could pursue them any time he wanted to. The night had played out just as he'd instructed her it should.

Rora might resent herself for following his plan, if she didn't hope that Strike had just given them exactly what they were looking for. If the DARPA device was in Opal, then this could be over for Junker and he'd be out of danger.

As soon as they got inside their hotel room, Rora went to the coffee table and turned Opal upside down. "I need a screwdriver," she said, stroking the underside of the laptop.

"What? Why?"

There was too much adrenaline still in her system. Her fingertips were trembling. "Just get me a damn screwdriver!" she hollered.

Although taken aback, Junker jumped into action and retrieved his tools for her, then sat to watch her work. A discomforting sensation of violation hung deep in her gut when she began to unscrew a panel on the bottom of the machine. It took her a minute to carefully remove all the screws.

Rora held her breath when she popped off the panel and… "Damnit," she said and sank back to sit on her feet.

"What?" he asked. "What is it?"

"He took it out." Slamming a hand on the table, everything jumped, and she leaped to her feet to pace away. "The bastard! Why the hell would he…"

"What? What did he take out?"

Turning to face Junker, she saw the open look on his face and decided to give him a little more of her trust. "The top-secret tech that you want to take from him, he did install it in his computer… I know because… I saw him do it."

It took a minute for his expression to catch up with his thoughts. "You…" He got up. "Why didn't you tell me?" She wanted to tell him she had a complicated reason, but she didn't. It was trust. Nothing more. The shock of clarity left his face in time with the anger that struck him. "What the hell else haven't you told me?"

He was entitled to be mad. So far as she knew, Junker had always been honest with her, and she hadn't confessed even an ounce of what she truly knew. Maybe it was that knowledge that urged her to make another hard confession.

"I was the willing civilian," she said and sighed. "Exile didn't tell me anything about the meeting before we got there. But I was the one who took the device from the government official… not that I knew that's who he was at first." She dipped her chin. "If I had, I might not have bit him so hard."

"Shit," Junker breathed out, putting a hand on his chest. "You've seen it?" She nodded. "And you thought it was in the computer, that's why you took it?"

Yes, that was why she'd taken Opal. Strike would believe it was because he'd told her to, but she wouldn't have done it if she hadn't believed it would be in her side's best interest. Rora was trying to figure this out one step at a time and making the right choices wasn't easy.

Dropping onto her knees, she cupped the open panel on the back of the computer. "He took it out."

Junker sighed. "He might have considered that leaving it in his primary terminal was too obvious," he said, coming to sit in the armchair at the top of the coffee table.

"He's a bastard," she said, calming herself before picking up the metal plate she'd taken from Opal. "I'm sorry, honey."

"What are you apologizing to me for?" Junker asked. Focusing on the task at hand, she didn't want to admit she'd actually been apologizing to Opal. "I can do that if—"

"No," she said, replacing the screws. "I want to."

He leaned forward to stroke her shoulders. "You've got a bullseye on you now," he said. "You told me not to touch his computer and then you went and stole it. He won't be happy."

There was a hint of pride beneath his concerned smile. "I had to do something," she said. "Exile was never going to listen to you and I couldn't listen to their mocking anymore… Why did he call you Redd?"

"It's my last name," Junker said, flopping his arms on the arms of the chair. "Guess he wanted to let me know he was investigating me."

"Like we didn't know that already," she said, turning Opal over when she was done. Smoothing her hands over the lid, it was odd to feel so protective of this hunk of metal as Bella had once called it. "I guess we can give it back… maybe he'll forgive and forget."

"Do you think so?"

Pushing her lips to one side, she shrugged, and got up to go over to the fridge. "I say this night calls for a drink. Might be my last chance to have one. What do you say?"

The whiskey bottle was on top of the fridge and she chose the hard liquor tonight.

"I don't know," Junker said, and she thought he meant the alcohol. "Maybe there's something of use on the machine."

"No!" she called, spinning around to see his fingers hovering just an inch above the keys. "Don't touch that."

With the whiskey bottle in one hand, she rushed over to him and slapped Opal shut. "What? There could be something on here that we can use. Something that will give us a lead on where he might have put the device, or what he plans to do with Benjamin's work."

"You can't," she said, stroking Opal's lid. "If you touch her, she'll hurt you… She might kill you."

"She?" he asked, squinting at her like she might have lost her marbles. "You give computers a gender?"

Not her, Strike, but Rora wasn't going to admit that she knew the name of his machine. "Just… don't open her, don't touch her. Trust me, it hurts like a motherfucker."

He was surprised, either by her language or the revelation of her experience. "The computer injured you?"

"More than that," she said. "If she doesn't kill you, she'll make sure you spend the rest of your life behind bars."

Sliding back in the seat, he rubbed the arms. "Is that what you meant about protecting technology without hiding it?" She shrugged. "Exile wasn't wrong about contingencies, was he?"

Junker's opinion of Exile was evolving, just as hers had once. "You don't know whether to be terrified or impressed," she said, rising onto the couch and taking Opal with her. "I know. That's kind of how I felt about it."

"Why would he… that's really how he protects his tech?"

"His laptop anyway," she said, noticing the time on the wall clock.

"How does it work?"

Even if Strike had wasted his time telling her, she'd never have understood what he was saying. "Damned if I know," she said. "Let's have a drink and get an early night. You take the bed tonight."

"No, I don't have—"

"It's ok," she said. "You need your rest."

Rora had no idea what she was going to do later, but she had so many questions without any chance for answers unless she took a risk. It was a hell of a risk to take, but at this point, she had nothing left to lose.

NINE

RORA AND JUNKER hadn't talked much beyond finishing their drinks. Junker had shared his impressions of Strike and Bella, but Rora had kept her opinions to herself. Once their glasses were empty, they decided to get an early night, so they could be fresh for the next day.

Lying on the couch, listening to Junker's quiet snore, Rora stared at the shadows on the ceiling, trying not to think about Opal being so close to her.

She'd hidden the computer in the room at Junker's behest. But after he was asleep, she'd got up and moved the laptop to a new hiding place. Junker thought they were hiding it from Strike, but Rora was hiding Opal from everyone.

It reeked of the Point all over again. What kind of a person was she that she couldn't trust anyone? She'd lied to Benjamin about hiding the Point. She'd lied to Strike about finding it. Now she was lying to Junker about where she was keeping Opal.

But that wasn't the only thing she was lying to her newest friend about.

Turning her head, she read the time on the wall clock and closed her eyes to give herself a pep talk before throwing back the covers and getting off the couch.

She dressed in silence, and crept toward the door, looking back at the sleeping Junker one more time before slipping out into the night.

Knowing the route to Apocalypse was an advantage, but she had no idea what lay beyond. Going on past the mouth of the Apocalypse alley, she carried on along the river until the lights of the city faded.

Following the path of the crude map she'd memorized, Rora went down onto a dock that seemed long abandoned. She was supposed to look for a warehouse and—

A whistle made her stop and turn. Movement at the end of an alleyway diverted her path. Heading toward it, she found his outline loitering in a narrow space between buildings.

"You made it."

Folding her arms, Rora went to him. "You can't leave me messages in cupcakes, Strike."

"Turns out I can, 'cause here you are."

What she'd meant was he couldn't do it anymore. They weren't on the same side and she wouldn't be his pawn. Rora felt guilty enough that she hadn't told Junker about Strike's plan, or that he'd been in their room, she couldn't compound that guilt with more secrets.

"You're a cocky bastard," she said, annoyed with herself for following his instructions.

She should've known when his direction to "steal" Opal had turned out to be fruitless that coming wouldn't be of any benefit to her. Ready to get the hell out of there, Rora turned, intending to return to her side of this war.

But Strike caught her hand, stopping her in her tracks. Damnit, when he touched her, she started to forget her rage… she started to feel.

Her breath blocked her throat, and it took her ten seconds to muster the courage to swallow it away. His thumb moved in a slow slide over her skin… the contact messed with her screwed-up head.

Lifting her eyes over her shoulder, she found him peering into her. "If you hadn't come here, I'd have come for you."

Words weren't as powerful as actions. "Like you did when Bella kidnapped me?" she asked, snatching her hand away from his. "You didn't give a damn about me then, did you?"

"I didn't know she had you," he said. "And the minute I did, I got you out."

"What the hell are you—"

"You think your bitch's anonymous tip was a coincidence? Who do you think blackmailed Bella's minions into standing down? Who do you think kept her busy while your bitch took you out of there? You don't think it was odd that you got away so clean?"

Junker had said he'd got a tip about her location. She'd been too out of it to analyze that information or to consider who his source could be. "I was…"

"You wouldn't have come quietly if I'd showed up," he said, proving he knew little of how out of it she'd been. "Soon as I realized you were off the grid I knew someone was holding you. There's no one capable of hiding you from me. You don't have a long list of enemies, and you know the list of people who are aware of the Point is short. Didn't take me long to figure it out."

He'd suspected that the Black Jewel was alive; he'd told her as much. Rora had thought it proved the sad state of her life that no one had cared enough to notice that she was missing… apparently Strike had noticed.

She was stuck in a state of disbelief, trying to put the pieces together, and trying to decide if she should believe him or not. "Why aren't you mad at me?" she heard herself ask.

He had to have realized that she'd conned him. "Same reason I came back for you when you got yourself arrested… Are you going to make me say it?" he asked. "Like you did in the loft?" Lifting his curled fingers to the underside of her jaw, he stroked her. "Are you sleeping with him?"

Shaking off her disbelief, she pushed his hand away, reminding herself of how he liked to use her weakness for him against her. The question annoyed her so much, that it was easy to regain her determination.

"None of your business."

"You can't trust him."

"Coming from you that statement works in his favor," she said. "Didn't you just say you trusted him to save me?"

Clenching his jaw, his voice dropped to a growl. "The bastard made no secret of the fact that he was looking for you. He sent out a damn beacon to everyone who wants what they think you have." The Point. "So, yeah, I knew he'd get you away from Bella, but that doesn't mean I trust him to keep you safe or to put your best interests first."

"Something you'd know all about," she said.

He ignored her jibe. "His name is Dexter Redd, he went to MIT, worked in the computer science research division. Except, he's—"

"He's suburban. I get it, Strike." Rora was getting tired of the games. "Why don't you tell me what the hell this is about? Why did you want me to take Opal? She doesn't have what Junk's looking for."

"I don't know what he's looking for. I could guess, but I don't care that much."

Didn't take her long to figure out that statement was a lie. "Yes, you do," she said. "But let's say I believe you, why tell me to take her?"

"I have my reasons."

Bobbing her head, she hated him being so cagey. "Ok, so why shouldn't I just drop her into a dumpster? If me bringing her inside has planted something in our room—"

"I was in your room," he said.

Valid point. He didn't need her to take his computer to spy on them, he could've planted something himself. If he hadn't hung around and left the cupcake, she wouldn't have known he was in there. Junker hadn't.

"You're such a creep sometimes, Strike."

"I'm a creep all the time." A noise made him stop to look up, but he took her arm and turned her around, putting her against the wall. "Did you tell him you were coming here?"

"No, I didn't," she said. "Then I'd have had to explain that you set me up to take a useless laptop."

"You didn't let him touch her," he said, his lips slanting.

Socking his shoulder, Rora didn't appreciate his look of satisfaction. Strike's implant would have notified him if someone unauthorized made contact with Opal's keyboard.

"I hope that wasn't what you were banking on. He's a good man, Strike. He's not from your world. He's just trying to do the right thing."

"I remember you were like that once," he said.

When he tried to touch her face, she ducked back and pushed his hand away. "I'm still trying to do the right thing."

"I know," he said. "Trying to stop my evil plan… You can't stop it. There's nothing you can do. I'm close."

That… that brought her up short.

"What?" she asked. Did he mean the Point? How could he be talking like he had the Point when he didn't? "Are you playing me?"

"Always, Cupcake," he said. "There's still space at my side for you."

Her jaw loosened. Strike didn't know he didn't have the Point!

Either he was lying to her or… he had never accessed the device. Her heart might as well have stopped, she was so stunned. He hadn't looked at what was on the USB. He wanted her to think he was working on perfecting the program, but she knew that was impossible because he didn't have it.

She'd told him if he used the Point that she'd be gone from his life forever. He'd put the drive into his machine but… he hadn't looked at what was on it. He'd chosen her. Rora was dumbfounded. For some reason he didn't want her to know it, but… he'd chosen her!

"Flame," she whispered, too shocked to realize she'd used the name of her lover, which he wasn't.

"That's better," he said, edging closer.

But she put her hands to his chest and tried to regain her senses. Strike didn't know that she'd double-crossed him. For now, that put her at an advantage. He believed he had everything he needed to enact his plan to use the Point if he chose to.

The fact that he hadn't done it suggested that either his decency wasn't as non-existent as he'd declared it to be, or that she had more sway with his conscience than she'd realized.

"I didn't mean that."

"I think you did," he said, his eyes growing heavier. "You're not done with me, baby."

Being pressed against him was too much for her bitter mind to deal with. "I am, I'm done," she said, but her voice was so weak it was just a breath.

She didn't even believe herself. Rora had been afraid to be near him again, thinking he'd be murderous after her deception. Learning that he had no intention of hurting her, and that her aversion to world domination had sparked a change in him, Rora was unsure of what to do.

" 'Cause you think you've got yourself a new guy? I can delete him for you, baby, slit his throat while he sleeps, then it'll be just you and me again."

All those days in Bella's basement, trying unsuccessfully to hate this man, came back to her. Maybe this had been the reason why she couldn't hate him; he hadn't really betrayed her at all. Maybe his feelings hadn't been as false as she'd feared. This was a lot to digest and completely unexpected.

Shaking her head, she licked her lips. "He's a good man and the Jewel is—"

"Crazy," he said.

"I'm crazy."

Saying it didn't sting as much as it used to, maybe because she was learning there were worse things to be.

"I'll make her pay for whatever she did to you, Cupcake. Your new guy's not capable of protecting you like I can. Will he go to any lengths to protect you no matter how naughty you are?"

Protection, something she craved, a partner who'd hold her up and stand to fight her battles with her. Sounded great, but Strike wasn't perfect. "He has a heart."

It made her ache all over when she gazed into Strike's eyes and felt herself falling all over again. Remembering the night they'd first made love, she thought about those eyes, about the way they'd made her feel adored. Could it have been real? Why did he have to ruin it?

"Can't claim to have one of those," he said. "I gave whatever was left of mine to you."

"Stop it," she hissed, the warmth of tears stinging the corners of her eyes. "This isn't you. You're manipulating me. I don't know why but I… don't do this to me again. Please, Strike."

The back of his fingers drifted up the side of her neck. He'd never been tender like this when they were together. But over the last couple of days it was like he couldn't keep his hands off her.

All she could guess was that he was trying to create a connection between them, and she hated him for it because she feared it was working. Rora wanted to feel those hands on her again, wanted him to tell her she was safe, wanted to look into his scowling eyes and smile just like she used to.

"Do you trust him, Ro? More than you trusted me?"

Rage and bitter heartache surged up inside her. "I want to trust him, Strike," she said, her eyes burning, her throat stinging and growing tight. Smacking his chest, she blew out her frustration. "I want to trust him. But I can't trust him. I can't trust anyone! That's what you taught me, Flame." She spat out the pet name like it disgusted her. "You taught me not to trust anyone! That everyone will screw me over because everyone's out for themselves!"

"You can trust me."

That was a gut punch. She lost her fury and just blinked at him. "What? No… No, you told me not to trust you. You made me walk away."

"You chose to walk away," he said. "You chose this."

Was he blaming her for killing their relationship? All she'd asked him to do was not put the supposed Point USB into the port and he'd done it.

"This was you," she said. "You chose the Point over me."

"You're stuck in the past again, think about the future. I want to know if you're fucking him."

Always back to the same point. It was so typical of a man to be more concerned about the physical than the emotional scars they'd caused. "Why should I tell you? Why is it your business if—"

"We said no one else."

On their first night together, when she'd thought they had a future. "We said no other women," she sneered. "Nothing was said about men, and you don't imply, do you? Maybe you should've been more specific."

"If he's touched you, I'll geld him, Ro… It's as simple as that. Think before you answer me because I'll take your word either way. If you don't answer, I'll do it just in case. Are you fucking him?"

If she needed any reminder that Strike was stronger than her, he was delivering the message. Fighting him would be the end of her, Rora knew it. She shook her heavy head. She was exhausted, physically, emotionally, in every way a person could be.

Almost ready to give up like she had been once before, she recalled that it had been this man who'd held her up.

"Strike," she whispered, wanting to believe that he valued her.

"You're not?"

"No," she wheezed out and surrendered to her urge to confide in him. "I think he wants to… he kissed me."

Why was she confessing this to him? Why did she feel herself leaning on the man who'd screwed her over? Maybe because she'd just learned that he hadn't screwed her over, he'd just used the Point to push her away and it had worked. Just like she'd said to Junker, Strike needed to believe he didn't need a human connection. One sure way to protect himself was to get rid of her and the Point had given him a way to do that.

There might be no hope for their relationship, but he'd just proved to her, without realizing it, that he wasn't as black-hearted as he'd wanted her to believe.

"Kissed you," he said, easing closer until he was pressed against her. Putting a fingertip to the underside of her chin, he pushed it up and lowered his mouth onto hers in a light brush. "Like that?" She shook her head. Kissing her again, harder this time, he held for a second and then looked at her. "Like that?"

"No," she breathed out.

His next kiss was a fraction longer, a fraction harder, and when his tongue touched her lip, she tried to lower her mouth, but he pushed her chin up again. "Like that?"

"Kind of," she said because kissing one man was nothing like kissing the other.

"So, not like this," he murmured and sank down to kiss her again.

Inhaling hard, his tongue delved into her mouth to twist around hers. He withdrew, and returned, teasing and tempting her. This was a bad idea. She shouldn't be standing here in this dark space alone with the man who'd stolen from her and left her tied to a bed.

The weight of his arm on the top of her head made her shift to accommodate his forearm at the back of her neck so she could rest her head against it. This was what she remembered, the strength of his arm hooked tight around her neck, the weight of his head suspended over hers as he pressed his mouth to hers and fought her tongue with his own.

But he bent lower and she didn't know what he was doing until his other arm hooked her thighs and lifted her up onto the utility box beside them.

"Strike," she said when he pushed up her skirt. "We can't."

Resting his forehead on hers, he stroked her thighs, dragging his fingers down her flesh and skimming them back up. "Say you don't want to… say it out loud, Cupcake. Tell me you haven't thought about having me inside you again." Clutching her face, he met her eye. "I need to be inside you, Ro… I'll spiral if you deny me, and that never works out for anyone."

Could she keep him grounded? Save his sanity by offering him her body? "I don't trust you," she whispered.

His expression became knowing, confident. "Never stopped you before. Do you want me?"

Damn him for being smug, even though he had every right to be. Her heart was beating hard, her chest heaving. Their panting breaths merged and when he tipped his head to join their lips again, her eyes closed slowly.

"Fuck you, Strike," she breathed. "Fuck you for what you do to me."

"Shh," he said. "I'm not listening."

"You never do," she panted, her fingers seeking his belt.

Desperately pursuing his kiss while pulling open his fly, she tried to maintain constant contact with his mouth. It sucked and licked at hers with a haphazard fury she struggled to keep up with, but her building need matched his.

Leaning away, she propped herself on an arm and lifted her hips to wriggle out of her panties. He wasn't patient, as soon as she had one leg out, he grabbed her thighs to yank them apart and hauled her to the edge.

Strike plunged into her. She tossed an arm around his shoulders, giving herself a leverage point to lift her hips in time with him slamming into her. Pulling her around to put her back to the wall, his fingers dug into her flesh, holding her at the very edge of the cool metal beneath her.

"Oh, fuck," she hissed. "This is so fucking stupid. What the hell am I doing?"

Pulling her pelvis up, he wrapped one arm around her hips to keep them engaged and grabbed her hair in the other to yank her head back so he could press his forehead against hers.

Their hot breath blended. "You're being bad," he said and ducked forward to let his tongue lap her upper lip. "Told you to get used to misbehaving."

Because he'd bring it out in her. Smacking his shoulders with both hands, she wanted to punch him for being him, as much as she wanted to feel his thick girth occupying her every minute.

"I hate you," she said, but couldn't tell herself to mean it. "I trusted you."

"Back then I told you not to. Now I'm saying different," he said. "You fuck with my head, Cupcake."

"Good," she said, squirming against his groin when he started rocking his hips again.

"I never needed anyone," he grunted. "Never needed a damn thing… until you came along."

"Stop it," she said, hating that his words affected her. "Stop trying to get under my skin again."

"Is that anger I hear in your voice, Cupcake?"

A tremor of arousal racked her when she recalled how he'd fucked her the last time she'd been vibrating with rage. "Yes."

"Hmm," he said and froze for a second, considering options.

Letting her fall against the wall, he grabbed the hem of her shirt and forced it up to expose her bra. Yanking the cups out of the way, he sealed his mouth around one nipple and the sensation of him sucking on her made her tighten her legs around his hips and moan. He moved to the other, licking it before he bit her so hard that she squealed.

Arching into the kisses he spread across her breasts, she hummed and whimpered until he rose to kiss her mouth again. "Fuck me, Strike," she panted, her eyes closed, her head rolling against the wall. "Oh, God, fuck me."

Thrusting into her, he didn't stop this time, didn't slow down until he'd brought her to climax and fired his seed into her.

"The Square won't ever kiss you like that," he said, his breathing heavy. What they'd just done went far beyond kissing. He stepped back, leaving her there in a mess, propped on the utility box and draped against the wall. "Keep Opal until I tell you otherwise."

He buttoned his jeans. Rora was still breathing through the aftershocks of her climax, so it took her a second to figure out what he was talking about. Forcing herself to get it together fast, Rora found that the lace on her bra was torn, but she hid it inside her top anyway and pulled her skirt down.

"Why did you need me to take her?"

"She'll protect you. You're safer together," he said and propped a fist on the metal surface at either side of her thighs, not touching, but coming close enough that she felt his breath on her face. "You need an ally and Opal's it. I'm telling you not to trust the square."

"I don't take orders from you, Strike," she said, putting her foot on his thigh to try pushing him away, but he didn't move.

"Trusting him would be a mistake. I don't trust him."

"You don't trust anyone."

"I trust you," he said.

When she searched for mocking in his eyes, she found none. "No, you don't." Rora swallowed. "You're just saying that."

"I told you to point a gun at my head. Told you to take Opal. And you're the only other one with access to her. She's at your disposal. Would I have done that if I didn't trust you?"

He seemed so certain, the guy barely blinked. "I can touch her?"

Tilting his head, he leaned in to brush his lips over hers. "Did you forget our first night together?"

No, she hadn't. Somehow, she could read his memories of that night playing behind his eyes and a bolt of heat fired through her. They'd just had sex, but she felt herself being seduced by him all over again.

"I… I assumed you'd reversed that," she said. All of this was more than she'd expected, his attitude, his words, his actions. She didn't get it. "You're manipulating me, you're trying to… I don't know what you're doing, but I don't like it."

"You can trust me, Ro," he said, skimming the back of his fingers over her cheek.

"Are you sleeping with the Jewel?" He didn't really shake his head, but it kind of swayed from one side to the other. Rora breathed out, letting her head fall onto his shoulder. "The stuff nightmares are made of."

Bending his knees, he put space between them and pressed his fingertip under her chin again. "Find out what you can about this guy. Facts I know, but read between the lines, try to figure out if—"

"I'm not your double agent," she said. "I did what I did at the meeting because… I wanted Opal."

"Bella, Opal," he said, narrowing one eye. "I said you had a thing for the ladies."

Smiling, she watched her fingertip move down his jaw. "Technically, I slept with both of them before I had sex with you."

When her eyes flicked to his, she dropped the smile. What the hell was she doing? She was acting like everything was normal between them and it wasn't. She couldn't be naïve enough to let him back into her heart without any explanations.

"One of 'em is welcome in our bed, the other isn't," he said, taking her hand off his face and putting it on her leg.

"You're not going to tell me not to flirt with you?" she asked, suspicious of his motives for being nice to her. "And we don't have a bed, not an 'our' bed."

"No?" he asked, pushing her skirt up the front of her thighs to expose her legs. " 'Cause you seemed at home raiding our stores in the loft."

"Our?" she asked, nudging him away when he kissed her collarbone. "What game are you playing, Strike? We broke up. Nothing is 'us' or 'we' or 'ours.' I know you say you trust me, but how can you when I took up with another guy and chased you across the country?"

"Trust you?" he asked and straightened to fold his arms. "You're not sleeping with him. You didn't take him into the loft. You didn't tell him my name. I'll bet there's plenty you haven't told him… Like it or not, Cupcake, you're still protecting me… protecting us."

But this time, she could take his certainty down a notch. "Maybe I'm just embarrassed to admit that I ever loved you," she said, sliding down onto her feet. "All those things are true, but I did tell him how to find you in Apocalypse."

But he was smirking again. "Then you came with him and stood between us to make sure no one got hurt."

She had done that, but he'd misread her motivation. "To protect him, not you."

"I am the better fighter."

He could turn anything to his advantage and it infuriated her. "You didn't have to hit him, that was just rude," she said. "I was so mad at you for that and I… I'd promised myself I wouldn't ever speak to you again and then somehow I was there at your table screaming at you."

"Turning me on," he said, moseying closer. "I love it when you turn that fury on me."

"Because you're a masochist. You'd probably have preferred it if I just walked up and punched you in the face," she said.

His brow rose in a way that told her she wasn't wrong. "Difference between you and Bella, you'll never hit back."

Hearing that made her feel angry and sick, but she just frowned at him. "Don't do that. Don't compare us… ever. And she'd actually like it if you hit her back. Me, I'd take the first opportunity I had to cut off your balls."

"Defend yourself or die."

Bowing lower, he tried to kiss her again, but she pushed him away. "I'm not what you think I am. None of this is what you think it is. I haven't kept all your secrets. I told Junker that you shot Bella."

"Saving you. After I found you in bed together. Did you tell him that?" he asked. Rora squirmed and his pride grew. "You told him just enough but not everything. What else?"

She'd made this evening too easy for him already; she wasn't going to keep on feeding him information. "I'm not going to tell you everything."

"You're right. We don't have time," he said, looking at his watch. "I should get back. I told Bella I'd swing by."

"Out of one pussy and straight into the next."

One side of his mouth rose, forcing his lips into a slant. "Envy is a mortal sin, Cupcake," he said. "We'll work on committing the others soon. Chin up."

Leaning forward, he kissed her fast and then turned to walk away. "Strike," she called out. "Strike, don't you…"

But he walked around the end of the building and she was left to stare at the black wall opposite her. What the hell had just happened and why the hell did she keep falling for this guy?

TEN

THE FOLLOWING MORNING was a tense limbo of talking and not talking. Rora and Junker agreed they would be safer if they left the city, but where could they go? Their mission wasn't over. But it was at an impasse.

So, they had to stay. But to do what? As long as they had Strike and the Black Jewel in their sights, Junker didn't want to lose them. The original plan was to monitor the pair, and he wanted to stick with that until they came up with a better idea of how to get the tech away from Strike.

Then there was the next debate: to return the computer or not to return the computer?

One thing was certain, Junker didn't know about her middle-of-the-night encounter with Strike.

But she did.

She couldn't get it off her mind. Rora was mad at herself for letting Strike kiss her. If he hadn't kissed her, they never would've… had they really had sex out there? Out there in the open?

Ok, so it was a secluded spot, but there was no denying that it was crazy to take that kind of risk. Didn't master criminals usually get caught, not for their primary crime, but for some stupid, insignificant act… like public indecency?

If they were both locked up, and Opal was out of Strike's control, how would they be able to get free?

They, them, we, us, our. Her mind connected them as a couple, a duo, so easily, and it wasn't meant to be that way. Rora had never made a conscious decision to connect herself to him like he was an extension of her, but somewhere along the way, it had happened and now she couldn't switch it off.

Beyond thoughts of her craziness and their relationship, she was preoccupied by his assertion that he had the Point. There was no way Benjamin had switched the drives out; he hadn't known what she'd done. Strike couldn't have it. He just couldn't.

And the more she thought about it, the more she figured if Strike had wanted to use the program, he'd have deployed it by now. He wouldn't be chasing Bella's requests or coming to meetings with her and Junker if he was working on the Point. He'd have worked every hour, every minute, tirelessly, until he got it perfect and then he'd have set it free in the world to work for him.

So he hadn't used the program, hadn't figured out yet that she hadn't given it to him. Their relationship, whatever it was, might change when he discovered her double-cross. Unless she told him the truth first… but, yeah, she was in no rush to do that.

She and Junker had lunch and then dinner, watching the cameras and seeing nothing. Just as night began to threaten they saw a blurred figure enter Bella's hotel lobby. It went into the elevator, and the next they saw it, it was entering Bella's suite.

"There he is," Junker said. "That's him, right?"

Rora didn't want to watch the way Bella greeted Strike or how the beauty took his arm and plastered herself to him. "That's him," she sighed, swirling her wine in the bottom of her glass.

Strike had been in Rora and Junker's room yesterday, so he knew Bella's suite was being watched, that she'd see everything. Just as Rora began to speculate that maybe he was going to put on a show with Bella just to fuck with both women's heads, he took Bella's arm from his and pushed her away.

"Oh, she doesn't look happy," Junker said, and he was right.

But Strike bowed to whisper something to Bella and the woman grinned with delight. Whatever he'd said, she liked. Strike turned to leave Bella's side and the two went in different directions. He moved to the window and just before closing the drapes, he opened his hand in a static wave.

"Damn, was that for us?" Junker asked, hitting the table. "How do you think he knew we were watching?"

Bella popped into the bedroom and closed the drapes fast, blocking them out from every angle. Either the couple were about to have sex or Strike was going to kill the Jewel, but Bella probably wouldn't have been so happy about that, and she'd been fizzing with excitement after Strike whispered to her.

Draining her glass, Rora put it on the table and got up. "I'm going out."

"You're… what? We have to talk about this. How do you think he knew about—"

She opened her hands to the screens. "The cameras are transmitting to us, he can intercept the signals, I don't know."

Except she did because she'd seen him sitting in front of their setup, but she hadn't told her ally that. Strike had made a liar out of her. Made sense, she was corrupted in every other way a person could be corrupted. But that didn't mean she liked herself for it.

"We have his computer."

He'd been monitoring them since long before she'd taken Opal, but Rora couldn't tell Junker that either. "But not his phone," she said. "He has military-grade tech in the phone he built himself. It does things I didn't think NASA could do… besides, he can do wonders with any terminal he puts his hands on."

"That's not hero worship I hear is it?"

Junker's smirk was so different to Strike's. Her friend's smirk was usually a prelude to a laugh, whereas Strike's could be followed by a knife to the throat. At one time, she'd called Strike her God, but that didn't mean she considered him a hero.

When she turned her lip into her mouth, she was trying to hide a laugh and it wasn't one of shame. "Hero is not a word I'd ever connect to Exile," she said and went over to retrieve her jacket.

Checking her pockets for her room key, her new switchblade, and her cash, Rora started for the door.

"Wait," Junker said and jumped to his feet. But he didn't know whether to stay with the video feed or go with her; he looked from one to the other and back. "I… you might not be safe out there."

But she nodded to the image of Bella's closed drapes. "We know where they are. They're not going to hurt me while they're keeping each other entertained," she said. "I won't be long."

Stepping out onto the porch, she took a deep, cleansing breath and then started across the parking lot. Rora couldn't be in there watching those drapes, not knowing what was going on inside Bella's suite.

Not that she'd really necessarily feel better if she could see in the room. Rora had been that woman. The one beneath Strike, under his body, his hands, his mouth, his power… Watching him pleasure Bella would be the worst kind of torture she could imagine.

It wasn't fair of her to think that way, not when she'd told herself their relationship was over, and chastised Strike for acting like it wasn't. Strike was a free agent. But that didn't mean she wanted to see him take advantage of that freedom, especially with the woman who'd tortured her.

While walking down the block, she realized that she didn't remember how to walk slowly anymore. Lifting her chin, she started to do the standard scan that had become a part of her life, checking for anything sinister or suspicious.

One figure stood out.

Slowing when she spotted him, Rora began to curse herself for leaving the room. He tipped his head to the side and then slipped through a doorway.

Blowing out a breath, she considered turning and running away, but knew better. This guy wasn't going anywhere, and it was no accident that she'd seen him. Checking the street, she crossed and went through the doorway he'd used.

She was the rat following the moving cheese. The cheese stood at the top of a set of stairs. She rolled her eyes, but he didn't respond, he just carried on up the next set of stairs.

On getting to the top of that flight, she noticed him by a doorway at the other end of a corridor. He went inside what could only be some kind of apartment, and she started heading his way. Though she did think it would serve him right if she turned and walked away instead.

When she entered, she found herself in a living room set up with furniture so new it looked like it might just have been delivered. As far as she could see, the room was empty of people. But the door closed, and she turned to find her cheese behind the door.

"Torres," she said, folding her arms.

"Kero."

"You're looking good," she said, checking out the cargo shorts and the loud shirt. "Undercover?"

"Sometimes the best way to hide is in plain sight."

"Straight from the NSA handbook?" she asked and moistened her lips. "So, what am I doing here, Agent?"

"Thought we should have a catch up."

"A catch up," she said. "No police station? No threat of arrest? Just buddies shooting the breeze?"

"That's it," he said, going past her into the body of the room. "Would you like a drink?"

She almost laughed. "I'm not going to drink anything you pour for me."

Because there was no one to swoop in and save her this time. If Torres drugged her and she was carted off to some NSA stronghold, Junker would have no chance of getting her out. Though she'd probably be treated better as a government captive than as Black Jewel's slave… maybe.

Putting down the bottle he'd just picked up, Torres opened his hand toward a chair. "Then would you like to sit down?"

But she wasn't ready to relax. "Did he send you here? You got another little doohickey he passed to you? Whatever he wants—"

"This time it's for real," he said.

The ease of his form grew more serious in sync with his expression. He sat down and then gestured to the perpendicular chair.

Considering him, she decided she wouldn't drop her guard, but crept over to the chair he'd indicated and sat down on the edge. "What is it you want?"

"Everything."

Now she sank back in the chair. Crossing her legs, she folded her arms, a smirk tickling her lips. "Really?" she drawled.

"We've never been in this position before. He's never had a… you."

"I'm not a me," she said, her head buzzing. The NSA knew how to talk in riddles; she'd have to learn their language. "Whatever you thought I was, or I thought I was… I'm not."

He nodded slowly. "You bitter yet?"

A smile came before a whisper of a laugh and she slid higher to sit straighter. "Was… maybe… But then I remembered he is who he is and taking what he does personally would be… indulgent… of me."

"What happened between you?"

Her smile got wider and with her elbows on the arms of the chair, she linked her fingers. "Now we're girlfriends? You want to hear about a crazy, passionate affair fueled by crime and sex and debauchery?" His brows rose. "You'll be disappointed. It wasn't like that."

Though it wasn't far off, it might have been more like that if Strike had given in to his feelings for her sooner.

"What was it like?"

Impossible to explain to someone like him, not that she would ever share such a private part of herself with him. Rora maintained her glib façade. "They don't teach you how to ask more subtle questions?" she asked. "Whatever went on between him and me, I don't want to see him rotting in prison… He's too brilliant to be caged… Even if he is a prick."

The corner of his mouth curled. "He is a prick," he said and shifted closer, twisting toward her. "But you misunderstand what it is we want. I don't want him in jail… I want him on payroll."

She didn't expect that, but as she sat examining Torres, she could tell he was serious, and it made sense. "You want…"

"Think about it," he said. "Makes sense for both of you. You could have a life with him, Kero. A real life. A home. A family."

"Wow," she breathed out and he smiled, but she wasn't thinking about how great that would be, she was thinking about how oblivious Torres was. "You don't understand him at all." Torres' smile fell. "Do you know how bored he would be sitting in an office?"

"Doesn't have to be that way," he said. "He can work in the field. He can live his life just like he does now. We'd just toss him some assignments, set him some challenges."

"Give him rules," she said. "He doesn't react well to rules."

"We wouldn't expect him to wear a suit and park in his designated spot. Doing what we do can be quite exciting."

Her lips twisted. "So is what we do," she said, then corrected herself. "What he does."

"This deal doesn't have to include you. If you want to give us what we need and take off, that's fine too."

"But if I talk, you'd have enough to blackmail him into working for you," she said. "Work with you or go to jail, those would be his options, right?"

Rora didn't have it in her to ruin his life or to take control of it from him. If she told Torres everything she knew about Exile, Strike would suffer for his alter-ego's crimes.

Sure, they were one and the same man, but there was something in Strike that didn't believe himself worthy of the freedoms others took for granted. Like the freedom to love. He certainly didn't believe he deserved that one.

Pushing at her, provoking her, like he had when they'd got close the night they talked about his mother's suicide for the first time, it was his way of keeping himself isolated. That was the reason he'd held off from touching her for so long. Some part of her knew he believed if he just didn't give in to his feelings, they'd go away.

But they hadn't.

They'd embraced those feelings and then she'd given him a final chance to sever their connection when she'd presented the Point to him. Of course he'd stolen it from her and made her think he was evil. Of course he wanted her to think he'd betrayed her. If she hated him, he didn't have to worry about losing her love. It was all part of his need to be in control. If he betrayed her first, he didn't have to worry about her doing it to him later.

God forbid, he just let their relationship run its course and take the knocks as they came. He had to hold the reins, even if that meant she became a casualty of his unspoken insecurity.

Everyone had left him, starting on the day he'd been born when his mother killed herself. His grandfather had beaten him, passed him off to anyone who'd care for him and then just as he built a connection with a new family, his grandfather would come and steal him away from them.

Strike had never been allowed the chance to form a true, honest relationship with anyone. Even Bella had been a toxic influence in his life, he'd said that himself.

Rora knew he felt the way he did because she wasn't so different. It was the reason she hadn't trusted Benjamin or Strike with the real Point. Somewhere along the way, she'd come to believe that everyone in her life had the potential to snap and turn on her, just like Kyan had done when he exterminated their family.

"Give us everything on him," Torres said, pulling her from her reflection. "I can tell you're thinking about it."

He'd misunderstood her silence. Leaning closer, she waited until she had his complete focus. "I don't want him to change," she murmured. "You talk to me like I'm an ally, like I want him to have this personality overhaul. What you've failed to notice is that if I am what you say I am, I'm your biggest hurdle. I don't want him to change, Mr. Torres, 'cause frankly, if he was on your payroll, he wouldn't be in my bed."

That surprised him, and he didn't do a great job of hiding it. "I thought your story wasn't about crime and sex."

"It's not the crime or the sex," she said, sitting back with a dismissive wave of her hand.

"Then what is it?" he asked, shuffling to the edge of his chair and linking his hands between his knees. "Help me understand what it is that provokes this loyalty, 'cause if you're right that you wouldn't be on board, I need to work on flipping you."

That was funny, but she didn't laugh, she just shook her head. "I told you, I'm not what you think I am. I'm not a factor in his life anymore."

"Funny that you're both in the same city at the same time then," he said. Rora just raised her brows in response. "It's the Black Jewel. Has she got something going on with him?" Tightening her linked fingers, she raised her shoulders and stuck out her lip in a gesture meant to convey ignorance. "You do know that she's dangerous. Unhinged dangerous."

"Have you met her?"

"Not directly."

Rora adjusted her legs to fold them under her. "Then you have no idea, Mr. Torres," she said. "No idea what that woman is capable of."

Peering at her, it was obvious that he was trying to figure her out, and it was funny to see him fail. "I've met you," he said. "And I still have no idea what you're capable of… I haven't forgotten about that little criminal damage stunt. All your victims were miraculously compensated by the way… 'cept one of the drivers. He's going to be serving a serious amount of time in prison… Want to explain how that happened?"

She shrugged again, exuding feigned ignorance. "Sometimes people do bad things, Mr. Torres."

"But not you, you don't do bad things?"

Touching the center of her top lip with her tongue, she pouted. "Why don't you ask our mutual friend that question the next time you talk to him?"

"You've got quite the mouth on you, Kero," he said. "Should I ask Exile about that mouth too?"

Seeing an opportunity, she got serious. "That thing you gave me, the DARPA toy… What is it?"

Torres smirked in a way that made her want to claw his eyes. "He never told you?"

"He told me… in his own way," she said, rolling her eyes again.

"If I tell you, you'll owe me one."

Holding up a finger, she indicated one. "You answer my question and I'll answer one of yours. A who, where, why, or when question."

"Ok," he said and nodded once. "It's a processor… with apparent infinite capacity."

"It could be used to run any number of programs at a time?"

He nodded. "Or process infinite amounts of data… it's a prototype, not perfect yet, but better than anything that's available out there now."

Now she understood why Exile wanted it and why he'd been excited by the idea of the Point. With that device, he had the ability to not only process a handful of data, but a globe's worth, just like he'd said in the resort suite when she first explained what the Point was designed to do.

"Ok, what's your question?"

"What—"

"Ah," she said and held up her finger again. "I said, who, where, why or when, not what." His gusto vanished in a puff of breath and while he was deflated, she was triumphant. "You don't have to ask anything at all… I'll let you ask a how question if you want."

Bobbing his head, he got near to her and lowered his voice. "How do I turn him?"

Bowing nearer, she touched his knee with her fingernail and mimicked his tone. "That one's easy." His eyes widened. "You don't."

Springing to her feet, she started for the door.

"Kero," he called after her, but she opened her arms. "That's it?"

"That's my answer," she said, relieved when the door opened under her hand and she learned that she wasn't locked in. "You don't turn him. He doesn't want to work for you and he doesn't care enough about anything that he can be manipulated. Pursue him as much as you like, but the truth is, I'm not sure you'd want him… he's unwieldy."

She turned to go. "Kero?"

Rora turned back. Torres came across the room and held out a small circular metal device in the middle of his palm, no bigger than a quarter. "If you change your mind, press the button in the middle, it will send out a signal to tell me you want to talk." Peering at him, she didn't believe him for a second. "I promise, no tricks, it won't track you unless you press the button… and hey, free tech, right? Just… don't tell Exile."

Taking the disc, she inspected it as she walked out. But before she got to the street, she popped it into her inside pocket and went back to the hotel. Torres obviously knew where she was staying, so she didn't have to worry about being tracked to her hotel room.

When she went into the empty room, she heard the shower on and assumed Junker was in there. Although the bathroom door was open an inch, she didn't worry about making noise, presuming that her friend would guess she was back if he heard anything.

On the video feed, the drapes were still drawn over the windows of Bella's suite. Jealousy tasted bitter and she disgusted herself for feeling it about her ex… the ex she'd screwed last night.

Junker was busy in the shower, and thinking about last night made her realize this was an opportunity. Tugging off her jacket, Rora dropped it and retrieved Opal from the panel in the suspended ceiling. Taking the laptop to the coffee table, she knelt down, and opened the lid.

Rora took a breath and ran her fingers down the edges. "Ok, friend, don't kill me," she whispered to the machine and braced with her finger over the keyboard.

Her heart was hammering to get out of her chest, her head was screaming at her not to take the risk, and her skin chilled. Extending her index finger, she bared her teeth, breathed and touched a key… nothing.

Opening her eyes, her jaw fell, and she breathed out a sound of shocked relief. Strike had been telling the truth! She was still authorized. Glancing up, she couldn't see the bathroom door from here, but she could still hear the shower.

Typing fast, she found herself looking at more programs than she could comprehend. What did they all do? What would happen if she… One in particular caught her eye, it was serendipitous, but it gave her an idea. If that was what she thought it was… Oh, if there was one program she had to learn, it was that one… and she was a quick study.

"What do you say, honey?" she whispered to the computer. "What do you say we have some fun with Daddy?"

Ease of use wasn't something she'd have ascribed to Strike, but the simplicity was incredible. Maybe it was her determination that helped her figure it out, she'd guess that all his programs weren't like this one, or maybe it was just that she was starting to learn his mind.

She was so caught up in playing with the settings that she almost didn't hear the shower going off. She'd just closed the computer when Junker came into view.

When he saw her with it, he frowned. "Any luck?"

Rora shook her head. "I was just curious," she said and wiggled her fingers. "I still have all my extremities."

"If you've seen what it can do, I don't blame you for not touching it." She hadn't said that, but he had, so she'd leave him with his assumptions. "How was your walk? You want a drink?"

Shaking her head, she gathered up Opal and hugged the laptop to her chest. "I think I'll… get an early night."

He nodded. "Good plan, I'm going to stay up a while, see if we get any movement on the cameras. Your turn in the bed tonight."

Movement from the amorous couple? Yeah, she didn't need the reminder. "Ok."

She got ready for bed, taking her switchblade and Opal with her. She couldn't put Opal back in the last hiding place with Junker still up and around. So Rora chose to slip the laptop under her pillow.

Tucking her fist beneath the pillow too, she held her thumb over the button that would open the blade in the event she needed it, and let her eyes close.

ELEVEN

RORA DIDN'T HEAR any movement. There were no voices or sounds. She didn't even remember feeling her pillow move. All she remembered was the clench of panic.

Still lying in bed with her eyes closed, instinct made her catch the wrist of the hand that had just slid under her pillow. At the same time, her other hand shot out from beneath the pillow. Her thumb released the blade of her knife and she thrust its length against the throat of whoever the hell had invaded her space.

In such a deep daze, she had to blink and tell herself that this wasn't a nightmare, this was reality.

"Fuck," Strike breathed out, his eyes alight with arousal. "Do your worst, Kero."

"Damnit," she said, relaxing her hand but pushing his shoulder.

Rora still had the blade in her fist and with her heavy body in the transition from sleep to awake, she had to take some time to breathe.

Strike forgot about his intrusion to pick up her hand and expose his gullet. "Do it," he growled.

And the weird thing was, for half a second, she was tempted by the heat in his eyes to actually cut him. Pushing the blade forward, she could feel his breathing growing shallower.

The first bud of blood at the tip of her blade made her gasp. "Strike," she said, opening her hand to let the blade fall first onto the bed and then probably to the floor.

Panic at the sight of his blood made her push a hand to his forehead to force his head away so she could lunge forward to press her mouth to the wound.

"Blood play," he said, smoothing a hand down her hip and over her ass. "Naughty, I love it. Drink your fill, baby."

She hadn't meant it to seem like she was drinking his blood, she meant to kiss the wound better, to apologize for her moment of weakness. But before she could vocalize that apology, she spotted lower legs flat on the floor behind Strike. The sight of those feet made her forget about whatever was happening between them.

Shoving Strike away, Rora clambered off the bed and dashed over to Junker who was lying flat out on the floor by the door.

"What the hell did you do to him?" she asked but didn't know what to do with her fury when she noticed the blood on the front of Strike's shirt. "Oh my God." Leaving Junker, she dashed back to Strike and pushed him down to sit on the floor against the bed. "What happened?"

Grabbing for his shirt, she tried to pull it up to look for a wound, but when he touched her chin to marry their eyes, he shrugged. "It's not my blood."

Ok, so she didn't have to be worried about him being mortally wounded, but that didn't quell her worry, though it was suspicion, not concern, that came out in her voice.

"That's not what I asked, Flame… What happened?"

"Flame?" the croaking voice came from behind her, from Junker, and though pained, the voice was aware.

Flipping around, she crawled away from Strike and scrambled over to Junker who was trying to sit. "Don't sit up," she said, pushing his shoulders to put him back on the floor. "Just stay still a minute."

"He came here," Junker grumbled, his eyes closed, and he settled onto his back again. "Exile. He just walked right in."

"He does that," she said, stroking his hair from his forehead. "Just lie still."

"He'll want the computer, he'll want—"

"Motherfucker!" Strike's voice made her whip around again and she saw him on the floor with Opal propped against his pulled-up knees. His glare snapped up to her. "What the fuck did you do?"

Junker rolled over and leaped to his feet, grabbing for Rora to put her behind him. "Stay away from her! Take the computer! Go! I won't let you hurt her!"

"Junker," she said, smoothing a hand down his arm.

Her friend thought he was making a heroic show, but her ex just ignored it. "You fucked with my machine, Ro," Strike declared, fuming at her without ever even acknowledging that Junker had spoken. "What the hell—"

"That's right, I did," she said, without hiding her triumph. Slinking around Junker, she started toward Strike who inhaled and shot to his feet, leaving Opal on the floor. But as he was about to talk, she held up a finger. "Ah!"

"What the fuck, Ro? Don't you dare think about—"

She clamped a hand over his mouth and tried her best to match his growling expression before curling her fingers around the back of his neck to pull him down so she could whisper in his ear. "I was handed something tonight. I don't know what it is. Will you shout at me after checking it out?"

Drawing back, she waited for his single nod before leaving him to retrieve the token from her inside jacket pocket. "What's going on?" Junker asked. "You're not afraid of him?"

She put a finger to her lips to indicate her friend should be quiet and diverted to get Junker's kit of mini tools from the box by the dresser. Rora took both to Strike who sat on the edge of the bed and used one of the tools to pop open the device on the nightstand. She turned on the lamp where he was working and stood there by his side, watching him examine the piece.

"Does it have an active tracker?" she asked, resting a hand on his shoulder.

"You can tell everyone else to shut up, but you're allowed to talk?" Strike muttered.

She bumped his shoulder with her hip. "Does it?"

He picked something out and flicked it onto the nightstand. Bending down, he retrieved her knife from the floor and raised it high to then stab the tip of the blade into the piece he'd pinged out, embedding the knife upright in the wood of the nightstand.

"Not anymore," he said and scooped the rest of the pieces into his palm.

He got up, walked away from her into the bathroom and a few seconds later the toilet flushed. Strike came back, taking off his jacket as he crossed the room. "Where'd you get it?"

"That friend of yours I bit," she said, watching as he took off his tee-shirt. His interest was just a glimmer before he went to the dresser to pull out one of Junker's tee-shirts. "We had an interesting conversation today."

"I'll bet. You don't mind, do you?" Strike said, but barely bothered to glance at Junker let alone wait for a response about the tee-shirt. "Did you roll on me, Kero?"

"Yep," she said, sitting down on the bed and pulling up her knees to her chest. "Told him everything… He's going to descend on us with his helicopter any second."

Strike went to the fridge and opened it to poke inside. He pulled out a beer and popped the cap to tip the liquid down his throat. "I've missed your sense of humor, Ro."

"I wonder if he has a helicopter," she said, turning her eyes up. "That would be hot. Helicopters are hot."

He took the bottle from his lips just long enough to ask, "Hotter than a motorcycle?"

"If we were traveling cross country again? Yes… and better for my ass."

He shrugged and trashed the beer bottle before taking out another. "Then I'll get us a helicopter."

"You cannot fly a helicopter," she said. "Can you?"

Strike turned to stroll over to the living room to examine their setup. "What you running here?" he asked, taking a mouthful of beer.

"Whoa, whoa, whoa!" Junker said. Rora had almost forgotten he was there, he'd been quiet, but he looked so stunned and confused that she guessed he'd been processing. "What the hell is going on? Isn't he the bad guy? The enemy? And you're letting him drink beer?"

"Shit, you are a square," Strike muttered and turned around to face her. "Hey, I almost forgot, what did you do to my girl?"

"We made friends," Rora said, bending down to pick Opal up from the floor. "Turns out your women have a thing for me too."

She put the computer in the middle of the bed, and then lay down beside Opal, smoothing a gentle hand over the keyboard.

"Whoa!" both guys said together and then glared at each other.

"I thought you said no one could touch the computer," Junker said, storming toward her. "That it would kill anyone who tried."

She winced in apology. "I said you couldn't touch her... that if you did, she'd hurt you and might kill you." Lifting her head, she saw Strike standing on the other side of the couch, frowning at her. "I wasn't lying about that, was I?"

"No," Strike said. "Don't know why you think he'd trust my word though."

Fair point, appealing to him probably wasn't wise. Rising to her knees, she focused on Junker. "I really wasn't lying."

Junker looked more surprised than angry, but she'd guess this was all a lot for him to take in. "But you can touch her—I mean..." he said. "Why didn't you tell me that?"

Now that she'd started, it felt right to keep telling the truth. "I didn't know it," she said. "Not at first."

"Then how did you figure it out?" Junker asked, his tone becoming less patient and more angry.

Oh, she wasn't sure if the truth-telling extended that far. Rora couldn't tell Junker that she'd met with Strike in secret… that she'd had sex with him.

Strike actually saved her from having to lie by speaking up before she had to decide what to say. "Listen, Square, there's a lot of shit you don't know 'bout me and my girls," Strike said.

Ok, she wasn't sure that really helped at all, especially not if Junker's reaction was any measure.

"Your girls?" Junker asked, horror leaping to his face.

Rora gasped and rose higher on her knees. "I am not his girl." She glared at Strike. "I am not your girl."

"No, not while you're fucking with my tech, what did you do?"

It felt good to check Strike. It might be an underhanded move, locking him out of his own machine after he'd been kind enough to allow her access. But he'd hurt her, and he understood the physical, so this gave her vindication.

"She needs a rest," Rora said, happy to advertise her pride in herself.

"So it's about spending more time in bed," Strike said and smirked before taking a drink.

She faltered. "It's nothing to do with bed, and don't pretend to be mad. You don't get mad when I act out, you get turned on."

"That's what you were going for?" Strike asked. "You want me turned on and in bed… You're not subtle, Cupcake."

He'd done it again, he'd managed to take her triumph and turn it into his own.

"Cupcake," Junker exhaled. It made her feel horrible to see him so shocked, but at least that distracted her from Strike's conceit. "Aurora, what… I… what?"

As usual, she'd had no time to figure out what she'd do if she was faced with these two men at the same time. "Look, this is a good thing," she said, trying to find a way out of this conundrum. "Exile is here, we can talk to him, properly. The Jewel isn't here and… wait, where's the Black Jewel?"

"Gone," Strike said, enjoying more beer.

"Gone where?" she asked. "We didn't see her go anywhere."

"What do you know? You were asleep," Strike said. "And your boy here was too busy drooling over you to be monitoring the feed."

"I…" Junker gasped. "I wasn't!"

"Yeah, so how did I get to sneak up on you? Ro's working for me even when she's asleep."

"I do not work for you," she snapped. "Can we please sit down and talk about this? Junker, you wanted to work something out with the pig-headed idiot, now's your chance… he's here."

Strike scoffed. "He doesn't want to work out a damn thing… Doesn't matter anyway, the Jewel knocked me out, took the only useful piece of tech any of us need."

Her ex could steal her anger faster than anyone else. "She knocked you out or one of her guys did?" Rora asked.

Strike's well-being rose on her priority list.

"Bitch stuck me with one of her little darts; you know how she likes her drugs… I might have gone too far with her punishment."

Rora wouldn't let her nausea show on her face, but that didn't mean she didn't feel her guts roiling.

Climbing off the bed, she passed Junker to go around the couch to Strike's side. "You were having sex with her?"

Strike held up his hands in innocence. "Didn't get as far as sex, didn't intend to… didn't let her know that."

Snatching the beer out of his hand, Rora bent over to slam the bottle onto the table. Strike took advantage of the opportunity she'd inadvertently presented to him and snuck a hand under her camisole to touch the lace edging of her panties on her ass. Rora swatted his hand, catching it and twisting it around to link her fingers between his. But she wasn't being affectionate, or even familiar, she made him turn and then thrust him down onto the couch.

Kneeling on the couch at his side, facing him, Rora pulled at his eyelids to open them wider. "Why are you drinking beer when you're under the influence of God knows what?" she asked. "I know what that stuff is like, I've been hit by it too. I think it sends you over the edge."

"I went over the edge years ago," he said, sliding his hand up between her thighs, but she shoved it away.

"Stop touching me."

"You're the one who told me to get used to us touching," he said. "Guess I got used to it."

He could try to logic her into it all he liked, but things weren't the way they used to be and that had been his choice, not hers.

"I meant what I said," Rora asserted. "I am not yours. Not anymore."

"Anymore?" Junker asked, coming to stand at the back of the couch, scowling at each of them. "But you were… Oh my God, you said flame… You were calling him Flame, weren't you? He's the one…" When she saw how interest lit Strike's eyes, she put her hand over them to block him out. "The one you keep calling out for in bed!"

Strike's lips curled in the most authentic smile she'd ever seen on his face. "Ha! You call my name in bed with this schmuck? I'm insulted. I'm way better than him."

Rora let her hand fall to his mouth to cover his smirk, but that meant looking at his smug eyes, so she covered those with her other hand and glared up at Junker. "I am not calling out for him."

"That's exactly what you do," Junker said. "Every time you wake up. Every time you have that nightmare you won't tell me about."

Strike pulled her hand from his eyes and she read only concern. "What nightmare?"

"I'm not going to talk about it," she said, hating the shiver of awareness that trickled up her spine when Strike's lips moved on her palm. "I think we have more important things to talk about. Jewel is in the wind with a seriously game-changing piece of tech… Did you injure her? Is that her blood on your shirt?"

"Some of it," Strike said. "Couple of her guys tried to get involved. When I was taking them down, she hit me with the dart. She took the device and split."

Rora pushed her fist into his chest. "Why did you have it on you? Wasn't that stupid?"

Leaning over her, he took his beer from the table. "No," he said. "I planned to kill her."

He maintained eye contact with her as he took a drink. Rora couldn't believe he'd really planned to kill Bella, not when he was sitting there like he'd just admitted to finishing the milk and not giving a damn about it.

"Do you kill many of your exes?" Junker asked.

That question was relevant to her, but she'd guess everyone was thinking something different. "Only the ones who hurt my Kero."

Lifting a scolding finger, she kept a stern tone, and snatched his beer away from his lips. "I am not your anything." He kissed the tip of her finger. Surprise made her wipe the moist spot on his shirt. "You're manipulating me," she grumbled. "Stop it."

"Why would I do that?"

"Because you want me to fix your baby."

Strike tilted his chin like he couldn't deny that.

"I don't trust him," Junker said, drawing her attention up.

"Feeling's mutual, Square," Strike said, sliding down in the seat to prop his feet on the coffee table.

"We have to go after her," Junker said. "I'll figure out where she is, just like we did before. We'll have to follow her."

"If she can take Exile down…" she said, hating having to admit that her former lover was more capable than she and Junker put together. "And she'd let him get closer than either of us."

"I don't know about that, Ro," Strike said. "You're her ex too."

Junker stumbled back a step. "You were with her?"

"No," she said, leaping off the couch to rush toward Junker. "No, it wasn't like that…"

"You seemed pretty cozy when I walked in on you two in bed together," Strike muttered. "When she asked me to join you."

Rora squawked and marched over to him, using her shins to pressure his legs off the coffee table so she could stand in front of him. "What are you doing?"

"Am I lying?" he asked.

Gritting her teeth, she wanted to scream but couldn't. Junker was there at the back of the couch again, shock and confusion all over his face, while Strike sat there like the cat who'd got the cream.

"Why are you doing this?" she asked her ex.

Any amusement left on Strike's face faded. "Because this is serious now, and I don't think we need the square. I came here to get you and my machine. That's it."

It might be easy for Strike to categorize Junker as irrelevant, but he'd risked his life to save her.

"Junker is not a square, he has supplies, skills, contacts... he's my friend. I've always been nice to your friends, haven't I?" she asked. "Except that one I bit..." Strike's jaw worked, telling her she knew she was making progress with him, so it was the perfect time to hitch her chin and knee his knee. "Besides, I have control of your BFF. Don't forget that."

Strike's tongue slid to the corner of his mouth and he pushed it out just a fraction. "Proud of yourself, aren't you, bad girl?"

That was as close as she'd get to a concession from Strike. So leaving him, she rounded the couch to stand in front of Junker. "You know he has skills, and he knows the Jewel better than either of us... We need him."

Junker squeezed his lips together. "I don't trust him. If we get this back, he might take it from us. How can you be sure he'll do the right thing?"

Given that she'd done nothing but tell Junker Exile wasn't righteous or moveable, that was a difficult point to argue. "We can work on that," she said. "This is the closest you're going to get." In the corner of her eye, she saw Strike lay his head on the back of the couch to peek back. Without looking, she drove her fingers through his hair to push his head forward again because she didn't need any snarky comments from him. "Please." Taking Junker's hand, she gave him a squeeze. "Please."

"You should've told me you were with him," Junker whispered, though there was no way Strike couldn't hear. "I trusted you, Aurora. What else have you hidden from me?"

Too much, but she couldn't voice that thought. "I'm sorry," she said. "I was embarrassed. I didn't exactly come out on top when it ended."

"How did it end?" Junker asked. "He seems to think you're still an item."

Strike turned his head, angling his ear to hear better, though she knew the show was meant for her. He had no trouble hearing. "It did end. It's over. And he's kidding himself."

Rora tightened her fingers in Strike's hair when he tried to tip his head backward again.

"Were you in love with him?" Junker asked, moving closer. "Are you still in love with him?"

She inhaled and squeezed both of his hands. "We don't have time to get into all the details now, Junker," Rora said. "You're right, we have to go after Jewel. She has a head start and we don't know where she's going. We have to get moving. Right now, we have a shared goal—we all want to find the Black Jewel. It's better to have Exile working for us than against us, don't you think?"

Junker thought about it for a second. "Ok," he exhaled. "But how are we gonna find her?"

"That's easy," Strike said, drinking his beer, and proving that he'd been listening the whole time. "Rora knows where she's headed."

"I do?" Rora asked and had a thought that chilled her. "She's not going to—"

"Wonderland? No," he said, sitting forward to twist and look up at them. "We left that place in ashes… Jewel doesn't know where she's going exactly, she has to do her research and that could take a while depending on how smart Gallagher was."

"Benjamin?" Rora asked, turning to the couch, more confused than ever. "I don't understand what you mean. He's dead."

"His ex-wife isn't," he said, putting his beer on the table before twisting to make eye contact with her. "What's the point? She thinks Leandra Gallagher is going to give her the answer."

"Oh my God," Rora breathed out. "You didn't tell her?" He shook his head. "And now the Jewel thinks… They divorced before Benjamin wrote it! Leandra has no idea… about any of this, but… she'll kill her!"

"Torture her first. I'd guess, pretty bad. Leandra can't save herself if she doesn't have the answer… So, Cupcake… where's Leandra?"

A new question and a new dilemma. Processing what would happen if Bella found Leandra, Rora stood dumb. It was almost unfathomable because Leandra was innocent and would never stand up to a woman like Bella.

"Leandra knows nothing."

"No point in telling me, Cupcake. Jewel doesn't believe that," Strike said. "And since you won't give her answers, she's going a different route."

"She didn't ask me," Rora said.

"When she held you captive—"

"All she wanted to do was talk about you," she said, staring at the screens displaying the streets. "Or Benjamin… or sex…" She was trying to process everything fast, and to play through different scenarios and possible outcomes. "She still needs you to fix it, I mean… isn't that what Jewel thinks?"

"One problem at a time with her," Strike said.

Rora pinned him with suspicion. "You don't have some deal with her, do you? You're not planning to follow us around for a while and then meet up with her after she's tracked down Leandra?"

"No," he said. "Why would I have to do that?"

The way he raised his brow made her suspicious for a different reason. They hadn't confronted the fact that he didn't have the Point yet. Rora still wasn't even sure if he knew he had a dummy device.

"With you I never know," Rora said. "Do you have an arrangement with her?"

"No," he said. When her expression made it obvious that she didn't believe him, he twisted further toward her. "No, Cupcake. Quit looking at me like that."

"It doesn't make sense why she'd ditch you when she needs you. If you were unconscious, she could've taken you with her, even if it was against your will."

"She doesn't have the resources to hold me, especially not on the move. She's losing her grip and Jewel doesn't like to be out of control. Besides, when her and I get… fractious… it's best we take a break from each other."

"A break?" Junker asked. "Is that what you call this? Blood all over you, drugs, the Black Jewel stealing and running off? This is normal?"

"For my life?" Strike asked. "Yeah. And I'm not talking to you." Shifting her hand to the back of the couch, Rora dug her nails into Strike's forearm. It was her intention to convey her displeasure, but he growled. "Starting something, baby? Want to sink your teeth in? Go for it." Picking his arm from under her hand, he held it up, offering it to her, but he glanced at Junker. "She has a thing for biting… Have you had the pleasure yet?"

"I am not a biter," she said, pushing his arm down. "And neither is Junker."

"Know that, do you?" Strike said.

"If you ever want to touch your baby again, you're going to stop being so snide," she said. "This thing with the Jewel is serious… If she goes after Leandra…"

"How well hidden is she?" Strike asked, all business.

"Well enough that the last I checked, she was still where we put her, but… I don't think anyone's looked for her."

"You tell me where she is, and I'll tell you how long it will take the Jewel to find her."

Grasping her forehead, Rora was getting overwhelmed. "Stop asking me… I don't know if I want to tell you."

"Then give me my girl and I'll find her myself."

If this had been just a few weeks ago, she'd have told Strike everything without pausing for breath. He might be saying the right things recently, but there was still so much that hadn't been said. Rora was keeping secrets from everyone and she was losing track of her trust levels in each of the men in her life.

"How do we know this isn't a trick?" Junker asked, planting more doubts in Rora's mind. "The Jewel wants to know where Leandra is, so Exile comes over here to sell you this fairytale, and then you just tell them what they want to know. Seems a bit convenient, doesn't it?"

It did. Both she and Junker turned to look down at Strike, who was scowling again. "Jewel and I are not in cahoots," he stated.

"How do we know that?" Junker asked. "You'd say that anyway."

Strike's frustration edged into anger and that put her on alert because he could choose to vent that anger at any second. She didn't fear for her physical safety, but she wasn't so sure about Junker's.

"If we were, she wouldn't have taken off without me, she'd be waiting in the parking lot. And she's not a happy Jewel right now. In fact I'd say she's about ready to kill me and probably will as soon as she gets what she wants."

"Why?" Rora asked. "She would never kill you. She loves you. You know she does."

But he shook his head and retrieved the beer. "Not anymore, least she hates me more than she loves me… And I'll be watching your six damn close too."

"Why? What did you say to her? What did you do that upset her?"

"I confirmed her accusation, the one she made when we were all in bed together in Wonderland," he said, looking into her. They hadn't been in bed together, but Rora knew what he meant. "I told her where my loyalty lies."

Rora remembered how Bella had reacted when she'd accused Strike of being in love, so she could believe Bella hadn't had a great reaction if Strike confirmed it and told her his loyalty lay elsewhere. But even if he'd said those words to

Bella, Rora couldn't be sure they meant anything real; this could be another maneuver on his part.

"Ok," she said, but not to him.

Strike thought she was talking to him and asked with hope, "Ok?"

Rora turned to Junker. "Will you pack up all the tech? I'll pack everything else." Spinning, she looked to Strike. "St— fuck."

He smirked. "Not easy, is it, Kero?"

"Get your pack, anything you need. This place is compromised. We're moving out tonight."

Junker immediately jumped to action and went to start shutting all his equipment down to pack it away.

"You're hot when you give orders," Strike said, raising his beer toward his mouth.

Rora bent over the back of the couch to snag the bottle from him before he could drink anymore. "You already have drugs in your system and I might need you to drive later. Will you please lay off the alcohol?"

"Blow me," he said. She sneered at him, but his eyes widened. "I'm serious, blow me and I'll do whatever you want... You remember how our exchanges work? Like our bargain when you had a particular metal box in those hungry little hands of yours and I asked you to hand it over. I believe you said, 'I want something.' Well, Cupcake, I want something."

She finished his beer and turned to toss the empty bottle across the room into the trash. Then with cool eyes, she put a hand on the back of the couch and bowed closer to him.

"Keep dreaming, Exile," she purred.

There was no way that dealing with two such different men was going to be easy for her, but they weren't going to ditch Junker. Rora had a feeling that her newest friend was going to have to act as conscience and chaperone for her and Strike.

If she'd learned one thing since Strike had been back in her life in the last few days, it was that she wasn't very good at resisting her attraction to her ex. Without Junker around, she couldn't tell how this situation might turn out, or if she'd still be whole at the end of it. Not that she felt whole now.

It might not be a fun job for Junker, but he was Benjamin's friend. If Leandra was in trouble, he'd be as motivated to save the woman as Rora.

Rora needed Junker's guiding force or she'd be seduced by the darkness, and as Strike liked to remind her that never worked out well for anyone.

TWELVE

LEAVING THE HOTEL room as a threesome, Rora and Junker started toward his truck, but Strike went the other way. She slowed to a stop and called after him. "Where are you going?"

"We're not taking his truck," Strike said.

Junker had stopped a few paces ahead of her, so here she was, equal distance between the two defiant men.

Huffing, she dropped her pack and went to Strike, getting up close to murmur. "You think it impedes your masculinity somehow to get in another guy's truck?"

"That what you think of me?" he asked.

If this battle of wills kept up, they'd never achieve anything. Working as a team, they'd be formidable, but if they did nothing but butt heads, they'd be their own worst enemies.

"Junker is not a bad guy," she said, resting a hand on Strike's upper arm. "You have to be reasonable about this. The truck is spacious, it carries everything we need it to."

"Then I'll get you another truck."

She bit her lip because as logical as he thought it was, it wasn't that simple. "Strike," she whispered. "Junker's not... he's not a criminal. I don't know how he'll feel about getting in a stolen car."

Strike widened his stance. "He was fine with you stealing from me."

Time for another admission, and she was ashamed of this one too. "He didn't really know I was going to do that until the last minute and then… I kinda didn't give him a choice."

"Then we won't give him a choice."

This time, Strike's intention wasn't to frustrate her. This was just about two men coming from different worlds. Strike saw an objective and did whatever he had to in order to achieve it. Junker was more process orientated. To him, the ends didn't justify the means, but Strike just didn't understand morals like that.

"He has a sister," she murmured.

His mouth slanted. "Thank you, baby. Now I know where to squeeze," he said and started to turn away.

Rora grabbed his jacket in both hands to pull him back. "That's not why I told you that. I don't want you to squeeze. I don't think he wants her to visit him in jail. He has a life. A family. He's not like us. He has something to lose."

Strike moved nearer until their bodies came into such close contact that she had to tip her head back to meet his eye. "I have something to lose," he whispered. "And she's standing right in front of me."

It made sense he was all bravado in front of Junker. But he had to know things weren't the same between them. This seemed simple to him too, and he was so damn calm, but her emotions and sanity were all churned up.

"Why are you doing this, Strike? I'm not yours anymore. You know I'm not yours," she said. "And Junker doesn't know we had sex the other night… I'd appreciate it if you didn't tell him." It took every bit of confidence she had to lay her hands flat on his chest to put some distance between them. "And we can't get in a stolen truck with Junker. It's not fair to force your way of life onto him."

"I forced it onto you," he said. "Getting in his truck has nothing to do with anyone's masculinity. That vehicle is marked. It's as compromised as your hotel room. Every player's seen it and if Torres is in town, he knows who you're with and the vehicle you came in. We need something clean and it's too late to go to a dealership."

"Ok," she said and bit her lip again. "But you do it, you drive, and if we get into trouble, you have to bail him out like you'd bail me out."

"Pretty tough without Opal," he said.

She smiled. "Good try," Rora said and prodded a finger into his navel through his tee-shirt. "You'll get her back… on my terms… when I forgive you… *if* I forgive you."

"I think I preferred it when you just marched into places and demanded an apology. It was much easier, and I got laid faster."

Since almost the day she'd met him, she'd wished to be with him when he let his playful side out. At most, she'd seen glimmers of a sense of humor, but he'd never relaxed with her enough to be himself unguarded. Seeing it now, having him this open with her and willing to push his own comfort level, it humbled her.

Yet, every time she started to let herself believe that he was being sincere, she remembered how their relationship had ended.

He could be playing her to get what he wanted. They had to talk about the Point. She had to find out why he wasn't mad at her for lying and why he hadn't confronted her about the bait and switch. If it was true that he didn't know, that he hadn't accessed the device because he'd chosen her, she had to know why he hadn't declared it and tried to claim her back.

"Strike…"

"What?" he asked when she didn't finish. "What is it, Ro?"

But Rora had no idea what to say. He was Strike, the man who'd saved her, the one she'd fallen in love with and made love to. But he was also the same guy who'd killed in front of her, who'd stolen from her, who'd broken her heart.

Rora wanted to be with the man she'd fallen in love with. She did. And everyone deserved a second chance. But Strike hadn't asked for one, he hadn't offered any explanation for what had happened or told her what he wanted for the future.

If he fooled her again, it would be on her head, and she knew he was capable. Strike could mean every word, he could love her through to his very bones. But he could be just as easily manipulating her for his own ends. She didn't know what to think.

Her mind wandered. "I keep thinking about the night Benjamin died," she whispered. "About the look in your eye when you put the gun to your head and I squeezed the trigger…"

Because he hadn't shown any fear. She'd believed that he really wanted her to kill him if it was her intention to follow.

"There isn't anywhere you can go that I won't follow," he murmured, his voice soft.

"I was so scared, Strike…" Her eyes found his. "But you were right there with me. You were… weren't you?"

It couldn't have been a lie. Those feelings. Surely, he couldn't have faked that depth of sincerity and with a gun to his head, who'd take that kind of risk?

"I was there, Cupcake… I'm still here."

When he raised his curled fingers to her jaw, she pushed them away. "We have to… talk."

"About?"

She shook her head. "Not here like this. There's too much to say. Can you just… do what needs to be done and come back here to get us?"

"Sure," he said, and turned to go.

Rora watched him walk around the end of the building and that was when Junker came up beside her. "Where's he going?"

She cleared her throat and tried to shake off her melancholy. "We need another vehicle, something that's not associated with me. Exile's going to get his."

That wasn't exactly true. The vehicle would be his for as long as he needed it, but it wasn't exactly his.

"I knew you'd been lovers," Junker muttered. Rora wasn't sure she was ready to return to this topic so soon, but it seemed that Junker was. "I don't know how, I… I could tell but, I guess I didn't want to believe it."

Turning to face him, she hated to see the sorrow in his eyes. Guilt filled her again. "I'm sorry I didn't tell you. I was embarrassed… I didn't want to admit it."

"Why not? I wouldn't have judged you."

"I judge me," she confessed. "He's… wrong, in every way a guy can be wrong. There isn't a guy who better fits the bad-boy description and I should've known better than to fall for him. But it was… easy to get caught up in him and I… I enjoyed it. I enjoyed the thrill of him and the… intensity of being near him, never knowing what was going to happen, but always hoping that it would end with me being close to him. It was this… simmer that was constantly between us and then…"

"What?" he asked, tucking her hair away from her face. "What happened between the two of you? How did it end? The Jewel?"

"No," she said, shaking her head. But all the motivations, the chain of events, it was all blurred now, and she couldn't figure out which butterfly had flapped its wings or how they'd all come to be here at this place in time. "Maybe. I don't know everything that went on in his head. All I know is, he broke my heart and I felt sick and… I wanted to hate him, but I…"

"You said he would kill you."

She had. Rora had started her journey with Junker telling him that Exile wanted her dead and then he'd seen them interacting in the hotel room without any hint of violence.

"I thought he might," she said, glancing around when she heard an engine approach. "I thought he would, for sure… But it turns out…"

"Turns out what?"

"I have a secret," she admitted in a whisper. "One I haven't told him. I thought he knew, but he doesn't. I think that maybe once I do tell him… that's when he'll kill me."

"I won't let that happen," Junker said, stroking his palm across her cheek to push her hair back.

She smiled. "You're very sweet."

"I mean it," he said. "You're right that we need him. We'll need him to get us close to the Jewel, and I want to get to know him, to get into his head. But once we find the Jewel… we won't have to worry about him anymore."

The truck pulled up to the stairs of the porch. Junker bent to pick up her pack and took her hand to pull her along to the new truck. The men loaded up as she got into the backseat.

This was going to be an interesting trip and there was a high chance they'd leave as three and come back as fewer than that.

***

RORA WOKE IN the back of the truck with a start. "Flame?" she called out, clenching her abs to rise a few inches from the seat.

"I'm here, you're safe," Strike said.

Her eyes were still heavy, and she was happy to stay on her back with her knuckles on her forehead, until she heard the second voice.

"She knows she's safe," Junker said. "She's not asking for you."

"I think we established last night that the guy in the dream is me," Strike grumbled.

Sitting up, she saw Strike in the driver's seat with one wrist draped on the top of the wheel. Junker was on the passenger side, as far from Strike as he could get. Both men were rigid and scowling.

Uh oh. Talk about tension… and not the good kind.

Rora gasped when she saw the redness on Junker's cheekbone. Lunging between the seats, she scooped his face toward her so she could inspect the wound. "Oh my God, what happened to you?"

"There was a disagreement about the radio," Junker said.

Flipping around, she socked Strike's shoulder. "Stop hitting him, would you, please? Goddamnit." Dropping into the backseat again, she sighed. "Can't you get along for a minute? You two are worse than high school kids."

"That your fantasy?" Strike asked and made eye contact with her in the rearview mirror.

She narrowed her eyes on his. "You were never this attentive when we were together. I preferred it when you ignored me and I had to work to get your attention. What is it about having another guy around that makes you want to piss all over me?"

"Pissing? More kink," Strike said. "I'll do whatever you need."

"Where did that come from?" Junker demanded.

"What? We're discussing etymology now?" Strike sniped back.

"That's a big word for a guy like you," Junker said.

"Want me to spell it too?"

"Stop it," she said, putting her elbows on the back of their seats to boost forward. "What is with you two? Have you been like this the whole time I've been asleep?"

Both mumbled but said little.

"We agreed not to talk after the radio incident," Junker said.

They all slid into silence again for a minute after she sank back.

"Tell me about the nightmare," Strike said, glancing at her in the mirror again.

"I don't want to," she said, folding her legs on the seat.

"I want to," he said. "Is it a sex dream? Is that why you don't want to talk about it in front of the square? 'Cause the way you called it out just now didn't sound the same as when you climax in reality... Maybe dream orgasms are different."

She bit her lip. "Would you please not talk about me like that?"

Strike grunted. "Now who's different 'cause there's another person around? Since when did you become reserved? If it's a sex thing tell me it's a sex thing. Your bitch knows we've had sex."

Now he did, but reminding Junker of what she'd kept from him wouldn't make him feel good. Still, arguing with Strike wouldn't get her anywhere and God only knew what he might blurt out next.

"It's not a sex thing," she admitted and paused before clarifying. "It's not an *us* sex thing."

"I don't get it," Strike said.

This was as much public exposure as she could take. "I said I don't want to talk about it."

"And I'll keep going until—"

"The Black Jewel is there."

"Ah," he said, opening his mouth in understanding. "And I'm fucking her."

Breathing out, she figured getting the truth out would be the quickest way to shut him up. "Not at first," she said, her eyes drifting to the window. "I'm in the dungeon, where she kept me… She's reading me a fairytale, I don't know which one, but… you come in and you start kissing her… her arms, her shoulders, her neck, it's like… you can't get enough of her while she's telling this story… And then you're making love with her… You're in this chair she had down there, right in front of me and… both of you keep looking at me and laughing and…"

"How does it end?" Strike asked.

Creeping numbness encircled her, making her wrap her arms around herself. "You tell me I should've pulled the trigger… And she… she starts yelling at me, asking me why I let him go alone… accusing me of abandoning him and then… this gun appears in your hand and… you shoot me… at least I think you do, that's when I wake up."

She was still thinking about the dream, reliving it, and the men said nothing for a minute, probably reflecting on it themselves.

"Wow," Strike said. "Sex, cruelty, jealousy, death… Are you sure this is a nightmare? Sounds like a Saturday night to me."

After throwing him the stink eye in the mirror, Rora twisted and lay down on her back again. "And you wonder why I didn't want to tell you… Can we stop for coffee?" she asked just a fraction of a second before the truck stopped.

A crackly voice asked, "What can I get you?"

"Always one step ahead of you, Cupcake," Strike said before putting his window all the way down to order breakfast.

THIRTEEN

THE REST OF THE DAY was mostly silent. Rora hadn't told anyone exactly where Leandra was, and she was deliberately giving evasive directions because she just didn't want to give away the location yet.

There was a lively debate about stopping for the night. Some voted for. Some against. Then there was a lively debate about rooms, one, two, or three, how many did they need?

Rora should've known that doing this with two such strong-minded men would be difficult. But now that they'd made some progress, she voted to stop. If they didn't address some of their issues and have some time to reorient themselves, someone would die before daybreak. It was just too close quarters in the car.

It was decided that they should get one room with two beds. Neither of the guys wanted her to be alone, for "safety" reasons apparently, but neither trusted the other to bunk in with her. So it was decided that because no one trusted anyone else, they could keep an eye on each other if they were all in the same room.

They took their things from the truck and traipsed inside to the motel room that had two double beds, and a couch. Perfect.

Deciding not to leave anything of theirs in the truck, just in case, the guys took the heavy things inside, leaving her to carry Opal, who'd become something of a security blanket.

Going to the furthest away of the beds, Rora climbed onto it on her hands and knees, ready to flop down, but she noticed something missing. "Where's my pillow?" she asked, looking left and right.

"Pillow?" Strike asked. "There's a pillow right there beside you."

"Not that pillow, my pillow," she said and smiled when Junker held it up.

She clapped and opened her arms to receive it, so Junker tossed it in her direction, but Strike lunged over and snagged it before it got to her.

He came to her, holding it up. "What the hell is this?"

"My pillow," she said, trying to take it from him. "Junker got it for me because my neck has been sore."

Strike scoffed and threw the pillow away over his shoulder. "Sore, huh?"

When he grabbed her shoulders, Rora gasped and tried to pull away, but he held her tight, squeezing and massaging the muscles at the sides of her neck.

"Get your hands off me," she exclaimed, trying to wriggle away. "Don't touch me! I don't want—oh, God…"

Her gusto vanished when he squeezed the sore spot and it immediately relaxed.

"There?"

"Right there," she breathed out. Closing her eyes, she let her head fall to one side. "Mmm."

"Feel good, baby?" Strike asked.

All she could do was nod. He squeezed tighter and she felt his fingers all the way down through her body to her core.

A moan slipped from her lips. "Higher, Ex," she said. "Harder."

"Harder?"

"Yes, harder. I want it to hurt," she said, thinking that overwhelming the ache might erase it.

"You like it hard, don't you, baby?"

She actually started to agree with a nod and then realized what he'd just done. Opening her eyes, she straightened and grabbed his hands away from her body to spin and glare at him.

"You're evil, you know that?"

"You've told me before… How's the neck?" he asked, but the smirk on his face told her that he knew he'd worked out the knot. "Now I've done my good deed, what's my reward?"

"Trust you," she muttered, knowing nothing came for free with him. Of their own accord, her eyes dropped to his fly. "What do you want?"

Leaning over, he scooped a hand around to the back of her head, giving her the slightest tug toward him. "I was thinking tech time, but if you're thinking that…"

"I wasn't thinking anything," she said, but he curled his fingers, catching her hair in his fist at the back of her head. Just like he'd hold her if her mouth was open and filled with his—

"Why do you always want to hurt her?" Junker asked.

When Rora registered the tension in Junker's expression as he marched toward them, she drew Strike's arm down, taking his fingers from her hair.

"He's not hurting me," she said. "And my neck does feel better."

Though not completely appeased, Junker did stop his advance. "Do you want me to draw you a bath?"

"Thank you," she said, not that she really wanted to get into the tub, but she'd let Strike help her, so she figured it would be right to let Junker do the same.

He disappeared to the back of the room and into the bathroom. As soon as he pushed the door over, she wiped her smile and sagged.

Flopping onto her back, Rora planted her hands on her face. "Oh, Strike," she exhaled.

"What do you see in that guy?"

When she felt him moving onto the bed, her hands fell. But her next breath was so sharp, it was almost a gasp. Strike had no shame about parting her legs and resting his hips between her thighs. She couldn't believe he'd be so brazen, but he compounded that act by stealing her wrists and pushing them into the bed so he could loom over her.

"What are you doing?"

"We're alone," he murmured, a sinister purr in his voice.

"It takes two seconds to turn the water on," she hissed and tried to struggle. "Get off me."

"I thought about getting you off first."

"Strike," she objected, but didn't want to raise her voice, if Junker thought Strike was forcing himself on her, there would be all out war. "You have to stop this. We have to stop."

"Why?" he asked, brushing his lips over hers. "Because it's wrong? Because it's bad?"

Both would only serve to turn him on more. "Because we're over," she said. "You were right to resist this. You didn't want us to be together and I pushed. I shouldn't have."

"Why not?" he asked. "What the hell's changed? The square? Tell me you want him and—"

"You'll leave me alone?"

"I was going to say I'd kill him," Strike said, his head tilting, but she wasn't sure he was joking.

Though he grumbled, he did get up off her. He'd just stood up when Junker came out of the bathroom. "There's bubble bath in there," Junker said.

"Party time," Strike mumbled.

"Thank you," she said.

Rora wanted to issue instructions for them to get along but thought that was likely to be inflammatory. So, instead, she gathered her nightwear and her toiletries, and slipped into the bathroom.

Tying her hair up on top of her head, she wiped steam from the mirror and washed her face.

When the bath was so full it was ready to overflow, she turned off the water, and slid into the soothing bubbles. With her eyes closed and her head propped on the back of the tub, Rora had to admit it did feel nice to be submerged in the warm water that was making her skin tingle.

"What did you want to talk about?"

Fright made her gasp. Opening her eyes, she sat up so fast that water sloshed from the tub. Strike took a single step backwards to avoid the water hitting his boots, managing, in his usual nonchalant way, to be so cool in avoiding disaster.

"Can I help you?" she asked, glancing down to see her breasts were exposed.

Sliding down in the water, she scooped some of the bubbles upward to conceal her chest. But this was Strike, he had no shame. He just sat on the toilet lid and propped his elbows on his knees.

"You said you wanted to talk."

"I'm naked, Strike."

"So?" he asked, his fingertips skimming the water to move some of the bubbles around, probably giving himself a view beneath the water. "You said you wanted to talk, whatever it is, we're alone, there's no clock, so talk."

"The point of lying in the tub is to help me relax, having you in here doesn't help me relax." Grabbing the neck of his tee-shirt, he pulled it off over his head. "What are you doing?"

"Lean forward, I'll give you a neck rub."

"You are not getting in this tub with me," she said, eyeing the door that was open a crack. "Junker is right out there."

"I say again, I'll take him out if—"

"It's disrespectful. Anyway, how many times do I have to say that we're not together?"

"It's a neck rub, not a ring," he said and stood up to slide the leather of his belt from its buckle.

Panic made her cling for the edges of the tub. It wasn't just a neck rub, it was a naked neck rub, and after how good his talented fingers had felt working her flesh out there in the room, she didn't trust herself not to get confused if he touched her.

"Stop it," she hissed. "Do not take your pants off."

"Talk or I'm getting in there," he said, "and I'll make sure your little buddy out there knows exactly what's going on in here… and what we did the other night."

Narrowing her eyes, she resented how easily he could push her buttons. "Fine, I'll talk," she said. Strike sat on the toilet lid again. But before she got underway, she had to check something. "Are you armed?"

That intrigued him. "No," he said. "Do I need to be?"

"I'm just thinking that after we start talking you might want to kill me."

He shrugged. "Then I'll drown you."

The water. She eyed the tub that she'd just been enjoying a few seconds ago, realizing it could be her coffin if Strike decided it should be.

"Ok, now I'm feeling vulnerable and thinking we should do this later… Take your pants off."

The side of his mouth lifted, and he got closer. "Now I'm too intrigued to fuck you… What did you do, naughty girl? Tell me and after I'll make you come so hard, your scream will melt the foundations."

"That's what I'm afraid of," she muttered and rubbed the side of her neck. "Strike, I… I want to be honest because I figure that if I just tell you, it will be better than you finding out on your own. But… this really isn't a good setup for me. I'm naked and slippery and you're stronger than me and—"

He breathed out a kind of laugh. "You're actually worried about this? Geez, Cupcake, I'm not gonna kill you. Why would I dispose of your body? Playing with it is too much fun."

"You say that now, but…"

Her eyes wandered away from him. "This is about the Point," he said.

Her attention leaped back to him. "How did you know that?"

"It is, isn't it?"

Could he know? No. He'd said he was working on it. For a minute, she let her jaw move, but resisted telling the truth. But she couldn't resist forever. "I lied to you. That… What you took from me at the resort wasn't the Point."

"I know," he said, so calm and collected while she was the one left stunned. "It was a test."

"You… you know?" she asked almost not recognizing the man sitting with her. "Why are you not mad?"

"The day you left me… I put the device into Opal, you walked out the door, and… something happened that's never happened before."

"What?" she asked, twisting to hook her hands on the side of the tub closest to him. "What happened?"

"I felt guilty," he said. "Took me a minute to figure out what it was, but I actually cared that I'd hurt you." He shivered, like the very idea of guilt made him feel sick. "I was on autopilot when I left you tied to that bed and as soon as I started driving, I knew something wasn't right… it was like there was this weight in me… I didn't get it."

"That's why you went back to Buddy's? You hoped I'd come to you and we'd make up?"

He shifted an elbow onto the side of the bath. "I don't know what I was thinking. I told you that you fuck with my head… When you showed up, I saw what I was doing to you, but I wanted to win. That's what I always do. I do what suits me and I win… I'm used to toxic, like with Bella." He'd told her. "I didn't think you'd really go, I figured it was some kind of game, but you did go. I thought I was prepared to lose you, but when you walked out, I didn't feel like I'd won."

"You should've talked to me," she said, sliding down the edge of the tub to get closer to him. "Told me what you were thinking. I thought you'd played me all along, that telling me you loved me, that our whole relationship had been a con for you to get your hands on the Point."

"I saw a chance and I took it. It's a way of life for me, baby. It's the way my mind works, I wanted the Point and I saw a way to get it… Whatever you do to me, baby, no other woman's ever done it… I guess I couldn't figure out how to handle it… how to handle you."

"So you pushed me away?"

Scooping her hand from the enamel, he laid it between his two hands, his chest resting on the back of his own hand when he hunkered down. "I didn't understand why you were so mad, I didn't get it. But it was my fault, I didn't tell you what I wanted…"

"From us?"

"From the Point," he said and sneered at himself. "It was never about taking over the world. I hate people, you know that, and as long as we have enough money to live, I don't give a damn about dough. Hell, you've seen the kind of place I setup camp. I could reserve rooms in the Plaza and not pay a dime, but I pick a secluded, dingy hole because I like it."

The loft wasn't dingy. It wasn't water-tight, but there was something appealing about its earthiness; something beautiful about finding love in an abandoned place. The loft was an embodiment of each of them. They'd each known what it was to be built up and then condemned and forgotten.

"I don't understand," she said. "If it wasn't about the money or power… then what was—"

"The tech," he said, his thumb brushing across her knuckles. "Tech turns me on, Cupcake… I had to see it."

Sincere, yet hard, she doubted he expected her to swoon, but she did a little. "You're a big kid, Stryker," she whispered and boosted herself closer to kiss his shoulder. "You wanted to play with a shiny new toy."

Slipping a hand out from between his chest and her hand, he cupped her face and tried to draw her mouth up to his. Rora parted her lips, her heart pounding; doubt, confusion, love, all of it bounced off each other in her chest. Before their lips could meet, she lay back, taking her head from his hand.

"What's wrong?" he asked. "I'm sorry, baby. Ok? I'm stubborn. I'm impulsive… This won't be the last time I'll hurt you. But the way I feel about you hasn't changed. It won't ever change. And my loyalty to you won't change either."

"I don't want you to hurt me, Strike. I wanted you to love me… more than you loved the tech."

"And I warned you… I'm weak."

In so many ways, he was the strongest man she knew. That was part of the reason it wrenched at her heart to hear that the only thing he couldn't be strong for, was her.

Rora tried to put it into perspective for him. He saw it as wanting to experiment with a new toy, but she saw it as a betrayal, and he had to understand her point of view.

"And what if next time it's not tech, it's another woman?"

Startled, he recoiled at the suggestion. "A woman?" he asked and sat upright. "Shit, baby, you don't have to worry about that. My dick's easier to control than my intellect. You remember the blonde? You served her up to me and I didn't follow through."

"Says you."

"I don't lie to you." Her brows rose because she couldn't contain her incredulity. "Ok, so I don't lie to you about that kind of stuff. Being faithful, I can handle, women never really interested me anyway. You have your obvious uses but…"

"It's those obvious uses that worry me."

"Bella put it on a plate. She offered me both of you, together, didn't take it, did I?"

"Because you can't stand her," she said, rolling to her back and folding her arms beneath her breasts. But Rora breathed out to confess. "I'm not really worried about you sleeping around, it took me long enough to get you into bed, but… I'm trying to make you see why I was hurt. Prioritizing something else over me when I've told you the opposite is important to me… You broke my heart, Strike. I don't know what to believe. I don't know if I can take the risk that you might do it again."

"We both know that you love me," he said, in a quote from their first night together.

Being led by her heart would be easy, but she still needed answers. "Why did you let me think you were working on the Point?"

"Wanted to see if you'd tell me the truth," he said. "You didn't."

She stuttered. "I was shocked. I thought you'd want to kill me for misleading you like I did. I really thought that you'd have accessed the Point, seen it wasn't what you thought, and come on the hunt for my blood."

He hunkered down. "After you walked out of Buddy's, I sat forever just looking at that front door."

She knew what that was like and a burst of satisfaction curled her lips. "I sat staring at that door in the weeks after you walked out on me. I was staring at that door when I decided to go bust up all those cars to get your attention."

"If I thought it would've worked, I'd have put a hole in the Earth to bring you back to me. Playing with a piece of tech wasn't worth losing you… but I didn't know that until it happened. Seconds after you left, I took the USB out of Opal and waited. I was sure you'd come back. When you didn't, I went on a binge, got myself good and drunk. I didn't know how to pursue you, I'd never cared about chasing a woman down for anything except business before. I thought you'd come back to me… you didn't."

"In my defense, Bella had me locked up."

"I know that now," he said, leaning closer to pick her hand out of the water to press it on the edge of the tub again. "And I'm sorry I let her hold you. I wanted to be the one to come for you, but if she'd found us both in that room together, she'd have locked the door and made us do things to each other, and to her that—"

"If you'd walked into that room, I'd have thought my nightmare was coming to life," she said, but he didn't respond to her attempt to joke.

Probably because it wasn't much of a joke. Bella would've used their love to play them off each other and Rora's nightmare probably would've come true because if it meant saving her life, Strike would've had sex with Bella in front of her, and he wouldn't have had a choice.

"I'm still sorry, Cupcake."

Something dawned on her. "If you took the USB out of Opal without using it, how did you know that it wasn't the Point?"

"Because I tried to do what you asked me to do. After the first week, it struck me that maybe if I destroyed the Point, you'd be happy. You'd know I was for real and didn't give a fuck about it. So, I did. Except it took no time at all to wipe the USB and that was when I knew you'd conned me. Something as powerful as the Point wouldn't have slipped away in seconds. I'd used an atom bomb to destroy a grain of rice… I don't know why it didn't occur to me when you were telling me at the resort what you'd done to Benjamin. You did the same thing to me. Suddenly, I don't know, everything fell into place. You took me to the same place you took Benjamin when he thought he was hiding the Point with you?" She nodded. The corner of his mouth lifted. "Damn, you're good, baby."

The last thing she'd expected was to see him relaxed about it. "You… you're not mad?"

"Proud," he said. "You proved something to both of us… You said in the loft that I had to trust myself. I would never have been able to do that if you hadn't given me temptation like that. And yeah, I failed at the first hurdle, but ultimately… I chose you, baby. I chose you over the tech… That's how I know this is different. That's how I know you can trust me… because finally I can trust myself… when it comes to you anyway."

Rora still wasn't a hundred percent sure that the story was true, he could be trying to manipulate her into giving up the real Point or Leandra's location. But she'd never seen him like this. There was a new kind of optimism in his eyes when he looked at her, like he really could see his redemption in her.

While she was still trying to figure out how to respond. There was a noise from beyond the bathroom.

Sitting up straight, she listened to the scuffle and the mumbled voices. "Strike," she said.

Up on his feet, he went to the door to try to peek out, but the angle wouldn't give him a great view.

"Stay in here, Cupcake," he said, and opened the door to slip out.

FOURTEEN

SCREW THAT. If there was something going on out there, she wasn't going to sit in there and wait to be attacked by a random assailant. Getting out of the tub as quickly and as quietly as she could, Rora grabbed her nightdress and pulled it on although her body wasn't completely dry.

Leaving the bathroom, she could still hear some kind of kerfuffle, but there had been no gunshots and it didn't sound like physical fighting. Someone was on the bed, a man. She could only see his legs because Strike and Junker were at the bottom of the other bed arguing and shoving each other.

"And I say we kick him out," Strike said.

"He's bleeding," Junker said. "This man needs help."

Pushing between the two men, Rora cared less about their argument and more about whoever was strewn out.

"Oh my God," she said, climbing onto the bed to crawl up beside Torres who was laid there, and just like Junker said, he was bleeding. "What happened?"

His face was red, his eye swelling, there were cuts and bruises all over like he'd been in a fight.

"Burke went rogue," Torres said, wincing when she started to help him take his arm from his jacket. "Killed four of our guys and then called it in accusing me."

Getting his jacket off, she dropped it onto the floor and then started to unbutton his shirt to find out why Torres was cradling the rather nasty patch of blood across his opposite shoulder and arm.

"Burke?" she said. "Why would he want to—"

"He's going after the Black Jewel. He's got her scent, he's tracking her."

"That makes no sense, why give us the tech if he was going to go after it himself?"

"She has the answer to the question," he croaked, sagging onto the bed when she took his arm from his shirt sleeve. "The tech meant nothing until we found out it was important to the question."

It was easy for her to almost forget that there were still people out there seeking the Point. Rora was so caught up in what it had done to her and Strike that she forgot about the world at large.

Glancing over her shoulder at Strike, all she got from him was a shrug, which she couldn't interpret as good or bad.

"Doesn't matter, we're bailing out," Strike said. "We don't trust this asshole."

Peeking at the wounds on Torres' arm and shoulder, she figured they did look like gunshots. The one on his arm was a flesh wound and it looked like it had stopped bleeding. The other wasn't so benign.

Balling his shirt, she pressed it to his shoulder and put Torres' hand over it. "Press hard," she ordered and turned around to climb off the bed. "You two come with me."

There was blood on her hands, so she couldn't grab hold of anyone, but she marched to the bathroom, hoping Strike and Junker would follow. She went to the sink to wash her hands, as soon as she saw Strike over her shoulder, she raised her brows.

He put his hands up in surrender. "I didn't tell her," he said. "I'm thinking Burke's making assumptions because, uh…"

Knowing that tone, she spun around, grabbing a towel from the rail. Junker came in and closed the door. "What's happening?" Junker asked.

Strike turned a scowl on him. "You don't need to be here. This is where the grown-ups make decisions that save lives."

Grabbing his arm, Rora turned Strike back to her. "Because, uh, what?"

"I put word out that she knew," he said.

Her mouth fell open and it took her a minute to return to reality. She smacked his shoulder. "Oh. My. God," she said, hitting him with each word. "I can't… I don't even know where to start."

"Look, it's no problem. The more people looking for her, the easier it will be for me to track her. She had you for over a week, people believe she got the truth out of you."

"That's not the point, S—" Sealing her lips, she breathed out through her nose.

"What are you talking about?" Junker asked. "What does this Burke think that the Jewel knows?"

Rora took a deep breath, prepared not to lie to him anymore. "The project of Benjamin's that you thought Exile had," she said and winced when she made eye contact with Junker. "It's called the Point and Exile thought he had it too. But he didn't… because I lied to him… no one knows where it is… except me."

Junker blinked once, but he stood completely still for at least half a minute, looking at her like he didn't recognize her. "You've… you've known this the whole time?" She nodded. "And he knew this?" She nodded again when Junker pointed at Strike. He ran his hands through his hair. "This is why you thought he wanted to kill you?" Junker looked at Strike. "If you hurt her—"

"If I hurt her, what, Square? Rora is my woman, and our shit, is our shit, and there's no one on this earth less capable of hurting her than me. You on the other hand—"

"Ok," she said, laying a hand on Strike's chest to stop him advancing on Junker. "Let's save this for later… What do we do with him out there?"

"Put him out of his misery?" Strike said.

Junker scoffed. But she chewed on her lip, keeping her eyes on Strike's. His brows rose slowly, and he tilted his head in a sort of shrug.

Junker looked between them. "Aurora, you cannot be thinking—"

"Ok," Strike said, spinning to face him. "Let's get one thing clear now, if you use her name again, I'll cut out your tongue. Call her Kero or you'll call her nothing."

"Kero?" Junker asked.

"That's right," Strike said and then glanced at her. "Should I just cut out his tongue?"

"No!" she said. "You know Torres will put all of this together, he must know who I am."

"You don't exist anymore," Strike said. "And Benjamin Gallagher's assistant is not famous. Even if he suspected it, he doesn't know it and we don't tempt fate around here. Besides, that goes away if you let me put him out of his misery."

Strike was capable, she knew it, and if she agreed, he'd end Torres' life now. Rora wasn't sure she liked having this kind of power. "You can't kill a man in his… profession," she said, because offing an NSA agent, whether he was rogue or not, would have serious repercussions.

Her ex stayed loose. "We can make it look like suicide… You and I have some experience with that," he said, which she didn't appreciate.

Putting her hands to her face, she covered her glare. "No, we're not talking about this. Either we help him, or we abandon him."

"He's here for intel," Strike said. "He thinks if he hangs around long enough that you'll start to feel sorry for him or he'll learn something useful that he can use to put us away."

"I already told him I wouldn't flip."

"Yeah, and how did that work out the first time?"

"You mean the time you set me up?"

"Ok," Junker said, stepping between them, taking a turn at being peacemaker. "We're not going to leave a bleeding man to die. The longer we stand in here talking, the more blood he's losing."

"And he figured out my evil plan," Strike said. "Maybe he's not so dumb after all." Rora smacked his chest, Strike's hand rose to the spot she'd struck. "You're hitting me a lot these days, Cupcake, even for you. Sexual frustration?"

She smiled, but not in happiness. Rora was smug. "I like doing it because I know you won't hit me back. It frustrates you to be out of control."

"Oh, I'm in control, baby. And it turns me on whenever you use those hands on me." Moseying closer, he pinned her to the vanity. "You remember the first time you saw my scars?"

She shivered and tried her best to swallow away the awareness tingling inside of her throat. "Yes."

"I told you it wasn't happening back then," he said, grabbing her shoulders to spin her around. Tugging her hair, he yanked her head aside and dropped his lips to her carotid before lifting them to her ear. "Now I say it is."

"Uh, excuse me," Junker said and grabbed Strike's arm to try pulling him away.

Instead, Strike growled at him and grabbed him by the throat, thrusting him back against the wall by the door. "Touch me again, Square, and I'll break every one of your fingers and then your face."

"Flame," Rora soothed, drawing his arm down from Junker's neck. "You need to calm down. And Junk, Exile really doesn't like to be touched."

"We have a man out there, dying!"

Junker was right. She and Strike were distracted by each other, and it would be kind of unholy if Torres died just because she liked it when Strike kissed her neck and touched her body.

"Good luck with that," Strike said, turning his back to the vanity behind her to lean against it, folding his arms.

Rora turned to make eye contact, beseeching him without words for half a minute. "Baby, you have to help him."

"Me?" Strike asked and pointed past her to Junker. "What about him? This is his great plan."

"He's right, I can handle this," Junk said. "We have a med kit. I can sew up a wound, it's not that hard… right?"

"I don't know, I've never done it," she said. "I guess we can figure it out." Strike mumbled something, making her turn. "Something to say?"

"Goddamnit," he said, marching past both of them to leave the bathroom and return to Torres. "If you sew up the wound with the bullet still in there—" he bent to grab the comforter and pulled it hard to drag Torres to the side of the bed closest to him "—he'll die of infection. Get me towels, water, and whatever med supplies you have."

Rora ran off to get everything and when she came back, he had a small black case on the nightstand and a syringe in his hand. "What is that?" she asked, climbing onto the bed on Torres' other side.

"Morphine," he said, taking a bottle from the small zipped case.

"You carry morphine around with you?" Junker asked. "Talk about never meeting your heroes, he's an addict!"

"He is not an addict," she said and watched Strike put the needle in the bottle to drag out some of the liquid. "Have you ever tried it?"

"Try not to ask me questions in front of the narc, huh, honey?" he said and put the needle in front of Torres' face, though the guy was half out of it. "I stick you with this, the pain goes away, and I patch you up. Your alternative is that I don't, and we leave you here to bleed out."

Torres sucked in a breath. "Lidocaine."

Strike hissed. "Sorry, fresh out of the sissy drugs and I'm not raiding a pharmacy for you. If it's not bad enough for this, then we leave you here to bleed out."

"What about doing it without?" she asked, looking around. "I'm sure we still have liquor."

"Fine, then you take responsibility for my murder charge," Strike said. "If I dig that bullet out, it'll hurt, and he'll lash out. What happens when men lash out at me? What's my patience level like, babe?"

She considered it for a blink and then looked to Torres. "Take the morphine."

Torres looked at them both and clenched his teeth to breathe through a bite of pain. He nodded. Strike stuck him and less than a minute later, Torres' body relaxed.

Strike went to work, and she bounced off the bed to grab jeans and a sweater that she pulled on over her nightdress. When she was dressed, Rora returned to the bed, kneeling on the mattress next to Torres.

"I'd have raided a pharmacy for you," Strike said, holding up the bullet he'd just dug out of Torres' shoulder to show her it.

"That's disgusting," she said of the bullet and then made eye contact with him. "And I'd have let you stick me with the morphine, I don't need any sissy drugs."

Turning his smirk back to the wounds, Strike got back to work. "You remember what I did when Jewel drugged you in Wonderland." She did and didn't have to say it because he carried on. "Next time, I'm doing the opposite."

Instead of protecting her virtue, he'd take advantage of her incapacity? He'd warned her about that during a conversation before they found her former workplace in flames.

"Then I better make sure not to get myself hurt," she said and slapped a hand to Torres' uninjured arm before climbing off the bed. "Come on, Junk. Let's get some food and some ice for his face."

"Can we leave him alone with Exile?"

Going to Strike's jacket first, she pulled some money from his pocket. "Exile isn't subtle," she said, pulling on her own jacket and grabbing a scarf, aware that Strike could hear them. "If he was going to kill the patient, he'd have done it already."

"Kero," Strike called when she opened the door. "Show me your blade." She took it from her pocket to prove she had it. "Defend yourself or die... and you know what happens if it's the latter."

Spinning around, she left with Junker on her heels. "What happens?" Junker asked.

"Never mind," she said, stopping to give him some money. "Go and get a couple of pizzas."

"Where are you going?" he asked as she walked away.

"To raid a pharmacy," she said, striding away from him.

FIFTEEN

ON RETURNING TO THE ROOM, Rora found Torres still unconscious on one bed, Strike sitting on the other, and Junker pacing the room. But the moment the door closed, both conscious men stopped to focus on her.

"What?" she asked the two men who were fixated on her, making her squirm.

Junker was still just gaping when Strike got up from the bed and came to her. Braced for whatever reaction he might have to the bag of supplies she was carrying, she didn't fight him when he took it from her.

Strike opened it, looked inside and then threw it aside to grab her face and haul her up to kiss her. She was so shocked by the kiss that she froze for a minute and didn't respond. He pushed her jacket from her shoulders and rushed her back against the door.

"You naughty, naughty girl," he said, shoving her head back to suck on her neck.

"Stop," she said, pushing at his shoulders, but her knees were starting to buckle. "Don't."

Junker came up behind Strike and she had to shove harder to make the man kissing her back off. "You can't support this, Exile," Junker declared. "I can't believe that even you—"

"I can't be mad at her when she misbehaves," Strike said, clasping her throat then letting his hand drift down over her torso. "Fuck, I love it when you're bad."

"Someone had to do it, Junk," she said, touching the spot Strike had marked on her neck. "Exile did the heavy lifting with the patient."

Strike glared at Junker. "Yeah, what do we need him for again? You and me can rely on each other to do whatever's necessary. We don't need a square or a narc."

Leaving the door, she went toward one of Junker's packs. "Can we use one of your laptops, Junk?"

"Uh, yeah, I—"

But she had already taken one from its case. Strike came over. "One of?"

"He has three," she said, grinning at him as she held it up. "Guess some guys carry a bigger wad than others."

"Guess some need to," Strike said. "Mine's all-purpose and obviously more powerful. Guess his doesn't measure up."

Presenting the laptop to him, she smiled. "I was careful. But will you cover my ass, please, Flame?"

"Oh," he said, folding his arms. "You want me to use his kit to clean up your mess."

She thrust the computer toward him. "A mess made for your friend."

He pushed the computer back to her. "I don't have friends."

The tension in the room didn't need to be fueled, but as they stood toe-to-toe with this computer between them, she could feel the air begin to crackle. "So, what am I?" she asked.

"You're my girl," he said.

Pushing the laptop against his chest, she didn't mind jolting him. "I am not your girl."

"Yeah? So why keep calling me your flame?"

" 'Cause I can't use your real name and I feel stupid saying Exile… It's a stupid name, by the way."

"You know his real name?" Junker exclaimed, but she didn't respond.

Rora wasn't going to break eye contact with Strike; no way was she giving him the satisfaction of winning this stare down. "Yes, I do, and I'll be happy to start using it if Exile keeps screwing with me."

"Someone's crabby," Strike said. "Guess I won't be getting any this week if it's that time of the month."

Rora hated that way he looked into her, he knew she was getting riled and he took great pleasure in being the one to push her buttons. But then again, no one could press her buttons the way that he did.

"Would you take this and do your job, please?" she said, picking up his hand to put it on the laptop she'd pressed to his chest.

"Give me mine and I'll do it," he said. She sneered at him. "Tick, tock, baby, you could be creeping onto the wanted lists right now."

"Do you want me to check if the robbery has been reported?" Junker asked from somewhere in the periphery of the room.

The corner of Strike's mouth rose, but there was no joy in his conceited expression. "There you go, baby. The square will check for you."

Strike dropped onto the couch, opening his arms along the back. "Uh," she said and licked her lips when she turned to Junker, deliberately stepping on Strike's foot as she did. "Thanks, Junk, but Exile does a little more than just check."

"What does he do?"

"Yeah, Cupcake, what do I do?"

Narrowing her eyes on him, she hated that he got such gratification from her need. Instead of fighting him, she surrendered. "Fine," she said, bending over him to put the laptop on the end table next to his chair. "Don't do a thing."

Walking away, she headed for the door.

"Whoa," Strike said when she pushed Junker aside and grabbed the door handle. Rora rested her weight on it as she twisted around to look to him. "Where are you going?"

"To get myself arrested," she said. "Maybe I'll try solicitation this time. Let's see how much you get while I'm in jail."

Pushing down the handle, she was about to go out, but he rushed over and put his hand on hers to try prying it away from the handle. "Baby," he murmured, trying to slide an arm around her waist, but she pushed it away.

"No," she said, giving him a push. "No, go away."

Crowding her, he kept trying to pull her into his arms and she kept pushing him away. "Cupcake," he mumbled into her hair and tried to duck down to kiss her, but she twisted away from him. "You want me to apologize, huh?"

Lifting her chin, she looked right past him. "Try it, see what happens."

Easing himself closer, he slid his arms around her, pulling her hip to his groin. "I'm sorry, babe," he said, crouching to nuzzle her neck through her hair. "You were so bad. You know what it does to me when you're bad." Yeah, it turned him on. "You make me want to be bad too. We're so good at being bad together."

Recognizing the growl in his voice, she smiled and tried again to push away his embrace. "Don't start that," she said.

Strike yanked her to him. "Let's fight, baby. I love it when you're angry."

"Yeah, because you usually get some," she said, trying to wriggle out of his arms, but that just made him hold her tighter. "Ok, I get it." Matching her eyes to his, she used the heat she saw in his to her advantage and stopped fighting him. "Do you have my back?"

"Always," he said, and leaned in for a kiss.

Avoiding his mouth, Rora ducked out under his arm and slipped away to go to Junker. "I think we'll have to pack up here and move on."

"He's out," Junker said, nodding at Torres on the bed. "And we just got here."

Rora felt Strike's eyes on her as he passed, but she just smiled and ignored him. He went back to the armchair and picked up the laptop she'd tried to give him before,

Junker's laptop. Weird as it might be for him to work on a different machine, and for her to see him on a different one, it impressed her that he could pick it up and do what he needed to without skipping a beat.

"We don't have to go far, just away from here. Pack up the truck and we'll worry about moving him when it's done," she said.

Junker accepted this and got to work.

They'd need to know where to go and she needed to get a better lay of the land. Because she needed to make some decisions about direction, and because she knew it would irk Strike, she retrieved Opal from beneath the pillow she'd been secreted under.

Instead of sitting on the bed, Rora went over to the dresser and sat on the floor against it, straightening her legs to prop her feet up on the chair Strike was sitting on, resting them between his thighs. It was nuts that she was using Opal for something as basic as checking maps, but when she peeked up and saw Strike fixated on her, she felt a surge of satisfaction that made it worth it.

"This machine's a piece of shit," he said.

"Bad workman blames his tools."

"I'm doing the job, I'm just not impressed," he said. "Good call bailing out though."

"How do you think they found us? The authorities have never been this close to our ass… have they? All this time I was impressed by your skills. Are you showing me now that without Opal, you can't keep me safe?"

Sliding further down into the chair, his groin bumped against her feet. "You're safe. Torres is clear of trackers," he said. "What about your new buddy?"

"How would they know to track him?" she asked.

Strike shrugged. "He's not as vigilant as you."

"Someone used to call me paranoid," she said, remembering what had happened in a certain convenience store parking lot after she told him she had a creepy feeling.

"Whatever," he said. "The square might not notice someone pinning something on him."

"Well we can't ask if—"

Strike rose, putting the laptop onto the chair and a hand on her head when he lifted his leg over her. "Yo, Square," he said just as Junker came back in. "Come here."

Closing Opal, Rora leaped to her feet and put the laptop on the dresser before darting over to get between the men. "What are you doing?" she asked Strike.

"Don't worry," he said, taking something from his back pocket. "It's painless." He began to wave the device in his hand up and down over Junker. "And saves me from having to touch the guy."

"What's he doing?" Junker asked.

Strike put a hand on her stomach and eased her aside to move around to Junker's back. "Just go with it," she said.

To her surprise the device bleeped when Strike moved it over the back of Junker's neck. "And what do we have here?" Strike muttered and ran his thumb up the inside of Junker's collar to pull out a miniscule flat square. Holding it up on a fingertip, Strike showed it to her.

"Wow," she said, getting in close. "It's so tiny."

"Now I get to hit him, right?" Strike asked. She tutted at him. "What? He endangered you."

Dropping the device to the floor, Strike stamped it with the heel of his boot. While she was still examining the shattered remains, Strike lunged forward and threw an arm around Junker's neck, pulling him backwards and locking the unsuspecting man in a chokehold.

"Flame!" she screamed.

Junker choked, coughing and clawing at the arm Strike had clamped around him. "He's a liability," Strike said.

"Please," she said. "Let him go! He didn't know! Please! He didn't know!" But Strike had determination on his face and Junker's hits were getting weaker. "Goddamnit!"

Grabbing Strike's forearm, she leaped up and sunk her teeth into the side of his hand. "Fuck," he called out and let go of Junker who fell to the floor. "Jesus, baby!"

Dropping to the floor, she checked on Junker; he was still conscious, just wheezing and coughing. "He's a maniac," Junker croaked, rubbing his throat.

The air rushed from her lungs when Strike grabbed her and hauled her up to her feet. "I'm gonna muzzle that mouth," Strike hissed at her, snatching her close to him.

"We have to get out of here," she said, willing to take any punishment he dished out, but the anger in his eyes was too aroused to be a danger to her. "They know we're here."

"Let's split," he said and started to pull her, but she yanked him back.

"Help Junker take Torres to the truck."

Tugging her hard so she fell against him, Strike was losing his patience. "No way," he said. "We're with each other, that's it."

But she curved her arm around her waist, pulling his arm with hers. "Junker is helpful. Like it or not, he can be useful."

"And him?" Strike asked, nodding at the bed though he didn't take his eyes from hers. "What do we need him for?"

"Burke needs his fall guy," she said. "And if we cross his path, we might need—"

"Leverage," Strike said, and he dropped his forehead to bump it on hers. "Fuck, baby, that's cold. I love it." Kissing her hairline, he let her go and went to haul Junker off the floor. "Move, Square, help me get this prick in the back of the truck."

Junker was still recovering from his own Strike encounter, but he stumbled along to do what was asked of him. She didn't know if Junker had picked up on much of what she'd said to Strike. Rora wasn't sure if she would be able to hand over one man to another who wanted to ruin his life. But, for now, it kept them all together and the sad truth was, if it saved innocent Leandra, she might be capable of it.

Torres had training and could be a plant, she hadn't eliminated that possibility, but for now, she didn't know enough to come to that conclusion. She and Strike knew how to limit what they said in front of Torres and as long as they told Junker not to talk too much in front of the narc, she hoped they wouldn't lose any ground.

This was a chance to gather some intel of her own on the men around her. One of them would be her path out of this, but as of this minute, she didn't know which one of them to trust, so she wasn't ready to call any of them out of the running.

SIXTEEN

SITTING ON THE EDGE of a bed in the new motel room they'd travelled to, Rora appreciated the skill of Strike's hands that were massaging the side of her neck again. All this driving and the lack of sleep was starting to take its toll, she wasn't used to being awake for such long periods of time.

Squeezing her shoulders, he worked the tension out of her taut muscles. "I swear I'm going to keep looking until I find a skill you can't master," she said, moaning at the pleasure delivered by his strong fingers. The TV was on in the background, but the volume was low, so she couldn't really hear it. But when her eyes opened, she saw the cute creature on the screen and smiled. "Sloths are cute, don't you think? If we were together, would you get me a sloth?"

"Sure," he said. "I let you have a pet square and a pet narc, a pet sloth is nothing."

His hand slid down inside her top to cup her breast. Rora curled her fingers around his wrist and drew it back out. "Don't get fresh, Mr. Exile."

"Why not? We're alone," he said, dipping down to kiss the back of her neck.

"What do you call that?" she asked, opening her hand to Torres who was sleeping on the bed next to the one they were seated on.

"He's out."

But the moment he said that, Torres groaned. Strike wasn't put off because he kissed her neck again. "Flame," she whispered, twisting to peek at him. "You can't risk touching me like that in front of Torres. If he's here for information—"

"What?" he asked, running a hand over the hair she had piled on her head. "He calls me your boyfriend. He knows we've fucked."

Taking his hand from her hair, she twisted around to look him in the eye. "I told him I wasn't a factor in your life anymore."

"Won't be the first or the last time we'll give him misinformation," he said, kissing her shoulder. "I don't give a damn what you say is for the best, Cupcake. I know that him thinking you're important in my life is vital to your safety. I love you and I don't play games with that. And I don't think you get it."

That was the first time since… before, that she'd heard him say those three little words. That his tone was so matter-of-fact gave her shivers, but she feared being sucked into his orbit again, she wasn't sure she'd be strong enough to break free.

"Get what?" she asked, surprised to see how quickly he became stern.

"We're not just together, we're the same. I've opened myself to you, Ro, and there's no way you're getting back out. I don't care how long it takes, I'm not leaving your side."

Glancing at Torres, she couldn't tell if he was still out or not, but he looked to be. "If you want to let him believe we're together, I don't care."

"But you're still going to play hard to get," he said. "This is some kind of payback, isn't it?"

"Payback?"

"For me trying to ignore what was happening between us for so long."

Could be. Letting him wonder about her motives for a while would be a novelty. "I always knew you were damaged. I never asked you not to be. I'm damaged too, it's one of the reasons we worked together."

"But?" he asked, brushing his lips across her shoulder.

Grabbing his hair, she pulled his mouth away from her skin. If she kept letting him get away with these subtle, intimate caresses, she'd be naked beneath him before she realized she'd been seduced.

"I was on my knees, begging you to choose me and you didn't."

"I did, baby. I did choose you."

She knew that now, but that didn't erase the memory of how it felt to have him rip her heart out. "Ultimately," she said. "That's what you say. How can I trust that? How can I trust you?"

"Don't worry about that," he said. "I've got a long time to make it up to you. I'm not going anywhere. You're not done with me."

Torres groaned again, and this time blinked open his eyes. Rora was watching him taking in what he could see of the ceiling and the bed when Strike began to massage her neck again. A kind of panic seized their patient and he tried to sit up.

"Don't sit up," she said, and when she tried to get up, Strike held her down.

Torres' head rolled on the pillow. "So this is what crime's power couple do of a night?"

"Save helpless strays?" Strike asked. "No, but you've got Kero to thank for your life… I'd have killed you." She swatted Strike's stomach as he passed her to climb off the bed. He opened a bottle of meds and shook a couple out to hand them to Torres. "There's water by the bed."

"You have no bedside manner," Rora muttered and got up to help Torres put the pills in his mouth and then she cradled his head to help him sip the water she held in her other hand.

"Does this make us even for the biting?" Torres asked her.

"Maybe," she said, returning the glass to the nightstand. "But I still haven't forgiven you for copping a feel."

"Whoa, wait, what?" Strike asked, putting a hand on her shoulder to drag her back against his chest.

"Never told him about that, huh?" Torres asked, shifting on the bed.

"If I had, you definitely wouldn't be here. Are you hungry?"

Torres shook his head. "Let's get back to him copping a feel," Strike said.

"Let's not," she said, patting his stomach and turning away to return to the bed she'd left.

Junker came out of the bathroom where he'd been in the shower and getting ready for bed. Strike was narrowing his laser focus on Torres who was squirming under the scrutiny; he wasn't exactly in a great position to fight back if Strike thought to put a pillow on his face or a bullet in his brain.

"How are we going to do this?" Junker asked, looking at each of the beds and the couch, clearly trying to figure out the sleeping arrangements.

Strike turned his back on Torres. "You're on the couch, Square," he said, grabbing the back of his tee-shirt.

From her place kneeling in the middle of the free bed, Rora held up both hands to him. "Stop," she said. Strike paused and tipped his head in question. "Keep that on."

Torres laughed, pained though it came out. "You're not getting any tonight, Exile."

"Don't bet on that," he growled and stepped forward to grab her wrist and haul her to the edge of the bed. "What's your game, Kero?"

Stroking a hand down his face, she drew him down to whisper in his ear. "We're not revealing our identifying marks to the feds, Flame."

Leaning back, he found her eyes. "You are something else."

She shrugged, taking her arm from his grip to loosen her hair and pull back the covers.

Rora had just slid beneath them when Junker came to the end of the bed. "You're happy with this?"

If this descended into another pissing contest, she'd probably end up walking out and abandoning them all. "Everybody's tired, can we please just sleep?" she asked, fed up. Though she didn't care where everyone ended up sleeping, she couldn't let Strike get into the bed just yet, and presented her palm to him when he tried to get in. "I'm not comfortable with the narc being free like that. Can we… I don't know…"

"Cuff him?" Strike asked, opening the nightstand drawer to pull out cuffs like he'd been going to restrain their prisoner whether she asked him to or not. "You got it, baby."

"Hey, now, wait a minute," Torres said when Strike went over to attach a cuff to his wrist. "What do you think I'm going to do? I'm sworn to uphold the law!"

"Yeah, when it suits you," Strike said.

Scooching over in the bed, Rora made herself comfortable on the furthest side. "I was more worried about you snooping than anything else, but now that you mention it, you are the only man in the room who's violated me against my will."

"Yeah," Strike sneered. "And we're gonna talk more about that soon as your wounds heal and you can stand up and fight like a man… What the fuck gives you the right to touch my woman?"

"It wasn't like that," Torres said. "And no way you haven't assaulted her. No fucking way. I know the stories about you."

Angered, Rora pushed onto an elbow. "I've welcomed his caress every time he's touched me," she snapped. "I crave having his hands on me, you prick. I beg him to get rough with me and trust him to push my limits because a real man gives his woman what she needs… not that you'd understand that."

She hadn't meant to sound quite so vehement, or defensive, or to inadvertently confirm that she belonged to any one man. When Strike tipped his head in her direction, she flopped onto her back, too afraid to see the look in his eyes. Either he'd be aroused or grateful, or both, and she knew better than to confront that kind of want when it radiated from him because she struggled to resist it.

"I said you had a mouth on you," Torres said. "You are some fucking woman, Kero."

"She's *my* fucking woman," Strike spat. She peeked around to see him pull Torres across the bed and cuff him to the radiator that was beside it. "You fucking move, and I'll put a bullet in you," he said and spun around to stalk over to her.

Sliding into bed beside her, Strike lay down, locking his fingers together over his chest.

"You know what occurs to me," she said, lifting her temple to her fist when she turned onto her side. "You once told Torres you'd take down his organization if he hurt me."

"Yeah," Strike said, fixated on the ceiling.

"His organization is the federal government."

Rolling his head toward her, his scowl hadn't moved. "Yeah."

He might think it the most obvious thing in the world, but to her it was still profound that he could threaten something so massive in such a casual way and be capable of following through. Shit, he could turn her on even when he was just being him.

"This is uncomfortable," Torres said, breaking their stare. "And this isn't the same motel room we were in before, is it? Where are we?"

Strike pulled his phone from beneath the pillow and pressed some buttons, making all the lights go off. "Go to sleep Torres," he grumbled.

The arm he'd attached to the radiator was Torres' uninjured one, so he couldn't gripe that they'd been unfair, he'd have done the same thing to them if the situation was reversed, no doubt about it.

"Are you ok, Junker?" she called out.

"Better than our patient."

"Damn right," Torres mumbled.

"What a happy little family," Strike mumbled.

She poked his ribs but moved over to pull his arm around her. Rora might be unable to trust him but sleeping with her head on his chest still made her feel safer than to be without it.

"You're just in a bad mood because your friend is still under my control."

"Thought you didn't have friends," Torres said.

Strike didn't want to be lying here with her, he wanted to be up doing whatever he usually did with Opal. But for now, Rora was keeping that particular game piece under her control. She'd relinquish it eventually, but she wanted Strike rested, and out of contact with the world.

"I remember when I had to beg you to lay down with me," she mumbled, sliding a flat hand up the front of his tee-shirt.

"How things change, huh?" he asked, threading his fingers through her hair. "Ask me if I wanna and I'll give you a different answer to last time."

She smiled, but relaxed, having no intention of seducing him. As much as Rora wanted to trust him, she had to be cautious. If this was all some gambit cooked up by Strike and the Black Jewel, Rora wanted to do all she could to make sure they couldn't coordinate and that meant keeping him away from Opal.

***

THE FIRST THING she was aware of the next morning was a sting of pain on her arm. Dazed as she woke and opened her eyes, she felt Strike move on top of her.

"Ow," she mumbled, her morning voice croaky. "What are you doing?"

"Getting up," he said, kissing her lips the moment her tired eyes closed again. "You got something else in mind?"

He rocked his hips, rubbing his morning wood against her, but she grumbled and shoved at him. "Bring me coffee," she sighed, still half asleep.

"Caffeine over cock?" Rora's eyes stayed closed, but her brows rose because, yes, that was pretty much exactly what she was saying. He brushed his lips across hers. "Shower first."

Strike climbed off her and left the bed to head into the bathroom. Rora was still at the confused end of the spectrum, but yawned and made herself wake up. Clasping her wrist, she sat up and looked around, trying to remember what was going on.

Torres appeared to still be sleeping. Junker was sitting up on the couch that faced away from the end of the beds and was watching the news on the TV at a low volume.

Slipping her legs out of bed, she pulled the tie from her wrist to put her hair up. She had no idea what time it was and there didn't appear to be any sign of coffee around. Yawning, she heard the shower going on, and dragged herself onto her feet.

Going to her pack, she pulled out the first dress she found and pulled it on under the tee-shirt she had worn to sleep in. Slipping her feet into Strike's untied boots that were by the door, she unlocked it and went out into the cool day.

Being outside in the fresh air was cleansing. She leaned back on the wall under the awning of the porch and blew out a breath.

But Rora was barely alone for a minute before the door opened at her side, forcing her to stand upright. She sort of expected to see Strike, but it was Junker who came out.

"Hey," he said, closing the door at his back. "How are you doing?"

"Just getting some air," she said.

"You've been through a lot in the last few days… probably the last few months. Have you stopped since Benjamin went missing?"

That felt like another lifetime. Thinking of herself after losing Benjamin and during her period of fervent determination to find him, was like looking at a different person. Back then she'd been full of hope, and now she felt that she'd lost her way.

"No," she said, but didn't elaborate.

"You and Exile, are you back together?"

Breathing out exhaustion and amusement, she sank back against the wall by the door. "We're not back together," she said. "I don't know what we are."

"You seem close."

She felt like the world just wouldn't stop and she needed it to, just for a minute. Her head bumped back against the wall and she closed her eyes. "Exile and I are complicated. We're as broken as each other and in that way, it works. What we are, works. And if this was just about me, if it was just about us, I'd probably have thrown myself back into our relationship. Yeah, we have issues, but, you know, what do I have to lose in loving him? Only my life, and he's never threatened that.

"I could lose my dignity, my heart, but I don't have family to lose or friends he can hurt. I don't know, Junk. I don't know who to believe or who to trust and I feel this burden on me. Leandra's life is on me and if I make one wrong move, she's dead… I remember thinking how much I needed someone to lean on when I was trying to find Benjamin. I wanted a partner to help me make the right choices, who I could rely on."

"That's a normal thing to want," he said, moving around in front of her. "Everyone needs someone in their life who they can trust no matter what. You trusted Benjamin."

Did she? Rora would've said she did, except if that was the truth, she wouldn't have lied to him about the Point. "Maybe I'm just not capable," she said. "Or maybe it's just not for me. Maybe I'm not supposed to have a rock like that in my life."

"I don't believe that," he said. "You're an incredible person and you deserve that kind of loyalty. You do."

Rubbing her arms, he tried to reassure her, but all she could think about was his naivety. Maybe this was how Strike had felt about her when they met. "I don't think life is a fairytale."

Pulling her forward into his arms, he held her close and it was nice to have the comfort of his embrace. Being in Junker's arms was the most consoling and unthreatening place. She felt warm and safe here. But it didn't solve any problems.

"It's not a fairytale," he said. "You're right. It takes hard work and tough choices. You have to be willing to make sacrifices and take risks."

Good advice, and the type Strike would give her too. "I missed out on a lot of life lessons. Everyone else gets how to do it and I just stumble from one problem to the next. I don't have a goal. I have no direction. I don't even know what I want."

Or what her life would be after this, if she still had it. There was nothing waiting for her. No Benjamin. No job. No life. What came next for her?

"Do you know what you don't want?" he asked. She didn't want to be alone, she knew that. "Sometimes that's the place the rest of us start from. Working out what you want isn't that hard. You just take a minute to think about your life and you figure out what's the one thing in it that's more important than everything else."

Like the Point would do for her. Except she didn't need the tech to tell her what she valued the most. Before the drama of his betrayal, she'd told Strike exactly what she valued. There was one thing in her life she'd choose over everything else. One person.

An odd kind of awakening quivered through her. "What happens when you figure that out?" she asked.

"People, for the most part, are selfish. Even those who believe they're selfless or who make all decisions based on integrity. All they've done is decide their self-righteousness is their most valued thing. So when you figure it out, you fixate on it, obsess about it, throw yourself over to it completely. You sacrifice everything in pursuit of it. You do whatever you have to in order to attain it. Sacrifice whatever you have to. Just keep your eye on that one thing. No one else will do it for you."

No. They wouldn't.

"Junker, you're a genius," she said, pushing out of his arms and running back into the motel room.

"What?" he asked, following her. "What's happening?"

But she didn't slow down to answer him; she needed to get answers of her own.

SEVENTEEN

RORA KICKED OUT of Strike's oversized boots because they slowed her down. Striding across the room, she went into the bathroom and closed the door behind her.

She didn't hesitate to cross the tile floor or to pull back the shower curtain to reveal a naked Strike. He twisted around, wiping water from his face with one hand while the other slicked back his hair. His scowl loosened when he identified that she was the interruption.

"Change your mind?" he asked, reaching for the strap of her dress.

Rora caught his hand before it could make contact with the fabric. "You led us to her," she said. "You were the reason Junker knew that Bella was going to be checking in to that hotel. You made sure we knew it with enough time to get there before her and set up."

"Yeah," he said, reaching for the soap. "Should I shave?"

"No," she said and folded her arms. "Why would you do that? Since the day we met, you made it clear that you only do things if there's something in it for you. Telling Junker where I was makes sense if you were feeling guilty about choosing the Point over me…"

He stopped soaping his body to make eye contact with her. "Momentarily."

"Right, but why lead us to the Black Jewel after I was free of her? You knew Junker was wrong. I know you said you didn't know what he wanted, and maybe you didn't, but you work off assumptions. You had to know that the Black Jewel had nothing we needed. Junker was using her as a way to get to you, which he only wanted to do because he thought you had both the Point and DARPA's infinite-processor." He was startled by her knowledge. "Torres has a loose tongue." His chin rose in understanding and he went back to washing off the soap. "So, tell me why, Strike, why have you been leading us on this merry dance?"

"If I answer correctly, are you going to join me?" he asked. "What are you going to do if you don't like my answer?"

"What was in it for you, Strike? This isn't a game. We're not playing kiss chase. You want your processor back now, but before this—"

"You. You were what was in it for me. It brought us back together," he said. "I told you I didn't know how to chase a woman. Thought it would be easier if you were chasing me. I was meeting Bella, and yeah, I knew your bitch was looking for me. I thought maybe he was looking for me because you were."

"I know how to get your attention if I want it."

"But by your admission, you thought I wanted to kill you. Maybe you wanted to take me out first. I don't know, baby. I didn't overthink it. You were with the square, you were stealing money and heading off on a mission… I didn't want to miss out."

He was jealous? Was that it? He wanted to be a part of the next stage of the adventure? "Strike—"

"Look, bottom line," he said, turning off the water. "You needed something, and I gave it to you. That's your life now. If you need something, I will find a way to give it to you. Whether I agree with it or not. You weren't telling the square the whole truth. If you were, he wouldn't have been chasing me. I was supporting your lie."

Junker would've been after Exile because he wanted the DARPA processor. But Strike wasn't wrong, she hadn't told Junker that her ex didn't have the Point. She didn't even tell Junker what it was or that Exile was her ex.

Before she let herself be swept up by the romance of Strike's statement, she had to get the facts straight. "You said you were going to meet Bella, why?"

He got out of the tub and grabbed a towel to dry off. "I told you, I was going to kill her. That part you can't doubt. After what she did to you? Damn right I was going to make her suffer."

"Bella was looking for you, probably because she heard you had the Point or the processor, or both. You agreed to meet her because you wanted to punish her for what she did to me?"

"That about sums it up," he said.

Rora watched him dress. "And you led me and Junker to her because you wanted to keep me close and maybe because you wanted me to know what you'd done to Bella... for me?"

Folding his capable arms, he propped himself on the vanity and folded his ankles. "Baby, you should know by now, I'll go to any lengths to get what I want. So, yeah, I thought if I paid Bella back in kind, you'd get that I was serious about you."

So she'd been supposed to swoon at the sight of him torturing and murdering the woman who'd imprisoned her... in its own perverse way, it was romantic.

She took a careful step toward him. "I don't want to be alone anymore, Strike."

Tentative hope seemed to flash in his eyes. "You won't ever be alone again, Ro."

"Can you keep Torres alive and find out why he's really here?"

"You asking about torture techniques? First thing we'll do is burst his stitches... reopen the wound."

"No," she said, shaking her head. "If I give you Opal, can you find it if there's any chatter about Burke? Any truth to what Torres told us?"

"You give me Opal and I can get you anything you want," he said. She smiled. But he grabbed her wrist when she started for the door. "But I don't want her back."

Rora's smile fell. Opal was the only bargaining chip she had. If he didn't care about that anymore, she had nothing to barter with. "What?"

His fingers dropped from her arm. "You told me I wouldn't get her back until you'd forgiven me. I don't want her back until I can have you both. Until then, the two of you stay together and I'm in the doghouse."

"You haven't… you haven't said that you want me back. You make it seem like you want to sleep with me, but… are you saying you want more?"

An almost smile touched his lips, but there was doubt in his eyes. "You know what I want, Cupcake."

Searching his face, she wanted to give in, wanted to run into his arms and embrace the love they'd found once before. But she was smarter now, and this time if she did it, there wouldn't be any backing out, no matter what. She'd be his or she'd cease to be.

"You say something like that and I…" His brow rose to prompt her. "I feel like I'm the one using you… But I suppose without Opal—"

"There are other computers," he said, seeming to reassure her. "I can still get you whatever you need."

Rora couldn't understand why he'd choose to use an alien machine over his own. "But you love Opal," she murmured.

"I love you too, Cupcake, and one of you is not worth having without the other."

"We're a family," she whispered. "That's what you're saying."

He lifted a shoulder. "I guess."

"Strike," she said, edging closer and curling her fingers over his forearms that crossed on his chest.

She wanted to touch him, to be near to him, to tell him that she loved him, but there was only one way she could be sure that this was real.

"Ro?"

Steeling herself, she had to take this first step. "I need to go away," she said, keeping her attention on her fingers even after he straightened up. "Alone."

"No way."

But she didn't let his obvious aversion affect her determination. "I need you to keep everything together for me here. Don't make war with Junker. Keep Torres alive… and only move if you have to. I'll find you or… I'll lead you to me."

She hadn't really thought this through all the way, but she was making plans as she spoke. "When?" he barked. "Why do you—"

"You know why," she said, her gaze ascending to his. "We can't move forward unless we trust each other, and we can never trust until we have it."

Understanding made him tense and his expression became sterner. "Aurora, it's dangerous. Let me come with you."

She smiled. "I don't think you've used my full name since the first time you told me you loved me."

The back of his fingers drifted down her jaw. "That's not true, I'm sure I barked it at you when we were shot at," he said, and took her hand. "But that should tell you how serious I am about this. Baby, let me—"

"No."

"Babe, you can trust me. If—"

"I know what I'm doing, Strike. I have to do this, and I need you to hold the fort here while I do. I'm asking you to help me, by staying here."

If she showed any weakness, he'd exploit it. He wanted to be at her side, whether for nefarious reasons or not, but Rora was determined to do what needed to be done without anyone beside her.

"Why now? Why not wait until after—"

"Will after be better?" she asked. "We're going to be confronted with all kinds of choices over the next few days, few weeks, however long this goes on. I need to know if I'm making those decisions alone, or if someone's at my back."

Determination burned from him, it felt almost as hot as her own. "I'll always have your back. Haven't I proved that?"

So many times, and the man who did whatever it took to protect her was the one she wanted to embrace. But until she could be sure he wasn't the man who'd tied her up and abandoned her, she'd never be able to trust him all the way.

"This is the biggest thing that will ever come between us and it will stay between us, in the way of us, until we face the demon…" But he didn't seem to be convinced. "Do you love me, Strike?" she asked, reading his undisguised displeasure. "Do you?"

"Yes," he replied with a clenched jaw. "I love you."

"Do you trust me?"

"Yes."

She stepped in against him to whisper. "Then give me the chance to do the same."

She kissed his arm and turned away, but he grabbed her and hauled her back, forcing his mouth over hers before she had a chance to breathe in.

Rora was still dazed by the devotion of his consuming kiss when he tore his mouth from hers.

"Defend yourself, Rora. There's no other option. Kill if you have to, I'll clean up the mess, but you get your ass back here in one piece… and soon."

She touched his jaw and nodded, feeling his overwhelming reluctance to let her go. Turning away from him was hard, but she was determined to get to work.

All along she'd been the key to this puzzle, now she was going to unlock it. Like Pandora's Box, she feared it may devour the world if not properly handled, but that was a risk she had to take… for love.

EIGHTEEN

SHE HADN'T DECLARED it to the others, but Rora's directions had positioned them only a day away from where she had to be. At the time, she hadn't been sure she'd be stopping for the Point, but Leandra wasn't more than a seventy-two-hour car ride from the secret everyone wanted to know, so coming this way worked out.

This one piece of the puzzle was always going to be important, no matter how events played out. But since her stay in Bella's basement, there had been a part of her that wished she could just forget the damn thing had ever existed.

Burying her head in the sand wasn't going to make anything go away. The damn problem kept chasing her, so she had to confront it.

Coming back to this location was eerie. At one time the building had been her home and now there was a stranger living in her apartment.

Rora didn't have to go inside, the storage unit she'd rented out back was filled with everything she had left in the world. At least, it was supposed to be. Rora didn't even care that when she opened it, the place was nothing more than a concrete shell. Of course the people who'd emptied

Benjamin's apartment would've emptied her storage locker too. That actually made sense to her.

Slapping her screwdriver against her thigh, she started forward. Whoever these people were, they would have a lot of high school yearbooks and paperback novels to trawl through to find that they had nothing at all.

At least, as she hunkered down to the concealed outlet at the back of the unit, she hoped that they didn't.

With Torres passed out and Burke chasing down Bella, Rora guessed that this was the closest she was going to get to a clear path to the thing everyone was in pursuit of. And she had faith that Strike would be keeping an eye on Torres and Junker, preventing them from pursuing her, though each man's interest in her would be different.

Popping off the front of the outlet, she ran her finger around the outside. Bingo. She plucked out a small USB storage device. This was it. The Point. Unbelievable that such a small thing could have such huge repercussions on so many lives.

It took little time to put the façade back on and slip out of the unit. While there might be cameras around, she couldn't be accused of stealing something from an empty unit. She had a scarf around her face anyway and had parked in an area without cameras, so she felt safe slipping away into the night.

Rora got back to the truck and considered her next move as she drove. She could go to Leandra on her own, but if she did that and Bella or Burke caught up with her, Strike wouldn't have time to get to her before something grave happened.

She couldn't really leave Junker and Torres alone for much longer anyway. It would only be a matter of time before Strike got bored of supporting them and split. He'd probably come after her. She didn't believe he'd abandon her, not if his recent declarations were true. But his patience for others was thin, especially others he didn't like in the first place.

Her intention had always been to retrieve the Point and return to the trio of men. It would be a miracle if she got back to find them without new injuries. All she could hope was that Strike had been so busy investigating Torres' story that he didn't have time to be aggravated by the others.

Glancing at the laptop on the seat beside her, she smiled. "Feels weird that he's not here, doesn't it, O?" she said. "I think he's using you to show me what I mean to him…" Her attention went to the road and she sighed. "I still can't decide if I should believe him or not."

Rora hadn't slept since she'd started this journey, it was approaching three in the morning and she considered stopping for rest. But she wasn't sure she'd be able to sleep with the Point burning a hole in her pocket.

Since Benjamin had written the algorithm, it had been a thorn in her side. For a while, after they'd hidden the USBs and split up, there had been a period of peace. Adjusting to working together and not being together had taken some time, but they'd been professionals and worked hard at it. And she'd always had such respect for Benjamin that she didn't think herself capable of walking away.

Someone, somewhere must have known the Point existed, but she'd never told anyone about it. Benjamin had been taken by Bella because the woman wanted the power the Point could give her. Now Benjamin was gone, but Bella was still in pursuit of her holy grail.

Bella was exactly the kind of person who shouldn't have control of such a thing. She'd exploit it to the maximum. Strike on the other hand, had said he wanted to explore the tech, but she couldn't see him building an evil lair into the side of a mountain and directing world affairs for his own gain. He might be one of the smartest men she'd ever met, but his needs were simple. The man didn't even sleep, for goodness sake, what would he do with jewels and gold?

"I suppose the problem would be if it got away from him," she said, not really thinking about the fact that she was talking to a machine. "We have to make a decision before we get back. Either we give it to him, or we don't."

Before she'd laid eyes on Exile, she'd been told he was an enigma. But she could never have imagined how she'd be drawn in by the man.

Her attraction to him had been undeniable from the beginning, but he'd been so resistant to it that she'd really believed he was indifferent to her. Now she understood that the man who'd claimed to be afraid of nothing, *was* afraid, of her.

Just like she'd thought in his presence once, fearing he could hurt her heart, he'd feared the same thing.

If Strike wanted the Point, he'd have come for her full-throttle. But now that she had it in her possession there was only really one way to find out where Strike's loyalties lay. Like she'd said to him in the bathroom the previous morning, it would always be hanging over them until she knew for sure.

She could hand it to him and ask him to destroy it. But she'd have no way to know if he really had. With all the tech he had at his disposal, it would be easy for him to tell her he'd destroyed it, but actually be copying it or sending it to himself for later use.

Trust.

That's what this came down to.

Rora hadn't trusted Benjamin not to return to the Point after they'd hidden it. That was why she'd switched the devices and hidden the true Point on her own. She'd trusted Benjamin more than she'd ever trusted anyone, but she'd learned even that trust had a limit when she chose to lie to him.

In truth, deciding to deceive him wasn't about his technical capabilities; she'd believed she was protecting him. Benjamin had a pure heart, but could be naïve, just as she had once been. If he'd kept the Point or used it with hackable networks, then others may have got hold of it without him knowing.

He might have returned to it, retrieved it, and believed that he was only accessing the code for educational purposes, but he didn't understand there were malevolent people out there.

"Strike understands it," Rora said, sliding a hand onto Opal. "He'd know how to isolate it, wouldn't he?"

Junker hadn't meant to give her such clarity. But he'd put it in such simple terms that she didn't know how she hadn't seen it before.

Holding onto righteousness was ridiculous. Who was she trying to impress? Her parents were gone. Her career was over. There was only one thing in the world that mattered to her and she'd lost that because of her own misguided integrity. But if she had the chance to fix that mistake, shouldn't she take it?

Was that it? Had she been the one to make the mistake by not trusting Strike's heart? Maybe he hadn't made a mistake at all.

This was a hell of a decision. To throw her lot in with Strike and trust him all the way or give up on any chance of having someone to rely on. If she couldn't make herself trust Strike when she loved him as much as she did, she'd never be able to trust anyone.

"Opal," she said and breathed out again, returning her hand to the wheel. "You have to help me out here, honey, we need a really ingenious idea, or I may as well drive both of us off the road right now."

Rora hadn't asked for this responsibility, Benjamin had given it to her long before he took his own life to protect it. Every day she missed him, or something reminded her of the man. But while she'd been with Strike, it had been easier; he'd carried some of the burden for her. But it was his motives that perplexed her... just what drove a man like Exile? Could love ever be his priority?

NINETEEN

IT WAS ALMOST MIDNIGHT before Rora got back to the motel room. Still hoping that the men hadn't killed each other without her around, she knew that leaving them alone had been a necessary risk. No one else could do what she'd just done.

Yawning, she started to regret not getting more sleep. She'd been on the road for almost forty hours, and while she'd taken breaks for power naps, and to grab food, she could feel exhaustion creeping in. Thankfully her addiction to coffee and loud music had kept her going for the last few miles, and adrenaline had a lot to answer for too.

The nearer she'd gotten to the motel room, the more concerned she'd been about what she'd find when she got there.

Her concerns turned out to be justified because when she opened the motel room door, every man she'd left here had a gun trained on another.

Rora's hand fell from the slightly ajar motel room door. "Seriously?" she asked.

Torres was still cuffed to the radiator, sitting on the bed that had been moved to the corner. But somehow, he had a weapon in his hand.

Strike was at the end of the other bed, and he had two guns, one pointed at Torres and another pointed at Junker who was closest to her, angled with his back almost to the door and a gun trained on Strike.

"Baby, come over here," Strike said, his voice low and his dangerous eyes creeping from Torres to Junker.

"No," she said, shoving the door into the frame and rounding Junker to stand in the middle of the triangle, no doubt blocking someone's shot.

"Ro!"

"No," she said and glared at each man in turn, but none of them were looking at her, they were all busy scowling at each other. "What the hell happened? I told all of you to get along, and this is what I come back to?"

Pinning Torres in her sights first, she crossed to him. With one leg hanging off the bed and an arm stretched to the radiator, he had to use his injured arm to hold the gun and it was obvious that it was beginning to tire from the shake in the barrel.

"Get out of the way, Kero! I will shoot!"

"Me?" she asked, walking right up to him until the end of the barrel almost touched her stomach. "You're cuffed to the wall. You put a bullet in me and both those men will empty theirs into you. What would be the point of that? Where did you even get a gun?"

"Your idiot bitch," Strike said. "Put his little friend on the nightstand."

The gun in Torres' hand did look like the one Junker had called his little friend. "You can shoot me, Torres, or you can help me diffuse this," she said. "Do you think Exile or Junker will try to shoot you if I'm standing in front of you?" She opened her hand. "Give me the weapon."

He didn't want to and didn't appreciate being the first one asked. But he huffed at her and slapped the weapon onto her palm. Proud that she'd achieved something, she spun around to switch her focus between the other two men.

"Junker, will you please—"

"He has two guns," Junker objected.

Strike did, though he'd lowered one to his side now that she was in front of Torres. "If Exile was going to shoot you, he'd have done it already," she said and then exhaled. "Will you put your gun down if he does?"

"I… I suppose," Junker said.

She nodded once and went to Strike. Without speaking to him, she slid a hand up his chest and around to the back of his neck. Though he resisted a little when she tried to guide him down, it didn't take him long to relent. When he bowed, she matched their lips and took her time about kissing him slowly.

With every second that passed, he relaxed more until they both sank into the rhythm of the kiss. When she felt his knuckles on her back, she eased away to smile at him. He might still be holding the guns, but they weren't pointed at anyone anymore.

"What would you do without me?" she whispered against his lips and then spun around to look at Junker. "Are we good?"

Junker had the weapon at his side and nodded. "Yes."

"Good," she said. "Does someone want to tell me what started this?"

"We had a… disagreement," Torres said.

"Yeah, no shit," she said. "About?"

A few tense seconds passed, and she wasn't surprised that Junker was the first to acquiesce. "Each of us has a different idea about our next move. I say we should get to Leandra, your friend Torres wants to go after his boss, and Exile—"

"Wants to go after the Black Jewel," she said, nodding. "You know, you can disagree with each other without shooting at each other… Maybe having guns around is a bad idea."

"Or bullets," Strike said, and she heard him opening a gun which made her turn. "We trash the ammunition and we can't kill each other."

He looked to Junker after emptying a gun, and though he hesitated, Junker lifted his gun to unload it too.

Strike emptied his other gun and all the ammunition was tossed onto the empty bed.

Rora looked at the gun in her hands. "I don't know how to do it," she said and passed the weapon off to Strike.

"Wouldn't want you shooting anyone by mistake," Strike said, unloading the gun for her.

With the weapons empty, they weren't much use, so while Strike went to stow them in a pack, Rora went to gather up the bullets, wondering if it was possible just to put them in the dumpster without causing problems.

"So we need a deciding vote," Torres said. Rora glanced around to see all three men were looking at her. "Wonder whose side she'll take."

He said it like her decision would be a foregone conclusion. She sank down on the corner of the bed. "I've spent a lot of time thinking about that," she said. "A lot of time…"

"And?" Junker asked.

"What did you decide?" Torres asked.

Her gaze floated to Strike who was peering at her. She hadn't come to any conclusions about where they should focus their efforts, though that might be because she was exhausted and kept talking herself out of her decisions.

"Can I talk to you for a minute?" Junker asked her.

She tore her gaze from Strike and forced herself onto her feet though she really just wanted to lie down on the bed and sleep for a week.

"Sure," she said, leaving the bullets on the bed and crossing to him.

Junker stepped back and opened the door, so she went outside onto the porch they'd talked on the morning she'd decided to go on her mission alone. Though she stopped just outside the door, he took her elbow and drew her down to the corner.

When they stopped, he moved in close. "I think we should leave."

"Leave?" she asked, trying her best not to sigh or fall asleep on her feet. "I think everyone agrees with that, but we need to decide who to pursue—"

"You know who we should pursue," he said. "But I wasn't talking about leaving as a group." The gravity of what he was suggesting erased some of her tiredness. "How could you kiss him like that?"

"Exile? You think we should ditch him... because I kissed him?"

"Because the man is unhinged," Junker said. "He has no conscience, no morals, no integrity."

All Rora could think was that she was too tired for this. "He has plenty of integrity," she said. "It just doesn't align with yours."

"You don't know the kind of man he is, you can't know."

She'd expected the big brother act from Junker a bit sooner. Then again, until now, she hadn't been as open to kissing Strike as she had just been inside. "I do know."

"And this mission, did you tell him where you went? Does he know what—"

"Yes."

"And what was it?" Junker asked, his patience wearing thin, and his anger beginning to bleed through. "What was so important that you had to leave the three of us together? You must have known it was a recipe for disaster."

"It was a risk worth taking," she said, reaching into her cleavage to pull out the USB. "This is what everyone is after and as long as it was out there in the world, it was at risk. Now I have it, we're a step closer to—"

"That's Benjamin's work," he said, his mouth open, his eyes glued to the USB. "The Point. Exile wants it. This Burke guy. Bella. All of them want it."

"Yes, I..." Despite her exhaustion, his words piqued her awareness. "You called her Bella... you've never done that." She took a step backwards. "Did Exile tell you her name?"

"I, uh... yeah," he said. "Yeah, he—"

"I'll ask him, Junker and he won't lie to me," she asked, her awareness edging toward panic. "How do you know her real name?"

Lunging forward, he grabbed her arm to pull her toward him. "You think this is what we should focus on now? I don't fucking know. One of you said it or—"

"You're lying to me," she said and tried to pull her arm away from him.

"Doesn't feel good, does it?"

Rora had never seen such dislike contorted on his face. "What are you doing? Who are you?" But the more she tried to pull away, the tighter his grip got. "Let me go. You're hurting me!"

"Ro?"

She managed to turn enough to see Strike thirty feet away, outside their open motel room door. Junker tugged her back to his chest and she squealed when a blade suddenly touched her neck.

"Back off, Exile!" Strike went from curious to irate in a flash and started toward them, but he only got a few steps before Junker pressed the blade deeper into her. "Stop!" Junker demanded. "Take one step closer and I'll gut her."

"You've just signed your own death warrant," Strike snarled, a malevolence in his tone that made even her cold. "Take your fucking hands off her and I'll give you a head start. You hurt her—"

"You did this!" Junker said, shaking her, but shouting at Exile. "I care for Aurora! I tried to protect her! This is you! This is all on you! You don't even see it! You fucking asshole!"

"What do you want?" she hissed.

"Let's start with what's in your hand," Junker said. "Give it to me. Slide it into my hand."

Holding her breath, she pushed the USB up into his palm, hoping it might loosen his hold on the blade, but it didn't. "You're going to regret this," she said.

"I could've helped you," he said into her hair. "I could've saved you…"

Shoving her, he spun and sprinted away. Rora stumbled forward a few steps, and a moment later was against Strike's chest, wrapped in his arms. "You good? You ok?" he asked her and eased her aside. "I'll catch that fucker and—"

"No!" she said, throwing her arms around him. "Let him go."

"What?" he spat. "He hurt you! He has the Point."

She smiled. "Does he?"

Strike's heart was hammering so hard against her chest that she knew adrenaline was coursing through him, so it made sense he wasn't thinking too clearly. Rora kept looking up at him until he caught on to her sly confidence.

He breathed out a laugh and brushed his knuckles against her jaw. "You switched it out," he said. "For me?"

"No," she said, shaking her head. "Because having something like that unsecured on a device that anyone could access was just insanity. Let him go. Let him find out on his own that he blew his cover for no reason."

Moving past him, she started for the motel room. "Ro… if he doesn't have it… where is it?"

Widening her smile, she didn't answer his question, just let him wonder while she felt pride in herself. "We have to get out of here."

"Torres was telling the truth, or some version of it," he said. "According to everything I've found so far, all reports suggest he's a wanted man. Could be true or Burke could be setting him up… or it could all be bullshit. I'm still looking."

"Ad-hoc us a car, would you?" she asked. "I'll start packing."

She started toward the room again but paused when he spoke. "I fucking love you, Ro," he said. "Every goddamn thing about you."

Smiling to herself, she didn't look at him, but continued walking toward the room. She was exhausted, but she'd sleep once they got on the road, and then she had to talk to Strike, *her* Strike, about so many things.

TWENTY

TORRES DIDN'T GET a choice about being put in the car. His hands and ankles were tied, and he was given a shot to make sure he was easy to maneuver. Strike packed up, leaving her to sleep in the front seat. She was already out by the time they got moving.

When she woke up, the sun was intrusive, blazing through the windshield. Rora whimpered and turned her head to bury her face in Strike's groin. But it was only after he reacted to her squirming that she realized she was rubbing her face on his dick through his jeans.

"You woke up in a good mood," Strike said, his fingers drifting through her hair.

Choosing to let her eyes close against the light, she rolled to her back and smiled up at him. "Killed anyone today?"

"Not yet," he said, his wrist resting on the top of the wheel. "I'm open to suggestions."

"Why are you always talking about hurting people?" Torres' voice came from the back seat. "Is that the only time you're happy? When you're hurting someone?"

"Only time I'm happy is when I'm inside my girl," Strike said, and she noted how his chin rose, so she'd guess the men were making eye contact in the mirror. "That's right, my girl, let that sink in, and don't forget it next time you get near her."

Rora rubbed her face, choosing to ignore the tension between the men. "We might need more help… now we're a man down," she said, waiting for Strike to glance down at her again.

"Anyone going to tell me what happened with Junker?" Torres asked, his tone suggesting he didn't think he'd get an answer, but he asked anyway.

Thinking about Junker, she had more questions than answers, and couldn't wait to get Strike alone so they might actually begin to make sense of this.

"We're going to have to decide how to deal with the Jewel," she said.

"What about Burke?" Torres said. "He'll be around with a squad of—"

"I'm not worried about the NSA," she said, stretching as she sat up. After running her fingers through her hair, she slid close to Strike and kissed his cheek, he turned to touch his mouth to hers too. "Are you worried about the NSA, Flame?"

The corner of his mouth quirked. "Feds? No, baby, I'm not worried about feds."

She twisted to look over the back of her seat to see a disheveled and disgruntled Torres. "You aren't used to being on the road." That observation probably didn't help his mood. "It doesn't matter. You'll get a chance to rest soon." Turning back to her love, she linked her fingers on his shoulder and pulled herself close. "We have to talk… alone."

With his eyes on the road ahead, he nodded once. "I'll drive another few hours. We'll talk when we find somewhere to stop for the night."

Rora agreed with that, it would be better that they had time rather than tried to rush a conversation at a truck stop. "You don't think he'll turn on you the first chance he gets?" Torres asked. "Trusting him will be your downfall."

Strike inhaled, but she whipped around to glare at Torres before her love could speak. "And just what is it that you're offering me? Seriously, Torres, I think you'd get bored giving the same speech over and over. I'm not interested in anything you have to offer."

"Guess one guy screwing you over wasn't enough," Torres said. "That is what happened, right? Junker took off. It's that or one of you killed him."

"Though I don't guess we'd admit that to you," she said.

"And this is the life you told me you wanted," Torres said. "I don't think you have the first clue what you want, Kero. You're sure not thinking about the future."

"I know exactly what I want," she said and fumbled for Strike's hand.

"One day his luck is going to run out," Torres said.

Strike picked up her hand to kiss her knuckles. "It's not luck, it's skill," she said, pulling Strike's arm around her so she could nestle closer to him. "And we like the quiet… so just keep your opinions to yourself, Torres. And don't forget that you came to us. You're an outlaw now, just like the rest of us. So why don't you think about what you're going to tell the court or your maker, who knows which one you'll meet first."

***

RORA WAS ASLEEP again when Strike stopped. She was still drowsy as she watched Strike drag Torres across the parking lot and into a new motel room.

She sighed. Motel room to motel room. Maybe after all of this was over, she'd ask Strike to take her somewhere tropical where they could just be for a while.

But there was no time to think about what would happen after this when there was no guarantee they'd live through it. She could suggest to Strike that they dump Torres and take off, but how long would they last after Junker found out he didn't have the Point. How long would Leandra last after Bella decided the woman knew nothing about the Point?

Watching through the windshield, she saw Strike come out of the room to return to the car. She admired the long, lean lines of his capable body. The curve of his muscular arms, the breadth of his chest and the certainty in his stride.

He approached the car and pulled open her passenger door. "You want me to carry you in too?" he asked.

Smiling, she shook her head and took his hand when he offered it to help her out. She clutched Opal against her chest and waited for him to grab a couple of bags out the back. He'd gone through most of Junker's stuff and decided what to keep and what to leave behind, and as she'd come to expect of Strike, he didn't trust much of the other man's possessions.

She was surprised when they went inside to find they were in a living room, it was small, but there were three doors at the back of the room and Torres wasn't in sight. "Where is—"

"Two bedrooms," he said, dumping the bags and going to open one of the doors to reveal a free bedroom. "He's in the other one."

That made her feel better, because she and Strike had a lot to talk about. After closing the front door, she locked it. Facing the room, she held a hand out to him, he came back to her to take it.

"Strike…" she breathed out, relieved that she could finally use his name.

"You want to talk," he said, leading her over to the couch. "Can't decide if this is going to end well for me."

"I don't know," she said, curling her fingers around Opal who rested in her lap. "I do need to ask you to do something that you're not going to like."

Her plan had come together in pieces between her bouts of slumber and consciousness on their trip here. "What?" he asked. "If it includes leaving Redd alive…"

"He's connected to Bella," she said, still trying to put the pieces together. "I don't know how, but… he used her name, and I knew you were too careful to have made a slip like that."

"Fuck," he growled. "I knew he wasn't to be trusted. He and Gallagher only connected a couple of months before Redd got in touch with you. I didn't know why he insinuated himself into Gallagher's life like that or how he gained the guy's trust so fast."

"Benjamin was a trusting person," she said. "But I was thinking…"

"Thinking what?"

"How did you hear about the Point? How did you know to ask the question?"

"Bella made a reference to it once," he said. "She was trying to turn me on and win me back with news she'd heard. Except she didn't know much about it and I was used to her being full of shit. I figured I'd keep an ear out, and if I got the chance I'd pursue it. But I wasn't going to throw in with her again, no way."

"That's what you meant about getting there first and about being uninterested in Gallagher."

"I think after I rejected her, she took Benjamin to try and show me she was capable and maybe in hope that I'd go help her torture the guy into giving up the truth," he said.

Twisting to face him, she pulled her knees up under her. "But you didn't?"

He shrugged. "I wasn't that interested. Don't think anything could've got me interested enough to go back to Bella."

But she had. He'd returned to Bella after Rora came into his life. Sliding a hand over his, she curled her fingers around his. "You offered yourself to her to save me," she said, watching their hands stroke each other. "In that room, you told her to let me and Benjamin go, that she could have you."

"You haven't figured out I was in love with you by then?"

She'd suspected it, but hadn't let herself believe it. "We hadn't even had sex then… when did you fall in love with me?"

"You got my interest the first time you almost slammed Opal on my hands," he said, making her smile. He curled a finger under her chin to draw her gaze up to his. "I fell in love with you the first time you threatened me… You didn't care about anything, not even your own safety, you had a goal and nothing was going to stop you. Nothing. Not even me.”

“I almost gave up,” she said. “Then you ambushed me in that alley and pointed a gun at my head.” They stared into each other for a minute. “You thought you could fight it. That if we didn’t get physical, you could move on and forget me.”

He nodded. “It was my way of being chivalrous, didn’t figure this was any life for you.”

It was one that belonged to her now, but there was something between them that didn’t. Letting go of his hand, she opened Opal, and slid the machine onto his lap. Rora took his hand again and it was his turn to hesitate when she started to lower his hand to the keys.

Making eye contact, she smiled, and though he appeared dubious, he let her rest his hand down on the keyboard. “I forgive you, Strike,” she whispered, laying her hand over his. “You can have both of us.”

It took him a second to absorb her words. “You’re sure?”

“Very sure,” she said, thinking her life reaped the biggest rewards when she took the biggest risks.

“You’re not worried that… ‘it’ will come between us again?”

“It doesn’t belong to me anymore,” she said and grinned at his confusion. “I told you Junker didn’t have it.”

“Right, but you didn’t tell me where it was,” he said. Lowering her attention to the computer on his lap, she peeked up at him, mischief in her eyes. “You… Ro, what did you do?”

“I told you the USB was too unsecure,” she said. “Opal and I were talking on the road and I figured that there wasn’t anyone capable of keeping it safer than she was.”

“You put the Point on Opal?” he asked, almost in disbelief, but she could tell there was a part of him that was humbled, and another that was impressed.

“She didn’t mind… I didn’t think for a second that it would be Junker, but I did think we might find ourselves at a crossroads eventually with someone threatening us for it. I figured Opal was the most secure place, you wouldn’t let anyone hack her and no one but us can touch her, so… I asked her to look after it."

"I'll destroy it," he said, but she laid a hand over his knuckles to halt him.

She shook her head, digging her teeth into her lip before lifting her eyes to his. "No," Rora said. "I want you to look at it… when you're ready."

He grew wary. "Why?"

Her lips lifted a fraction. "Because I want to lead you into temptation," she said. "I want you to look at it, play with it… refine it if you want… Play with your shiny new toy… but don't use it."

For a few seconds, he just looked at her. "How do you know I won't—"

"I don't," she said. "But I never will unless I take a chance. I am giving it to you, absolving myself of all responsibility and my only condition is that you never use it, or let it be used, in the real world."

Opening a hand on Opal, he stroked his fingers across the keys. "I can do whatever I want with the Point? It belongs to me now?"

She was biting her lip again but nodded and kept her smile. "I once told you that I didn't want you to change, that I would never judge you, and I don't plan to. But if I don't change, if I don't make myself trust someone, trust you, we can never work as any kind of us. So that's what I'm doing. I'm trusting you. Whatever you decide to do… it's on you."

"You're trusting me?"

"I'm trusting you," she said, and looped her arm through his. "Though maybe if you'd made it clearer to me in the first place that you were just curious, I might have been more understanding."

Rora couldn't guarantee that. But now that they were mending fences, she got a sense that if they came out the other side of this ordeal, they might actually be stronger and closer than they had been before.

TWENTY-ONE

STRIKE SURPRISED HER by closing Opal and putting the laptop on the table. "What are you doing?" Rora asked. "You just got her back."

"I just got you back." Scooping her into his arms, he stood up and carried her through to the bedroom. "It feels like years since we've been alone."

"Since we've been bad together," she said, tightening her hold on his neck when he laid her on the bed to pull him down with her. Maybe she had gone over the edge, but if she had then oblivion felt good. "I want you to corrupt me, Strike. I want to be bad with you. I thought I was lost, that I didn't know what I wanted, but I did. All along I knew what I wanted… you. You're the only thing I want." Invigorated, she pushed him onto his back and climbed up into his lap to rock her hips on his. "I'm so happy we're alone right now."

Sitting up, he touched his lips to hers. But rather than the deep, passionate kiss she was expecting, this kiss was short. "Wouldn't matter if we weren't," he said, stroking her breasts. "I'd have given Torres a shot of morphine before I gave up the chance to be inside you again."

She laughed, working her pelvis faster, whimpering at the feel of his erection fighting to get out of his jeans.

Their gazes locked.

Dragging her lip in her teeth, she chewed hard, not because she was anxious but because as she stared into him, she saw it. She saw what she'd spent her life looking for: her rock.

"We need to be naked," she said and leaped off the bed to begin stripping.

He didn't stand up, but pulled off his tee-shirt and kicked off his boots. She laughed at their haste and turned to toss her clothes away as he pulled off his socks and started on his jeans.

"What the fuck is that?"

She didn't expect him to be off the bed and so close to her when she twisted toward him. But he grabbed her arm and turned her away from him again. She saw in the mirrored closet door that he was examining her back, his face tensed in a scowl.

When his fingertips traced downward on her back, she figured out what he'd found. "Junker said most of them won't scar, but that one was the worst. It's taking the longest to heal, most of the time I forget it's there, but sometimes if the water in the tub is too hot, it stings."

The mark started beneath her shoulder blade and ran down about six or eight inches. She wasn't sure, she'd never seen it properly, only felt it.

Grabbing her arm tight, he flipped her to face him. Nothing but fury exuded from him. "Bella," he growled, his jaw clenched.

She nodded and tried to reach for his face, but he backed off. "Baby, it's fine," she said. "I don't care. I love you. As long as I have you, every second of pain was worth it."

"I don't think so," he said, turning his back on her. Rora had never seen him so tight with anger. "I will make her feel every second of agony she put you through. I'll make her pay for every moment she even thought about hurting you."

"Word is that's what you were doing when she ran off," she said, going to him to slide her hands up to his shoulders. "Don't be blinded by your hate, my love. That's living in the past, you never do that. Celebrate that we have each other. Celebrate the future we can have." Rising on her tiptoes, she moved around him to brush her mouth over his. "Celebrate with me, Flame."

Curling her fingers around his solid arms, she guided him to the bed, and held his hands on her waist, bringing him down onto the mattress with her. He scooped a hand under her jaw and tried to guide her mouth to his, but she pulled back.

"Did we lock the door?" she whispered, breaking eye contact for the first time.

But he grabbed her chin to pull her focus back to him. "I cuffed Torres. Doesn't matter anyway, in a minute your screams will keep everyone out of here."

Her smile grew but worry made her catch her lip in her teeth. "I don't trust myself not to scream your name too loud."

He kissed her, a slow but hard press of his mouth onto hers. "I trust you, Ro," he said and parted his lips to plunder her mouth deeper.

Kissing him really did have the power to set her alight, just like Bella had once said, except now this mouth, this man was hers. He belonged to her and had proved that her happiness was more important to him than even his own.

"I need you," she said, her fingers not working fast enough to free him from his jeans.

The moment he slid into her was the most freeing of her life. This joining was more significant than any they'd ever had before because as her body locked around his, Rora knew, no other man would ever occupy her like this again.

With his fingers digging into her ass, he pulled her up to meet every one of his thrusts. Rora let him take control of her body and instead focused on stroking him, kissing him, feeling him, enjoying every second with this man she'd missed so much.

"Fuck, baby, you feel good," he said and pulled her pelvis to his, clamping them together.

She was still writhing beneath him when he coiled his fingers in her hair and pulled her head back to open his mouth on her throat, dragging his teeth against her skin. The sensation of his wet mouth and the scrape of his teeth made her shudder.

"Strike," she whispered. "Oh, yes."

His teeth went deeper, and she grabbed for his waist, digging her teeth into his arm when orgasm clenched her whole body. He groaned and pulled out to drive himself back into her again.

Air was pushed from her throat as their bodies clashed together. Her whimpers became moans until the overwhelming pleasure was making her scream out.

"Fuck, yes, I need it. I need you!"

"You've got me, baby. You've got me," he groaned, shoving his dick into her and meeting her climax with his own when she called out until her throat grew hoarse.

He began to withdraw, but she grabbed for his shoulders and pulled him back to her. "No, no," she whimpered. "I'm not ready for you to go yet. Don't leave me, Strike."

Stroking his face, she tempted his mouth back to hers, but he leaned back when she tried to slip her tongue into his mouth.

"I'm not going anywhere, baby," he said, moving his lips back and forth over hers. "I'm yours, and any time you want me, you can have me."

"Any time?" she asked, running her hands down his arms. "And what if I want to touch you or flirt with you?"

Pushing her chin up with a fingertip, he kissed her lower lip. "Did it hurt? When you fell from heaven."

Laughing at his use of such a cheesy line, she patted his chest. "We'll work on that, baby."

Lying in his arms, she began to relax. They'd never really done this, never just held each other. But then they'd probably never appreciated the importance of their connection, not until they almost lost it.

"What changed your mind, Ro?"

That was a loaded question and wasn't an easy one to answer. "You weren't wrong, I was. I mean, you were in your methods, but I was wrong too," she said. "I thought I wanted to do the right thing because this is dangerous and that's what people do. But people are selfish. They go after what they want and say fuck the world. That's what I want to do, Strike. I want to say fuck the world."

He kissed her head. "Then you've definitely picked the right guy."

Burying her face in his chest, she breathed him in. "I don't doubt that."

His fingers coiled in her hair. "I can't believe you did it… you put the fucking Point on Opal… I'm still in shock."

She laughed and kissed his ribs. "Good. It's nice to know I can surprise you… in a good way."

"The way I did it wasn't good?"

Leaving her tied to a bed and running off? She bit him. "No, that wasn't a good surprise. Cupcakes and coffee are good surprises. Abandonment and betrayal, not good surprises."

"So, your plan… does it extend to what we do next?"

Rising to prop herself on an elbow, she looked at him. "You don't have a plan?"

"I have plenty," he said. "But I want to hear what you've come up with."

"Well," she said, trailing a finger across his chest. "One thing I wondered about was letting them destroy each other… What if we led Burke to the Black Jewel, let him destroy her, then we hand over Torres or threaten to blow the whistle. We'll have the processor and the Point, and the world will be at peace again."

"And we'll be together."

It felt so freeing to give in to her need for him. If playing with the Point was what her man needed to be happy, then it was her job to support him in the pursuit of his dream… and she had to have faith that he'd respect her reservations about using or bartering it.

"We will be together, my flame. I love you."

Both corners of his mouth rose, but even his smile was sinister. "You're something else, Miss. Maguire."

"I want you to be happy," she said, trying to kiss him again. "I need a rock, I need someone I can rely on no matter what. I thought that man was you before the Point came between us. Without that, I have no reason not to trust you. And if I'm wrong, I'll put a bullet in my head and be done with it."

"I told you that you had your one."

He seemed so inspired by her act that he was almost in awe of her and that was what she wanted. Rora wanted him to be proud of her. She'd told him that she would never judge him and that was why she needed him so badly because he would never judge her either, even when she wasn't following the rules.

"You told me there was still a place at your side," she said, taking that risk Junker had told her about. "Now you have the tech, you don't need me, but I'm asking you… can I be your one and only Queen?"

"There's nothing else you were destined to be."

She kissed his chest again. "Promise me you'll remember that while you're with her."

"Her," he said, tugging the strand of her hair he had coiled around his finger. "I'm not going back to the Jewel, Ro. No fucking way."

She didn't like to see him annoyed with her, and she couldn't think of anything she'd hate more, but their options were limited. "Junker has screwed everything up," she said. "Setting Burke after the Jewel could work, but what if it doesn't? What if Bella wins? And now we have Junker out there making alliances with God knows who, he knows Torres is here, and what he's told us. We need an inside man."

Rora was forced to move when Strike pulled his arm from around her, she lay down while he sat up. "You want to send me back to her?"

"Want to? No," she said and tried to take his hand, but he pulled it away. "But you're the only one I trust to make sure she doesn't get near Leandra."

Letting him think about it, she hoped he could come up with a better suggestion. They'd just found each other again and she'd handed him some pretty enticing temptation. Sending him off to Bella with Opal and the Point, he'd have the chance to retrieve the processor and then he'd have no reason to come back to her.

Funny, Rora had gone from one extreme to the other. This was another test, but it was real, and if he failed it, she wouldn't only have her heart broken, but the people of the world could be at Exile's mercy and it would be all her fault.

TWENTY-TWO

SHAKING THOUGHTS LIKE that from her mind, she recalled all those moments that had made her sure of their love, including the ones where he fought their craving for each other.

"What is it you want, Flame?" she whispered. "Talk to me."

Snapping out of his thoughts, he grazed a knuckle beneath her chin. "I want my toy back."

The processor, which could have so many more uses than just facilitating the Point. "Ok," she said.

"Ok?" She nodded. "If you don't want to—"

Boosting up, she grabbed his neck to pull him down for a kiss. When the weight of his body rested on hers, she didn't want to move for fear she'd lose him all over again. They were still enjoying each other's mouths when Torres called out from the other room. "Hey!"

There was a snarl in Strike's voice when he ripped his mouth from hers. "That fucker's got a death wish."

Stroking his face, she lifted her head to kiss him again. "Was I too loud?"

Some of the ire left his eyes when they met hers. "No, baby," he said and kissed her. "Bastard's probably jealous."

Next time he bowed to kiss her, his lips met her smile. Sliding her hands around his head and into his hair, she parted her legs, twining them around his, begging him to own her again.

"Hey!" Torres called out.

Strike's irritated groan made her laugh. "Maybe he needs to pee or something," she said. "We were driving for a while."

"I don't give a fuck what he needs," he said and kissed her chin then descended to begin feasting on her breasts. "If I fuck off back to Bella, what are you going to do with him?"

"Torres isn't going to hurt me," she said, moving beneath his mouth as he skimmed his lips from one nipple across to the other. "And unless he can convince us otherwise, we have no use for him."

He lifted his head. "You want to cut him loose?"

"Or take him with you, a prize for Bella, barter for Burke."

"And leave you alone?"

"I can take care of myself, baby," she said, letting her fingers run through his hair. "I'll go to Leandra, get her out before Bella can get to her… then you bring Bella."

"You want me to bring Bella to Leandra's location?"

"I'll make sure she's out before you get there," she said and licked her lips, watching her fingers move through his hair. "Leandra's place is isolated… very isolated."

His mouth relaxed. "The perfect place for a little payback." She smiled. "What would you do with Leandra? Where would she be safe while we dispose of Bella?"

"I thought maybe your friends could help us with that."

"My friends? I don't have friends, baby."

So he liked to say, but she knew that wasn't exactly true; he had friends, whether they were willing or not. "Before you go back to Bella, will you get me some backup?"

"Build you your own posse like I did for her?" he asked. "I don't know that we have time—"

"I had something more specific in mind," she said, and his head tilted in question. "X." Slowly, he tensed. "When we went to visit Shula, she said that that guy Thane was—"

"No," he said. "We're not getting them involved. We're not asking for their help… Thane wouldn't kill federal agents anyway."

"We don't need him to kill anyone. I meant we could ask them to protect Leandra while we deal with Bella and Burke. I'm not worried about the feds, but they do have access to manpower and I think Bella will pull out all the stops. Whether she gets to Leandra or not, Bella isn't going to stop until she has no more options. We need to limit her options."

"And you want me to find out what those options are? Bella's not going to let me waltz back into her life after I told her I was in love with you. She was fucking livid, Ro. She didn't care who I fucked, but finding out we were in love—"

"I know," she said. "But I trust you'll be able to convince her. Tell her it was a ploy. That you wanted to get my trust back so I'd give you the Point, and when Junker took off with it, you dumped me too."

"Isn't that what you thought when I first stumbled into your motel room? That I was playing you?"

Yes, that was what she'd thought, and it was what she'd feared up until she decided to surrender to her feelings for him. "I'm trusting you, Strike. I'm trusting that you love me more than you love her."

His expression hardened. "I don't love that witch. I want to put a knife in her eye for what she did to you."

"I know," she soothed, stroking his face and rubbing herself against him. "I know, baby. But let's not worry about that. The Point is out of play, all we need to do is get our hands on the processor and protect Leandra. I'm worried that when Bella finds out she can't have the Point, she'll lose what's left of her sanity… we could all get hurt. I trust that you and I can take it. And I don't care about Burke and Torres; they have their own safety net. But Leandra doesn't deserve any of this."

"So that's your plan? You just want to send me off to Bella with Leandra's location? You trust me enough to—"

"You are my love," she said, picking up his hands to kiss each of them. "If you betray me, if that's your plan, I can't stop you. But I've already told you, I don't have anything to live for but you. So if I'm being naïve, if you're playing with me, so be it. I'll take care of my own fate."

An angry look of sympathy crossed his face and rose up to brush his thumb across her cheek. "I'll keep you bound if you threaten to hurt yourself one more time, Cupcake."

"You don't hurt me, I won't hurt you," she said. If he didn't betray her, she wouldn't have any need to take her life. "Deal?"

"Deal," he said and lowered to kiss her. "But that works both ways."

In a moment of clarity, she understood the gravity of being responsible for another's life. If she hurt herself, Strike would do the same. But if he hurt himself… she wouldn't be able to take another breath; the pain would overwhelm her.

But it wasn't only Strike's life that she had in her hands at the moment. "We're going to need help," she said, threading her fingers into his hair again. "Someone has to protect Leandra, and I can't do that alone… Your X friends are the only ones I can think to ask. They have the manpower, right?"

"I can't endanger Shula, Ro."

"Do you love her?" she asked.

He'd said Shula wasn't an ex and that Thane would kill him for thinking about making a move on her. But he'd never explained his connection to the couple.

He shook his head, rising to sit between her legs. "It's not like that. I've known Thane a long time. I met him and his brother overseas while they were training with their father… We got involved in some shady shit together. Emeritus, that's Thane's father, he wouldn't let the boys come back until he was sure they were ready. Thane asked me to come back and watch over Shula, she's his Beloved, it's a thing in their cult."

"X," she said. "Shula said it wasn't a cult."

"To-may-toe, to-mah-toe," he said. "They say it isn't, I say it is. They have a council of ten men who make decisions for those below them. Their mission is to keep the city safe. Thane is the First, the guy in charge."

"So if you ask him—"

"He owes me. If I ask him to watch over my beloved, he will… but Leandra isn't my girl. If we ask him to endanger his men, out of his city limits, as a favor… there's going to be a price. You know how I feel about working under other people's purview."

"And if I know it, Thane knows it too," she said, but her thoughts wandered back in another direction. "Did you ever… think about it?"

"About what?"

Pushing her fingers into her thigh, she avoided looking at him. "You said Thane would kill you if you touched Shula… but you didn't tell me if you wanted to touch her."

"You think I'm harboring some hidden desire," he said, deadpan. "If another guy had been *our* problem, we wouldn't have had a problem. If I'd wanted to fuck Shula, I'd have fucked her. Thane would be worm food."

Feeling that there was something else he wanted to share, her chin rose to search for what it was. "You're not attracted to her?" she asked. "She's beautiful."

The look in his eye was sure, but hesitant. "She's my cousin."

"Oh my god. Your cousin?"

"Sort of. Her biological father and mine are half-brothers. Same mother, different fathers."

She sat up to grab for his wrist. "Does she know?"

"No," he said, pulling his arm away. "No one knows. It was no coincidence that I met Thane overseas. I found out who Shula was and that she'd been claimed by this guy, but she was still a kid…"

"You went to find out who he was," she said, understanding his thought process exactly. "You couldn't just walk up to the woman you're actually related to and try to form some kind of connection with her to ask about her relationship with Thane. Your way of showing your love was to track down her boyfriend and spy on him."

He wasn't contrite, in fact, his mouth slanted. "You know me, Cupcake. I got to know him and what his cult was all about. Thane sending me back to watch over Shula was just sort of… accidental."

"But it worked out because you did get to form a bond with her… even if you couldn't tell anyone the whole story… until me." Sentiment welled within her. "I love when you confide in me."

"You're the only one," he said, not resisting when she took his hand.

Much as she'd love to appreciate him for his faith some more, they had to deal with business first. "Do you think we can take Bella down alone? We don't need an army with us… do we? X could protect Leandra in their city, if I took her to them, maybe."

"Bella doesn't worry me, and I'm not worried about avoiding the feds or even fending them off if I'm alone… But you're asking me to leave you out there unprotected," he said.

It was obvious from the way his jaw moved, he didn't like the taste of that plan.

"If there's even a shred of truth to what Torres said, Burke won't have an army at his disposal. What did you find out about Torres?"

"Burke put in a report," he said. "Said he and Torres got into an altercation and the latter left. He's accusing him of going rogue… I don't know what his game is… I think it's a con, that it was put there for me to find. I've known Torres a long time and yeah, he bends the rules, but he also likes the protection of his home."

"Like I do," she said, sitting up to scrunch her hands in his hair to draw him in for a kiss. "I love you, Strike. I want both of us to keep loving each other for a long time… You have to make Bella think you're on her side, it's the only way we'll know what she's doing."

And if he was with her, he could make sure the Jewel wasn't close to catching Rora as she secreted Leandra with Strike's X friends.

"And if she wants to have sex?" he asked.

Easing back, she stopped nuzzling his mouth to search his eyes. "If you fuck her, you won't be fucking me."

There was a twist to his lips as he took his eyes to the side. "Remember how you reacted when you saw her make me bleed."

The memory of what happened in that Wonderland bedroom sickened and angered her at the same time. She yanked him close. "If she makes you bleed again, I'll skin her alive… Remember that if she starts to get close to you. Now, are you onboard, or do I have to find myself a man with the balls to be bad with me?"

Grabbing her hips, he hauled her against him, pressing his erection into her. "This is why you're my Kero." Because her actions set him alight. "I'm your slave, baby. Whatever you want, you get."

TWENTY-THREE

THEY MADE LOVE again, ignoring Torres' calls and surrendering only to each other. While Rora was so boneless that she was sure she'd never move again, Strike inhaled and vaulted off the bed, striding out into the living room in his full naked glory.

There was no one out there to see him, but she rolled to the edge of the bed to admire the view for as long as she could. When he came back into the bedroom, he didn't get on the vacant side of the bed. He put Opal on the nightstand and with his phone in his fist, he pushed her to the other side of the bed and then got on beside her.

"What are you doing?" Rora asked, tracing a fingertip up the front of his naked thigh.

"Shh," he said, wrapping his hand around her finger to hold it still while taking the phone to his ear. He listened for a few seconds before he spoke. "You secure?" His brow was set hard and it was funny to see how he switched from Strike to Exile mode so fast. "I've got work for you… You still First over there, Thane? Maybe I should be talking to your daddy or the woman who keeps your balls in her purse?" Rora rolled onto her back, but Strike didn't give her back her finger. "Yeah, she told me, just 'cause you're not fucking her doesn't mean she doesn't own your ass… Yeah… That's right, man. Simple as…"

Strike looked down at her, loosening his grip. Rora tipped her head back assuming he was going to tell her something, but he was admiring her chest instead. She guessed if Strike was talking to Thane that the woman they were referring to was Shula.

Rolling over to her chest again, she didn't bother with his thigh and instead ran her finger up the length of his dick then opened her hand beneath it to stroke his balls. If he could rib Thane about his need to keep Shula happy, Rora was going to remind him of just how close she was to his most sensitive parts.

He caught her hand in a fist and held it on top of his dick that was enjoying her attention. Smiling at the reaction, she wriggled closer and kissed his thigh.

"Hold on," Strike said into the phone, but only lowered the mouthpiece an inch to address her. "Go find out what our hostage wanted, Ro. Don't uncuff him."

Her smile became a grin. But she pulled herself onto her knees and climbed over him to straddle his thighs. "You just don't want me playing with your balls while you're playing the big man," she whispered and leaned in to kiss him.

As she carried on off the bed, he smacked her ass hard. "Play with my balls anytime you like, baby," he said without shame. "I just don't like hearing Thane's voice in my ear while you're giving me a hard-on." She grabbed his tee-shirt from the floor and tugged it on over her head. As she pulled her hair from the back of the neck, a look of pride grew on his face. "Yeah, man, that's her… love is the easiest part of being with her, it's the rest I'm calling about."

Rora blew her love a kiss as she crept from the room. Closing the door on that private conversation, she stretched her aching muscles before going to Torres' door and pushing it open, but she didn't go inside, she just propped herself on the doorframe.

He was cuffed to the frame of the heavy bed by both wrists, but he wasn't sitting on it, he was standing next to it, choosing to stand up. She recalled the bed he'd cuffed her to once, and thought it was some kind of justice that he found himself in this position now.

"What do you want?" she asked, annoyed at him for interrupting her cozy time with Strike.

"Oh, I'm sorry, are my basic human rights interrupting your sex life?"

Her grin was automatic. "Yes, actually," she said. "And if I were you, I'd expect Exile and I to be prioritizing said sex life for the foreseeable future."

Acting like the loved-up girlfriend complemented their plan. Torres would believe she'd been oblivious to Exile's apparent plan to screw her over if she played it innocent now. And it was easy to do because she was a woman enjoying her man.

What came next would rely on Strike's ability to sell his indifference to her, and it would help if he could claim to have used her for sex before dumping her… that was kind of his MO.

"What happened to your plan to save that woman from the Jewel?"

"I care less about plans when I have my man all to myself," she said. "And maybe we sent Junker off to deal with that problem."

He shook his head. "Something happened there, but we cleared out way too fast for it to have been an anticipated issue."

Leaning forward, Rora clutched the door handle. "Well, since your vast NSA training has taught you everything, I guess you don't need me to stand here all night—"

"No, wait," he said when she took a backwards step. "I'm hungry… and I want to use the restroom."

"The latter I can't help you with, but I'll order a pizza or something."

She started to swing the door shut again, but he called out. "You can't just leave me here. I'm not going to run anywhere, I just need—"

"Exile makes the rules around here," she said, narrowing her eyes on him. "And if he says no, then it's a no… I couldn't care less about you running. Where would you go?

You came to us. You running actually does me a favor… then no one will be around to interrupt my sex life. But, unfortunately for you, Exile doesn't trust you not to feel me up again."

Her next smile was tight, but she reversed from the room and closed the door.

Excitement was already bubbling within her before she got back to the other bedroom. But when she opened the door and took in the sight of Strike sitting up in bed, wearing his jeans, with Opal propped on his knees, her breath caught in her throat.

She must have loitered there longer than she realized because he looked over Opal's lid at her. "What's wrong?"

But there was nothing wrong, only happiness existed in her now. "I forgot how much it turned me on to see the two of you together… It's like the old days."

When his fingers returned to their work, flying over Opal's keys, Rora tiptoed over to the bed and climbed on, managing to steal a kiss from him even though his eyes never left the screen and his fingers never slowed.

"Everything's set," Strike said. "Thane's sending two guys down with orders not to leave your side and to follow your every command." She slid onto her back. "But this is temporary… they're not yours. This isn't like Bella's posse."

"Good," she said, stroking the seam of his jeans. "I don't want to know which of them has the bigger cock." His fingers stopped, but she didn't look up. "I think if you ever tried to build me my own posse, I'd get nervous. You only gave Bella hers so you could walk away from her. I don't want you to walk away from me."

"Don't ask me to rape a teenager and we'll be good," he muttered, returning to his work.

Rora was so shocked that she sat up slowly, gaping at him. "Is that what she did? She asked you to…"

"The girl was legal and all," he said, his focus on Opal. "But she was terrified. There was no way I was going to do it. Anyone who had the slightest clue about me would know that. But Bella got mad… as she does."

"Baby, I'm sorry," she said and leaned in to kiss his shoulder. "I can't believe she did that to you."

"That wasn't the only thing she did." Strike stopped typing to touch his knuckles to her jaw. "I don't have to tell you that she's dangerous… but I shouldn't have to remind you that you're nothing like her either."

"Hey!" Torres shouted.

His tenderness fled in a flash to be replaced with a scowl. "What the fuck did that bastard want?"

"Food and the bathroom," she said. "I told him I'd order pizza… but the second was up to you."

"I have to talk to him anyway," he muttered and tapped a few keys before putting Opal aside.

"Talk to him? About what?" she asked, watching him slide off the bed and head for the door.

"About why he came to us and what's really going on."

"We were the only people he knew in town and he needed someone to patch him up," she said and leaned against the headboard. "That's what I assumed."

"It's time to find out for sure. He's an asset or a liability. Until I know which, I can't decide what to do with him. Thane won't like the NSA in his business. So either we stash Torres, or he's coming with me."

Cutting him loose didn't seem to be an option, but Rora wasn't going to bring it up again. Strike would reach his own conclusions and when it came to law enforcement, and especially this particular agent, her love's experience far outweighed her own.

"But you have to talk to him first," she said and slid down onto her side when he opened their bedroom door. "You just remember what I told him. If you get a desk job, you won't be getting laid." She enjoyed teasing him. "I won't leave you, but your sex life will be greatly affected."

"Understood, Kero," he said and left the room.

Lying in their sheets, languishing in their mingled scents, fantasizing about her man, Rora didn't know how long she'd been there when she heard the first sound of distress.

Sitting slowly, she heard what could only be flesh on flesh, and not in a sexy way, in a much more violent way.

Clambering off the bed, she looked left and right, seeking out a weapon and recalled that her knife was in her jacket pocket. But her jacket was in the car and she didn't have the key, Strike did. Not only that, she wasn't dressed and didn't have time to—

"Kero!"

Strike's voice was unmistakable. She didn't loiter, she ran straight out of the bedroom to find her lover standing in Torres' bedroom doorway, his hand wrapped around his knuckles. "Baby," she said, rushing to him to pull his hand up to her mouth to cover it in kisses.

Strike eased her into the room. Torres was still cuffed to the bed, but not standing by it anymore, he was slouched down, against the wall, with blood trickling from his mouth.

"This bastard's got something to say to you before I kill him," Strike said.

Rubbing his knuckles on her cheek, she kissed them again. "If he hurt you, I want you to kill him slow," she murmured, tracing her lips back and forth on his fingers.

Torres spat blood and then scoffed. "Exile, are you asking your woman's permission?"

The mocking in his voice wasn't appreciated by either of them. Strike whipped around to stalk toward him. "You'd be dead if it wasn't for us," Rora said before Strike got to him.

Lunging down, Strike grabbed Torres and pulled him back to his feet. "You're still breathing because of her," Strike snarled. "I know you're full of shit. I know you... Don't you forget who you're fucking with."

"Then turn me loose."

Tossing him down onto the bed, Strike turned his back. "Not a chance," he said. "Apologize to my girl." Torres said nothing. "Do it!"

Even she jumped at the volume and venom in Strike's voice. "Sorry," Torres said. "Right? Shit! I'm sorry, Kero!"

She didn't really know what Torres was apologizing for, but it was nice to see her man triumph.

Satisfied, Strike came back to her and threw an arm around her neck to pull her face to his chest. "How's this, baby? There are no reports of agents going down. The rest of his story checks out, but scratch the surface and there's not one recorded NSA death for this whole last month."

"We don't advertise when our dirty agents murder innocent ones," Torres snapped.

"Yeah, and I don't look in the National Archives. There's nothing goes on in your agency that I can't touch."

Rora didn't doubt that. He'd only had Opal back for a short time, but he'd prioritized verifying Torres' story, she was impressed.

Snagging his belt buckle, she tipped up her chin. "He lied to us, baby?"

"Yeah, and we don't like it when people do that," Strike said, his venom fixated on Torres. "You're here for information."

It was something they'd considered, but having confirmation was appalling. Torres had come in bleeding, his wounds were real, putting himself through that showed quite a commitment to his cause.

"I'm not," Torres argued. "Everything I said was true and I came to you people as a last resort because I didn't want to bleed out in the street."

"That's not what you said a minute ago," Strike said. "What'd you say that made me hit you in the face?"

Taking a labored breath, Torres sank down to the floor again, his arms pulled over his head as they were still cuffed to the bed frame. "All I said was, I'm trained to gather intel. So since I was here anyway, I didn't keep my eyes and ears closed. I wanted to learn whatever I could… you'd have done the same thing if you were me, Exile, don't deny it."

"He's spying on you?" she asked.

"Worse than that," Strike said. "He's spying on you."

Rora felt sick. She tried to get a better look at Strike, but he kept her close and so she did the next best thing and looked at Torres. "What the hell?" she asked. "Why would you be spying on—"

"Because of what you said to him at your last meeting," Strike said. "You told him if you found out I was cooperating with him that we wouldn't be together anymore."

She remembered that, she'd just been joking about it with Strike a few minutes ago. Rora hadn't really thought that Torres would follow up with what he'd said about flipping her. Back then her relationship with Strike had been in flux, and she'd believed that she didn't have sway with her ex.

As it turned out, she'd been wrong. Somehow Torres had known that before she had because even Rora hadn't been sure of Strike's feelings until she chose to forgive him.

"You bastard," she murmured. "You really thought that you could gather some kind of intel on me that would change my mind? That I would turn on the man I love or convince him to come and work for you?"

Rora took one step, ready to fly for Torres, she wanted to do a hell of a lot more than hit him in the face. But Strike's arm strengthened to pull her back. "I love it when you're good and angry, baby," he murmured, rubbing his face in her hair. "But don't waste it on him, save it for me. This prick might think he can use us, but what are we going to do about that?"

Twisting her sly smile, she narrowed her eyes on Torres, and slid her arms around Strike. "We're going to use him instead."

"That's it, Cupcake," he said and kissed the top of her head. "We know he can't flip you or recruit me, but he does want to get back into his precious club. There's only one way that can happen, before he can return to work... he has to clear his name."

Torres hissed in a curse. "There's no way—"

"You want them to take you back, you need Burke's confession on tape. I can get you full live audio, video, whatever you want, and I'll air it on every network in the world if that's what floats your boat," Strike said, leaving her side to go to the middle of the room and crouch, bringing his eye level closer to that of the hunched Torres. "But if you want my help to get your justice... you have to help me and my girl get some of our own."

The men looked at each other for a second and it was clear Torres was intrigued. Strike looked over his shoulder at her and jerked his head to the side, telling her to scram.

"Don't be long," she whispered and appreciated his wink before leaving the men alone to come up with their own plan.

Approaching Bella wasn't going to be easy, but if Strike had a prisoner with him, one he might convince his ex he was willing to trade should the need arise, Bella would be more open to hearing him out. And if they could trust Torres, Rora felt better about her love having someone watching his back while he was there.

Returning to their bedroom, she called for pizza as she'd promised Torres she would and then pulled down the bedcovers to get comfortable. Strike would be in her bed for tonight, but their rediscovered love was going to be put on hold soon, and until then, she didn't want them to waste any time not enjoying each other.

TWENTY-FOUR

STANDING OUTSIDE their motel room, Rora stayed in the shade looking from one end of the parking lot to the other. Torres was in the passenger seat of the car in the far right corner. Strike was striding across the asphalt toward her having just spoken to the men in the truck parked in the furthest left corner.

She breathed in and blew out the air slowly, stealing herself against what she was about to do.

"You're all set," Strike said as he approached her. "Crescent's driving and Spear is his second. They're both high council, as close to Thane as you can get. They'll take Leandra back and she'll be under X protection until Thane gets the all-clear from us."

Her nerves were making it difficult to relax. She tried to dampen them, but this was beyond risky. Lives depended on them, they had a full operation running, but all she could think about was how much better she'd feel if she could do this with Strike at her side.

Raising his curled fingers to her jaw, he rested them there. "You have my permission and complete support to castrate any man who thinks about touching you, including them," he said. "They're both single, but have been warned. Don't let them play dumb."

He was trying to make her feel better while meaning every word at the same time. "They're your friends… by proxy at least. It's not my virtue I'm worried about… it's yours."

Stroking her arms, he pulled her closer. "We've been having sex for almost two days straight. My appetite is quenched." He leaned down. "At least until we see each other again."

She slid her hands onto his chest. "And Bella's appetite? How will you convince her to trust you without seducing her?"

"I won't deny it. If I could use sex as a tool, my job would be easy. But Bella's into games and loves a challenge. I'll tease her, tell her it's all business, but she'll push for more… and the more I say no, the more she'll want it. I'll tell her I'm swearing off women for a while. That you're all fucked in the head, you're too easy for me, you bore me. Seems like all I've gotta do is snap my fingers and you're all prepared to drop your panties for me. She knows I'm not into women like that."

"So you're going to call us whores," she said, but smiled. "I remember how disgusted you looked when that blonde stripper was rubbing herself all over you. Maybe that's why I thought I could tease you with her. I didn't think you'd follow through… I was devastated when I thought you had."

His hands slid around to splay on her back. "You play with me, I play right back," he said, leaning in. Rora leaned away, using his hands to support her weight. "What?"

"You just said you like a challenge. What kind of a challenge would I be if I let you kiss me every time?"

He yanked her body tight to his. "You are a challenge every goddamn minute. Since I met you, I haven't had a second of peace… and fuck, I love you for it."

Joy and attraction made her snuggle closer to whisper, "Those three words get you pretty much anything you want."

She parted her lips to accept his and probably could've stood there all day in his arms, making out with him, thinking about how close they were to their sex sheets.

But someone blasted a car horn, making her jump and Strike curse. He glared over her to the car in the right corner.

"Damn Torres," he growled. "I might kill him as soon as he has Burke's confession, just for kicks."

"Well don't do it before we're back together. I can't say I don't feel uneasy about this whole plan, but knowing you at least have someone at your back makes me feel a teensy bit better… even if he is a narc."

"You're sure Leandra doesn't have internet access?" he asked, centering her thoughts on the plan again.

"Definitely not. There's barely electricity where she is. I told you that after her daughter's death she became a recluse. That was why her and Benjamin's marriage broke down. But she didn't move out of the city until after Benjamin went missing."

"And if she's not where you think she is, if you can't find her, what are you going to do?"

It wasn't a question, he was asking her to recite their agreed contingency. "Go to Thane and stay with X until you come for me."

"That's right," he said and kissed her forehead.

Rora sighed. "I wish my directions were better. Leandra's is so off the beaten path."

"Don't worry about that," he said. One of his hands slipped from her back down to her wrist and he squeezed it in his fist before brushing his thumb up and down against it. "I'll always be able to pinpoint your location… Opal has the ability to train up to a dozen satellites on you at any given minute."

Leaning back again, she tried to figure him out. Strike kept caressing her wrist, but held up his own to show her, much like he had the time he'd told her about… Rora gasped. "Your implant," she said, and his thumb stopped on the center of her wrist. "Oh my god, you put something inside me?" His lips quirked, but she smacked his chest. "You're allowed to put *that* inside me. But this…" Pulling her arm from his hand, she clutched it to her chest. "I don't know how I feel about this."

"It allows me to protect you, that's all. I'll always be able to find you and monitor your life signs. It's my way of showing you I care."

His way of being romantic. "Will I get zapped if someone else touches Opal?" she asked, wringing her hand around her wrist.

"No, not unless you want to. I can reprogram it at any time to do pretty much anything you want."

Relaxing as she absorbed this development, Rora figured there was no point in fighting it, so she embraced it instead. "Will it tell me every time you get an erection?" she asked, her lips curving. "Or every time you put your dick in another woman's pussy?"

He lowered to brush the tip of his nose against her hairline. "I don't have a chip in my cock… but I guess that's something we can look into."

She shoved his chest but didn't really want him to go anywhere. Happy to settle into his arms when he pulled her to him again, Rora exhaled. "I love you, Strike," she said, closing her eyes and nestling herself against his chest, knowing their time was coming to an end. "With all my soul, I worship you, lord."

"And I love you, my corrupted queen," he said, cupping his hands beneath her jaw to draw her face up and join their lips again.

Neither of them wanted to go, but there was work to be done, and hopefully this would be over without any hiccups in less than a week. Afterwards, all they would have to look forward to was the rest of their lives together.

TWENTY-FIVE

"WOW, THIS IS SOME place," Spear said, leaning forward to look at the timber building emerging from the woods up ahead.

Set over two floors, the four-bedroom house was designed to camouflage with its surroundings and was set five miles back from the nearest road.

"There's space in the basement for cold storage and a dry store that can be stocked to keep this place going for two years," Rora explained.

"How did she end up here?"

"After Benjamin went missing, she got anxious. She's always been kind of a nervous woman. The cops didn't help with their constant questions. Though I guess I wasn't much of a help myself. When she hinted that she was thinking about disappearing, I jumped on the idea and convinced her to do it. I knew Benjamin would've wanted her protected... This was one of three places that Benjamin and I had discussed, you know, in case of emergency if we needed to get off the grid. So, I helped set her up here."

They stopped the truck near the corner of the porch, facing toward the road they'd just used, presumably to allow a quick getaway if it was needed.

"We have to do some recon," Crescent said, twisting to look over the shoulder of his chair at her.

"For Exile?"

Crescent nodded. If everything went to plan, Rora would convince Leandra to go with these men and then she would lie in wait for Strike to bring Bella to this isolated location, hopefully with the processor.

It wasn't possible for Rora to get a message to him from here, but if Crescent and Spear left with Leandra, they'd be able to get one to him when they were back on the road taking Leandra to safety.

Strike had tried to convince her to go with Crescent and Spear to safety, but Rora didn't want to miss out on Bella's demise. She also didn't want her man dealing with the crazy bitch alone; he needed backup.

Burke was out there somewhere, tailing Bella, waiting for the right time to strike, and they couldn't be complacent about that. If Burke thought Strike was going to damage his target, he might try to step in and take Strike down himself.

Even though Torres was supposed to be watching her love's back, Rora couldn't guarantee he'd go to extreme lengths to stop his ex-boss from killing Strike, if given the chance. Not that the narc could necessarily protect anyone, she'd never seen him in action in the field, so couldn't vouch for his skills.

"You ok?" Spear asked, and she realized she was the focus of both men's attention.

"I'd feel better if Exile was here," she said with a shrug. "No offence to your skills, I'm just... worried about him. I have you two at my back and we're in a secret place. He's out there in the open with a looney toon woman and I don't know for sure that I can trust his backup."

The men shared a look. "Why didn't he ask for more backup from Thane?"

She smiled. "We don't use force, we use manipulation. Besides, what we want to do, we want to do slow and I'm not sure your boss would condone it."

Thane didn't know what Bella had put them both through and if he wasn't the type to be comfortable taking down Feds, he probably wouldn't be comfortable torturing a woman either.

"We'll go in with you first," Crescent said. "To make sure the environment is secure and that we don't freak the woman out, skulking around the place. But after introductions, we'll do a perimeter sweep, take a few pictures, and survey the interior."

She nodded. "Whatever he needs," she said. "We want the works and I want him prepared when he gets here." The guys both nodded together and reached for their doors, but she spoke before they could exit, drawing their attention back to her. "I appreciate this. We both do. I know the trip has been uneventful so far, but… having you with me has made me feel safer and I know it puts Exile's mind at rest. You're probably irritated to be on babysitting duty, but the woman in there, she meant the world to a dear friend of mine who killed himself to protect a secret only he and I shared. It's only right that I do whatever I can to keep her safe… it's what he'd want."

Crescent offered a tight but comforting smile. "We do what our First tells us to do and we're never complacent enough to shrug any assignment off as babysitting or uneventful. We're ready to do whatever it takes to keep Leandra safe… and to keep you safe too."

"Yeah, and our High Priestess made it clear she'd kick our asses if you got hurt, so that guarantees you're getting out of this alive," Spear said to Crescent's amused nod, and they all climbed out of the vehicle together, sharing a smile.

Leandra was surprised to see them. To see anyone. Rora didn't blame her for that, the woman had only left the place once in all the months she'd been stuck there alone.

Rora did think that if it had been anyone else, Leandra might have died there on the spot. After the initial second of shock, she did look happy to see Rora until the two great hulks appeared like daunting menaces at her flanks.

Quickly explaining that they were friends here to protect her, Rora managed to calm the woman and sent her two bodyguards off to do their reconnaissance work.

Guiding her into the kitchen, Leandra talked about her life there while she made tea. She spoke of the plant life and her time in the forest and her love of the quiet.

It did seem that Leandra was better grounded than the last time Rora had seen her. But from her quick, almost constant speech, Rora did wonder if some part of the woman had missed having a human to talk to.

Once Leandra had brought the tea to the table, she settled down and began to pour. "Now, you must tell me, how is our Benjamin? Has he been injured? Is that why he isn't here? Maybe he's in hospital, but you're here to tell me he's going to visit me when he's released. I can't believe he got himself kidnapped like that, what a horror! Tell me the complete truth, Aurora, you know I can handle it. What did they do to him? How did he get away?"

Rora had known this conversation was coming, but that knowledge didn't make telling this truth any easier.

"Benjamin is dead, Leandra," she said, softening her voice.

Leandra had just put the teapot down but froze with one hand on the lid and another on the handle.

Swallowing her own grief, Rora felt her heart ache for the beauty who had had so much taken from her in her life. No wonder Leandra wanted to be alone. All she'd wanted was a happy family, but that dream had been torn from her piece by piece and now she was truly alone.

Even after the divorce, Leandra and Benjamin had remained friends, maybe sometimes more; Benjamin had always been cagey about just which of Leandra's needs he fulfilled. And he had fulfilled her. He supported his ex-wife; Leandra's adoration and gratitude was always obvious. It was just a shame that their relationship hadn't survived the tragedy of losing their daughter.

"I'm so sorry," Rora said and tried to reach for Leandra's hand, but the woman sat back, settling both hands in her lap.

"Was it quick? Did he suffer?"

"No," Rora said, having no intention of telling her of the torture he endured. "He didn't suffer. It was quick."

Leandra's eyes floated toward the window. Rora didn't know how to comfort her. How did she make the woman feel better about losing her great love? She knew how it felt watching Benjamin fall and how devastated she'd been by losing Strike, and there were no words that would've appeased or comforted her in those moments. Handling Benjamin's death had only been possible for Rora because she'd had Strike. But Rora couldn't offer Leandra comfort like Strike offered it to her.

"How did it happen? Where is he buried?"

Those were normal questions, but Rora had to be delicate about telling the truth. "He was shot," she said, which was true. She shifted to the edge of the chair and reached over to rest her hands on Leandra's on her lap. "The danger is still out there, and I'm worried about you."

"About me?"

"The people who took Benjamin didn't get what they wanted…"

It took a minute for her thoughts to catch up, but Rora saw the moment Leandra caught on. "That's why you came here? To warn me? But I… what do these people want? I don't know how I can—"

"Don't worry," Rora said, offering a tiny smile. "I came to make sure you got to safety. The men who brought me here are part of a group who can protect you. I know it's a lot to digest, but Benjamin would want you safe. So, I need you to pack your essentials as quickly as you can and go with them."

Leandra was clinging to her now, either trying to draw strength or to vent her growing panic. "Where will they take us?"

"Not us. I'm staying here," she said, and Leandra gripped her tighter. "Don't worry. They've been keeping me safe for days and I trust them with my life… Benjamin would too."

Leandra thought about it for only a few seconds. "I suppose I don't have a choice. With Benji gone, you're the only person left I can trust on this matter. But I don't feel comfortable leaving you behind, Benjamin wouldn't have it."

Benjamin had left her alone. But he'd expected her to follow him, so it wasn't clear who'd abandoned who.

"Don't worry about me. There's a plan in place to put an end to this once and for all. I have backup on the way, and I'm going to take care of this. Benjamin knew I could take care of myself that's why he reached out to me to help him. I failed to save him; I won't fail him again by letting you get hurt."

It was slow, but Leandra eventually managed a smile. "You're a good person, Rora," she said. "It's no wonder he loved you as much as he did."

"He loved you too, Lea," she said, resting a hand on her cheek. "And grieving him is one of the hardest things either of us will ever have to do." She pulled herself closer. "But the best way for us to honor his memory is to be safe now. We have the chance to end this. Let's do it… for Benji."

It didn't take Leandra long to pack. Most of her things were grouped in the same place and she hadn't brought much in the first place.

Crescent and Spear packed the truck and didn't waste much time in saying goodbye. They issued instructions to her, much as Strike had, and once everyone had said their piece, she watched them bundle into the truck and disappear from view.

Rora stayed there until long after the sound of the engine had faded. It was getting late and Leandra had left food in the kitchen for her, so she couldn't stay there in the fresh air all night, appealing as it might be.

Rora had to keep her strength. She needed to eat, to sleep, and to do everything Strike had told her to do to prepare for their final showdown with Bella. If all went to plan, her love would be leading their prey here in less than twenty-four hours and Rora was going to be ready.

TWENTY-SIX

RORA DIDN'T KNOW what had woken her up. But lying in the dark, she tried to adjust to the absolute blackness around her and remember where she was.

The first thing she did was reach to the other side of the bed, but when she found it empty and the sheets unfamiliar beneath her palm, she recalled that Strike wasn't there. No one was. She was all alone in this isolated place and alone was eerily unfamiliar.

It took her a second to read the glowing numbers on the clock on the nightstand and establish it was just after four-thirty in the morning.

Usually she only woke this early if Strike was waking her, either for fun or to flee. But she sank onto her back and closed her eyes again. Letting her fingertips brush across her thigh, this seemed like a rare opportunity; being all alone with thoughts of her man, she could enjoy a little quality time with herself.

She heard a creak and sat up immediately, clutching the blankets to her chest. Strike had warned her not to sleep naked, though she wouldn't have anyway, but instinct made her want to protect her body even though it was clothed.

She heard it again.

Quiet as she could, Rora crept out of bed and reached for the jeans she'd left on a nearby chair. She made little noise pulling them on but heard enough from outside the room that by the time she was done, she was sure there was another person in the house.

Strike wouldn't be so obvious, or make so much noise, if he was trying to sneak up on her and he was the only ally she had left who might be approaching this place that few people knew about.

Leandra hadn't mentioned any friends and Rora couldn't imagine anyone showing up for a social visit at this time.

Her switchblade snicked when she opened it. Rora crept forward, one careful step at a time, low, braced, ready for whoever might—

The bedroom door opened, and a bright white light suddenly blinded her. She held up a hand to try to block the beam, but couldn't make out who was there.

She was about to ask when she heard the unmistakable sound of a bullet being loaded into a gun barrel.

"Did you miss me, Aurora?"

Rora couldn't say that her fear lessened when she identified Junker's voice, but it did change hue. Her blade was going to make little difference in a gun fight, so she let her hands fall to her sides and straightened up.

"Junker," she said. "What are you doing here?"

"You led me to exactly what I needed. I always knew you would. Now tell me, where is he?"

"If you're looking for Exile, he's not here," she said. "No one's here, so if you're going to kill me—"

"No," he said with what could only be pain in his tone. "No, Aurora, I don't want to hurt you… I always felt sorry for you, I always…"

He exhaled, and the brightness of the flashlight beam vanished a breath before the overhead light came on.

The generator was rarely used, candles were preferred for light. But it was there, and although it was hidden at the far side of the house, she wondered now if it had been the generator starting up that had woken her up.

She'd been tearing around the country for so long that she'd lost any notion of familiar sounds or smells, she had to adjust to somewhere new almost every day. The only thing that she'd had with any kind of regularity was Strike and even he hadn't been a constant.

"I don't want to fight with you, Aurora. I want to make you understand… I don't like the way things ended between us," he said. "Will you let me explain everything?"

She hesitated. "You lied to me."

"I think we were both guilty of not being honest with each other," he said. "Let's change that. Let us go downstairs, have a drink, and lay all our cards on the table."

Rora wasn't going to confide in him, but Strike wasn't going to be there with Bella for hours. She couldn't let Junker leave, and it seemed unlikely that he'd want to. Keeping an eye on him was the smartest option.

He'd revealed himself to her, so he wanted something, and if she had to keep him talking until Strike could get here, that's what she was going to do.

****

THEY WERE WARY of each other. Rora tried to hide her suspicion, but this guy had already held a knife to her throat, she didn't know what he might do next. They'd both left their weapons in the bedroom and gone to the living room. Each sat in an armchair at opposite ends of the long coffee table that stood beside the rug in front of the fireplace.

"How did you find me?" Rora asked.

"I followed you."

"You didn't," she said. "There's no way—"

"Exile isn't the only one who can make technology work for him," he said. "I've been following you for a couple of days."

"How?"

He smiled. "Let's just say your new friends aren't as careful as your previous ones."

Meaning Crescent and Spear weren't as thorough as Strike in covering their tracks. She'd known they were reporting to their First, but hadn't thought to warn them to be careful about disguising their digital signature. Rora preferred to think Strike was monitoring them; it made her feel more at ease.

It hadn't occurred to her to think that Junker might be out there trying to track her down.

"What took you so long to get here?"

"I couldn't bring my vehicle down that isolated road. For one thing, I didn't know where it would come out, and I didn't want to give up the element of surprise."

It didn't make sense. She couldn't figure him out. "So you hid your vehicle and walked? But you missed Leandra, she's not—"

He scowled. "I don't care about Leandra."

"You don't?"

"Why should I?"

"I thought she was the point of… Wait," she said and shook her head. "Start at the beginning, you're clearly not who I thought you were."

Which meant speculating about his motives, or what she thought were his motives, was crazy. She had no idea who this man really was, and now was her chance to find out.

"Neither are you," he said, jumping onto the defensive. "I didn't think for a second you'd be nuts enough to get yourself involved with a person like Exile… not physically."

Not sexually, that's what he was saying. His face screwed up like he was disgusted by the idea. "So I don't have the smartest taste in men." According to him. "Everything else you knew about me was true. My search for Benjamin, my work with him, how much I cared about him. You lied about everything. Exile was the only thing I wasn't honest about."

"Don't you see, this has all been about him," he said, clasping his hands between his knees when he moved to the front of his chair to rock forward. "I started this. I'm involved because of him."

"Junker, I… I don't understand. All I know about you is what Exile told me. Your name is Dexter Redd, you studied at MIT, worked in their computer science division…"

"That's true. That's all true," he said, but she was ready for him to fill in the blanks. "What you don't know is about a year ago, my life changed… everything changed… when I found out who my father was."

"Your father… I don't…"

"And that I had a sister. I reached out to Benjamin Gallagher because of her." Rora waited. It was a technique she'd learned from Strike. Stay quiet long enough and eventually someone else would fill the silence. "Our father was always interested in technological innovation, that's why he had an interest in Exile, I guess. My sister, she had the same fascination. They believed that technology could bring rewards."

"Financial rewards," she said. "Is that what you mean?"

"There is a lot of money to be made," he said. "Maybe it's in our genes; maybe that's why I got into the industry… I'd been searching for my father for years, a decade at least. Obviously, I was devastated when I found out he was dead, him and the brothers I never knew I had… But when I found out about Bella…"

This was a clarity she wasn't sure she wanted. "Bella is your sister…"

"I knew she was out there, but I first encountered her on the dark web. She was looking for something new and exciting, something powerful. On the grapevine, I'd heard Gallagher was working on something world changing. Once you tell one guy in our field you've got something special, it spreads like wildfire."

And Benjamin was never the most discreet. Rora could believe he might have mentioned the Point to a colleague at a conference or during a late-night call. "You knew about the Point."

"I didn't know that's what it was called. But I wanted to impress her, to prove myself to her as a provider before we met. So, I swore to myself I wouldn't tell her we were related until I could show her I could provide for her like our father had before he was murdered… I sent her a message telling her about Gallagher. I didn't know him then, but I made it a point to connect with him, thinking I could get more information about this program he had. At first, I made it seem professional, but we built a friendship. He was vague about his work, but clear in how much he cared about you."

"That's why you sent me that message. Benjamin didn't ask you to look out for me at all," she said, trying not to be outraged, but he was turning everything she thought she knew on its head.

"He did. Connecting with you was more my idea than his, but it was easy to draw him around to my way of thinking so that he believed it was his idea. You know how easily he was manipulated, which was probably how Bella got him, I don't know how that went down. I thought you could be useful. You worked so closely with him, I figured that you had to know something."

Though he seemed sincere enough in what he was saying, she couldn't deny that there was something cold about the genesis of their friendship and it made her feel ill that Benjamin had been taken advantage of by someone he trusted.

"After he went missing," Rora said, trying to remember the sequence of events. "I didn't hear from you."

"They went off the grid. She had what she wanted, and she was just gone. Bella was good, I don't know who taught her, but she and Gallagher disappeared."

Exile probably taught her. Even if he hadn't meant to, Bella would've picked up a few hints. "And that's when you started to help me."

"The message you sent asking about Exile surprised me. But when you said you'd heard from Benjamin Gallagher that he needed Exile, I knew that meant my sister needed him. I had to help."

Feeling angry, and conned, Rora was too numb to really show her outrage. "That was why you helped me. You found Exile and made me lead him to Bella because she wanted him there."

Junker had been the first to use the words, 'Black Jewel' with her. He'd said that Exile had an interest in the Black Jewel and she'd had no idea what that meant. Now she learned it was the Black Jewel who'd had an interest in Exile, Junker had played her good.

"I didn't expect Exile to be as good as he was," Junker said. "After you connected with him, you vanished, and I didn't hear a whisper from any of you… that's when I cleared out Gallagher's place and yours… I got nothing and started to get worried. But then, you messaged me. The phone you used to send the message didn't move, but there was another in the same apartment a while later, I tracked it… until it vanished in the vicinity of a resort Benjamin told me you and he visited."

The man had done his research. Junker had probably been the one to torch her and Benjamin's old workplace when he didn't find anything. He'd have wanted to hide the evidence that he'd been there and probably cover his sister's tracks too. Junker was good with a computer, but didn't have great skills as a criminal.

"That's how you found me at the bus station?" she said. "You tracked me from the resort."

"I saw you hitchhiking. I almost couldn't believe my luck when I drove up that road and there you were. I considered stopping, but it was Exile I needed. I followed you from the bus station back to that apartment building, I didn't know what was inside, so I watched… I saw my sister take you…" His expression became contrite. "I'm sorry, but if you were what she wanted, I wasn't going to interfere."

He wouldn't have known Strike was in Buddy's apartment, wouldn't have known that if he'd just hung around he might have located his target. If he had lost track of them after she and Strike connected, Junker wouldn't have known about Wonderland, that Bella and Strike had already connected and parted, or that Benjamin was dead.

"But why did you rescue me from her?"

"Bella wanted the Point. Exile seemed to have disappeared. You knew about the Point, and what Exile looked like. All I wanted to do was help my sister do what she was struggling to do. I thought maybe I could use your trust in me, in our previous connection, to get Bella what she wanted."

"You told me you wanted to stop them. That Exile was dangerous."

"He is. And I didn't want him to use the program, I wanted Bella to have it and to be safe from him. If it had been up to me, I'd have killed Exile on the spot. But Bella needed him to fix whatever was wrong with Benjamin's work and he had the processor. It was my plan to wait until Bella had used him for what she needed and then…"

"You were going to kill him," she whispered. "It was all a lie. Why would you want to kill him? Your sister loved him! I think she *still* loves him."

Disgust made him shoot to his feet. "I didn't know that! I didn't know about her ridiculous infatuation with him… or yours! What the hell is it about the guy? How does he seduce smart, beautiful women into losing their minds? Why would you share your body with such a monster?"

"He's not a monster," she said, but couldn't be too vehement in her defense of the man she'd have to pretend to hate later.

"He's the monster who killed my family!"

Oh no. She chilled. At some point through all his investigating, he'd found out that his father and brothers had been killed by Exile. She swallowed. "That's why you want to kill him."

"And you could share yourself with him? My sister could? I don't understand it!"

"He has a way of making us feel… special."

Junker came to her and crouched down to gather her hands into his. "My sister is special," he said. "And so are you." He slid a hand onto her cheek. "You're beautiful, Rora, and you don't need him. You deserve better than him."

It was difficult to let him touch her and difficult not to argue for her love, but she held steady for the greater cause. "I thought we were friends, Junker," she said. "I thought I could trust you."

"You can," he said. "He betrayed you again, didn't he?" She averted her eyes, but he drew her attention back and rose higher to brush his lips over hers. "I'll never betray you, Rora… We can work this out together. I want to punish him for what he did to my father and brothers, for duping my poor, naive sister."

That was clear proof how little he knew his sister, but she tightened her hold on his hand. "That's why I'm here… why I stayed. I trusted him, and I know I shouldn't have, but… I thought I could trust him, he made me believe and…"

"You told him where Leandra was," he said, and she managed to conjure a few tears. "You think he's on his way here."

"I don't know. All I know is he left me, so I reached out to some people who can keep Leandra safe."

"He used you to get what he wanted. Just like he's using Bella now because she has the device he wants. He's a user… Bella wants the Point, that's all. But I won't let him hurt her again. I won't… You do see him for what he truly is now… don't you?"

So now she and Junker were allies again? Strike would come here unaware of Junker's presence. They hadn't discussed him at all. But keeping Junker close was the only way to play this. The whole situation was messed up. Strike was pretending to be Bella's ally and now Rora had to pretend to be Junker's.

Strike had betrayed her once, and it had taken a lot of emotional strength to forgive him. Rora had to be confident he wouldn't do it again or this wouldn't work. But the last thing she wanted was for him to think she'd switched allegiances and put any doubt in his mind.

But this whole situation had just gotten more dangerous, Junker thought he had the Point and that Bella had the processor, so the only part of his plan left was making the program work. After that, he intended to kill Strike. She couldn't tell Junker that he didn't have the Point, but she'd have to play this carefully for the sake of her love's life.

Rora nodded her head and let Junker keep caressing her face. "They could show up at any time," he said. "And we have to be prepared… How about I draw you a bubble bath?" He smiled. "I'll help you relax, like we used to when it was just us."

She hid her swallow and smiled instead. "Sounds good."

He rose and pressed his mouth to her forehead for way longer than she was comfortable with. If Strike was in the room, he'd have slit Junker's throat for sure. But she kept her smile in place and watched him go.

She couldn't run, she had to be here for Strike. She couldn't get a message out, there was no phone, so no internet. She had to keep her cool and wait. The clock was ticking, and it would take every ounce of her strength and Strike's to get through this.

****

IT WAS DIFFICULT to relax in the tub when she didn't know what Junker was doing in the house on his own.

Rora didn't do more than dip herself in the water, but wasted some time loitering in the bathroom to let him think that she was enjoying herself.

He was in the hallway when she came out of the bathroom and though she was taken aback to see him there, she'd be happy if that's where he'd been the whole time because it would mean he hadn't been snooping or setting traps.

Going to bed was slightly awkward because he kissed her head again and the way he held her hand made her wonder if he was waiting for her to say something. It was a look he'd given her before and she never knew how to respond to it.

Rora was glad to be in her room, but knew she wouldn't sleep much. Before Junker had shown up, she'd been anxious about Strike getting here, fearing how this all might come to a head. Now she was eager for him to arrive. Until she could look him in the eye, she didn't think she'd shake this foreboding from her heart.

She needed her man to anchor her. Sending out a silent message of love to him, she hoped he was safe, wherever he was.

TWENTY-SEVEN

"YOU KNOW, we could be here for a while," Junker said, drawing her eyes up from the book Rora had resting on her crooked knees. "We don't know how long it will take them to track us."

He left his armchair to come over to her. Resting an arm along the back of the couch, he picked up the ends of her hair from her shoulder, and watched his fingers play through it.

Since the first time he'd kissed her, he'd been more physically affectionate. He'd been tactile before that too, though when they'd first met she'd been naked and unable to stand on her own two feet, so the physical contact was more of a necessity than a choice.

"I guess."

The day hadn't been easy, mostly because she'd had to make it appear it was. If she hadn't known she needed her senses, she'd have been tempted to raid the basement stores for liquor. Rora's reserve energy was running on low, and just like she had before, she probably would've thought about giving up, if she hadn't known Strike was on his way.

Breakfast was lots of false smiles. Junker talked about how nice the house was and what a great hiding spot it was.

They'd spent a vast chunk of the day writing an inventory of what was in the store. Lunch was light, and then they went out to chop wood for the fire.

Using the axe had made her sore, but she'd taken her turns with it, preferring to have a chance with the weapon than to leave it in Junker's hands all afternoon.

"How's your shoulder?" he asked, his fingers drifting over to the spot she'd had issues with. "You should've let me deal with the wood."

"My neck's a little stiff," she said, thinking it wouldn't hurt if he thought she had a weakness. She'd prefer to be underestimated than the opposite. "But it's okay."

He shifted closer and her breathing slowed when he touched her face. "We have to make the most of this time we have… alone."

If he was suggesting what she thought he was suggesting…

After dinner, she'd tried to take her book up to the bedroom, but he'd asked her to stay with him by the fire. She'd had little choice except to agree and it did let her keep an eye on him… Rora wondered if that's what he was thinking too. Was he watching her? Wary of her? Or did he really trust her?

If he trusted her, he would've told her the truth about his sister's identity from the beginning.

She couldn't let her guard down. When he leaned closer, she tensed. If she had to push him away, she would, but it would anger him, and how would she explain?

"Junker," she said, moving a hand to his shoulder. "I don't think we should."

"Just relax, Aurora," he murmured, getting closer, his hand beginning to massage her shoulder. "I'll make everything better… I promise. You're so beautiful."

Growing rigid as he got closer, she held her breath, waiting for the moment she'd have to push him away and risk him exploding at her.

The sound of a gun barrel being loaded broke the moment.

Junker froze. Rora was already tense, so didn't have to react, though she hadn't expected the sound either.

"That's my job, Square," a sinister voice said, making both of them ease away to look over the back of the couch.

Strike.

Oh, fuck, yes. She tried not to smile, but her initial joy became alarm when she read the dark hatred in her lover's eyes. Smiling was the furthest thing from her mind when she registered that he had a gun trained to her head, and a second pointed at Junker.

Standing at the back of the couch, Strike looked from Junker to her. But his eyes didn't register her as anything more than an enemy. Rora wanted to be in his mind, just for a minute, she had to know he trusted her; that he didn't think she and Junker had set this whole thing up.

Strike whistled.

"We're late to the party," Bella's voice bled into the room before the woman slunk in from the kitchen to show herself. Obviously, Strike had been sent ahead to secure the scene. Tugging each finger from the leather gloves she wore, the Black Jewel glittered as she examined the couple on the couch. "You could've let them fuck before pulling the weapon, my prince."

No, he couldn't and Rora was grateful that he hadn't. Strike wouldn't look at her, his indifference made her heart race. Did he doubt her?

"Though I suppose…" the Black Jewel said, tossing her gloves aside and strutting to Strike to slide her body in front of his, though his weapons didn't move from their targets. With her back to his chest, the Black Jewel curled her arms backwards around Strike, holding his body against her as she smiled at their captives. "We could watch… and you could do me right here."

Bella bent forward, resting her elbows on the back of the couch and pressing her ass into Strike's groin. As she began to grind, Rora bit her lip, reminding herself not to blow their cover, not to grab the woman and claw her eyes out. Strike had a weapon pointed at her and she'd guess if she did anything to threaten Bella, he was supposed to shoot her, so she had to grit her teeth and let that witch arouse her boyfriend.

She was so busy concentrating on what Bella's ass was doing to Strike that she almost missed Bella's hand coming toward her face. "My Arousing Aurora," Bella purred, stroking her hair and curling her talons around Rora's chin to pull their mouths close. "I missed you, duckie."

Rora didn't move when Bella kissed her. Even after the Jewel's tongue slid into her mouth, she kept her focus set, and when Bella's head tilted to press their mouths closer, Rora's eyes met Strike's, which were cooler than they had been before.

Just the sight of his anger made her respond, but not in lust, Rora bit down hard, tasting Bella's blood a second before the woman hissed away and brought her hand across Rora's cheek so hard that she fell from the couch.

Leaping onto her feet, Rora jumped onto the couch and over the back ready to receive Bella who was swinging already. "Not this again," Strike said somewhere in the background as the women screamed and wrestled each other to the floor.

Fingers were lost in hair, nails scratched. Rora got Bella onto her back and grabbed for her throat. But the Jewel fought back, grabbing a handful of Rora's hair and pulling hard, making her scream. She fell to the side, and kicked out, but Bella's body disappeared from hers and when she spat her hair away she saw Strike holding the woman back.

Huffing and puffing, Bella's eyes were wild, but it wasn't fury for the blood on her chin, it was desire that burned from her. Strike couldn't have that tight a hold on her because Bella spun to face him and grabbed for his belt.

"Fuck off, Bell," he said, trying to push her away with his elbow because he was still holding a gun.

"I want you to fuck us both," Bella panted, yanking his tee-shirt from his jeans.

Strike pushed her away hard, and she fell against the back of the couch. Pulling the second gun from his waistband, he pointed the weapons at his victims again, which included her.

"And how the fuck do you want me to do that and keep these two from running off?"

Bella looked at Junker and then at her. "We'll tie them up," she said and dropped onto her knees. Crawling to him, the Jewel pressed her hands to his groin. "They deserve one last moment of pleasure before we gut them… don't they?"

Rora's sickness returned while watching the pair stare into each other. She tried to be subtle about moving onto her knees, preparing herself to attack Bella again.

Without looking, Strike pulled back the hammer of his gun and she froze. "Don't fucking move, Kero," he snarled.

He could've let her get to Bella, let her pull the bitch away from him. Instead, he'd chosen to protect the Jewel and keep her close, with her hands there… on him.

Bella's laugh made Rora grind her teeth. The Black Jewel spun away from Strike and on all fours crawled toward her. "He belongs to me, duckie," Bella murmured. "Just like I always told you he did."

She swallowed hard when Bella rose to kneel in front of her. She didn't kiss her this time, but she did caress her face, pushing her hair from her cheeks and brushing her lips along her jaw.

"We would've worshiped you," Bella whispered, undoing the buttons of Rora's vest over her chest.

There were only four buttons descending over her chest, but when Bella pulled the fabric apart hard, it ripped further, revealing her bra to the room. Bella ducked and kissed each of Rora's breasts.

Hissing, she shoved at the woman, but Bella caught her wrists to hold her in place. "Ah, ah, duckie," she said. "If I tell my prince to shoot, he will. You better do as you're told, or your fun will be cut short…" Her fingertip trailed into Rora's cleavage and down over the partially torn material toward her jeans. "What would you like… hmm? What's your favorite? I offered you the world once… I can offer you it again…"

Bella's voice was seductive, there was no denying the pull of that woman's sultry tone. Rora could understand how the oblivious could be pulled in by the beauty. But Rora saw only what Strike did, the Black Jewels' rotten core.

"I want nothing from you," Rora spat.

Bella just smiled and kissed her chin. "What about our prince? Would you like him to pleasure you? He could be inside you in a moment; it would take just one word from me."

Strike had already refused Bella's other advances, so how she could believe he'd perform for her on demand, Rora didn't know. But when her eyes rose, she didn't see Strike looking at her, he was focused on Junker, who was watching the scene unfold from the couch. High on his knees, Junker leaned against the back of the seat he'd been on when he tried to kiss her. But with a gun only a few inches from his head, it was no surprise that he hadn't moved.

"I don't want him anywhere near me," Rora hissed. "He's as insane as you are."

She couldn't think of anything she wanted more than to have Strike inside her now. Except in her fantasy it wouldn't be here in front of these people. They'd be somewhere safe, far from here, alone, without any of these troubles hanging over them.

"What you want is less important to him than what I want," Bella said, still stroking Rora's body. "If I tell him to force you, he will."

Letting a smile rise to her lips, Rora leaned in as if to kiss Bella, but at the last moment, she leaned back and spat in her face. "No, he won't. He's disgusted by you."

Bella screamed and leaped onto her feet. Rora remembered Bella's arm moving away, but she didn't remember the hit or any pain. Everything just became black.

TWENTY-EIGHT

THE NEXT THING Rora remembered was blinking open her eyes, fighting darkness that wanted to take her back, and a sickening moment of panic. For that breath, she feared she was back in Bella's basement, attached to the wall.

Except the scent of clean wood and warmth erased those fears fast. Orienting herself, she recalled that she was in Leandra's hiding place. Her wrists were bound by rope above her head. She was attached to one of the bannister spindles, with the empty space under the ascending stairs behind her.

Strike was holding one weapon and had another in his waistband. He and Bella were standing at the back of the couch, discussing what to do with Junker.

"I'll take him out, they'll never find the body," Strike said.

"We have to find out what they did with Leandra first," Bella said, her hands on Strike's hips. "Our duckie was naughty stealing that woman away from us…"

"You don't need her," Junker spoke up.

Strike's back was to her, but Rora didn't need to see his face to know he was angry. "Fuck you, Square. You're a walking corpse, don't push me to make any rash decisions. They won't work out for you."

"Bella," Junker beseeched the woman. "I have the Point. We have everything we need."

One of Bella's hands fell from Strike's hip and her chin rose. "We? What do 'we' need?"

"I'm on your side," Junker said, smiling.

More interest grew in Bella's expression. "So, I have all the men… that's good to know. Why should I believe you?"

"Maybe because men are groveling, pathetic idiots, just like you always said," Rora said, feeling nothing but disgust.

Everyone turned to her. "Ah, she's back with us," Bella said, turning to her, though there was a good twenty feet between Rora and them. "We were just discussing how you'd been naughty… Do you want to tell us where Leandra is? I'd hate to mar that beautiful body with the scars of torture, but my prince does have a way with a blade."

"Junker's wrong," Rora said. "He doesn't have the Point." Junker's optimism faded. "But if you give me your word that you won't harm Leandra, or even approach her, I'll give you what you want."

"Ah," Bella said, tapping a fingertip on her lip and then drawing the digit down the center of Strike's chest. "Do we believe their sudden change of heart? Weren't they the ones concerned with our decency?"

"I don't care about that," Junker said, a new kind of cynicism in his voice. Maybe her lie had been the final straw for him or maybe he was just reprioritizing fast. "All I care about is him."

Bella's surprise probably matched Strike's. Rora's heart began to race again. "I don't go that way," Strike said.

Bella laughed and threw her arms around Strike. "I love a man who's willing to experiment. But if you're implying an exchange, a sample of our prince in exchange for what I want, we will have to subdue him first. He's less open-minded than me and my duckie… You can have her too, she's already incapacitated… though she does have a habit of being rebellious… sometimes that makes it more fun." Bella turned to the side to lean on Strike who looked over his shoulder in her direction as Bella walked her fingers up Junker's chest. "And if you're not spent after—"

"He's her half-brother," Rora blurted out, her eyes matched to Strike's. Her love had to know, and she didn't care that Junker wasn't ready for the big reveal, telling Strike the truth was most prominent in her mind. "He knows you killed his father."

It wasn't exactly gratitude on Strike's face, but he did get a look of understanding. In a fraction of a second, she saw the flicker of a thousand calculations sprint across his gaze.

Bella and Junker seemed to be busy staring at each other. So Rora took another risk to mouth, 'I love you' though she had no idea if Strike saw it or not, he was too busy trying to figure out how this changed the plan.

"That we killed his father," Strike said, and for a second Rora thought he was talking to her, but his eyes slowly slid around to Bella. "Right, Belladonna? I killed him because you begged me to…"

"Oh my God," Rora exhaled, trying to play along with Strike's plan. "He's right. I… Oh my God, Junker, I'm sorry… I forgot, she… she did. She told me she did."

"No," Junker said. "You've got it wrong, Aurora."

"No, she doesn't," Bella said. Rora hadn't expected her endorsement. "I begged him to kill Daddy and my disgusting brothers." Pushing away from Strike and from Junker, Bella backed away a few steps. "And I might have my prince kill you too."

Strike raised his gun, adjusting his position to aim at Junker's head. "No!" Junker said. "No, you don't know… you don't know what he's like! He's bewitched you!"

"My prince loves me," Bella said. "He always has… You're a stranger to me, why should I trust your word?"

"Because I can get you what you want," he said, glancing at Rora. "Aurora will tell you everything you want to know…"

Bella turned to her. "Will you, Rora? And what's your price?"

"Leave Leandra alone," Rora said.

"And…"

"Let me kill Exile." Junker said.

That wasn't part of Rora's plan and panic made her start to sweat. Tugging at the rope that was cutting into her wrists, she tried to be subtle in her attempts to free her hands.

"But, Junk," Rora said, trying to come across as the concerned damsel in distress. "If Bella was complicit… she ordered her brothers' deaths. What if she turns on you? You could get hurt."

"I only turn on disgusting men who put their hands on me without permission," Bella said.

Though apparently Bella's permission extended to every woman on the planet. Bella had no problem with rape, and no problem threatening women with it. But it seemed to the Black Jewel that if she gave her permission for a man to touch a woman's body, even one that wasn't hers, it was enough.

This was arrogance above any that Rora had ever experienced. "No!" Junker suddenly called out and shoved away from the couch. "No! This is wrong! Bella! Bella!"

Marching toward the mantelpiece, he seemed to be losing his marbles, but reached up suddenly and grabbed something. Metal glinted, but Rora couldn't see what was in his hand. Bella screamed and lunged forward, pushing at Strike who fired a shot in the same instant.

Junker wailed, but didn't go down. He clung to his arm, but spun around with a knife extended toward Strike. A knife, Rora exhaled her relief, that wasn't as dangerous as a gun. Bella didn't seem to know that though, she'd plastered herself against Strike, protecting his body.

"You can't love him!" Junker called, blood running from the wound on his arm that suggested a bullet had just grazed him. "You can't have wanted our family dead!"

"I can!" Bella screeched. "And you will not hurt my prince!"

Finally, something Rora and the Jewel had in common. "If you ask forgiveness, if you tell me you're sorry…" Junker said like he was trying to make sense of this. "Get over your infatuation with him—"

Movement to the right made Rora take her eyes from the stand-off. Someone was in the kitchen.

"Burke," she said.

Strike turned to her, but she nodded sideways toward the kitchen. Strike pulled the second gun from his waistband just a second before the kitchen door opened and Burke came in brandishing a weapon of his own.

Strike backed away slowly, putting more space between him and the couch to better keep the two other weapons in his sights. He couldn't watch both Junker and Burke at the same time, not unless he got to the other side of the room and widened his view.

Bella, still working for her without knowing it, stayed against Strike, offering a shield.

Rora tugged at her bounds and felt one loosen. She was the only one restrained, and though she was in a corner, she didn't like being helpless.

"This is fucked up," Strike spat out.

She didn't envy his position, there were three guns and a knife in the room now; one man bleeding, one woman trussed up, and everyone wanted something different.

"Isaac Burke," Bella said and squealed. "We might have a present for you."

Torres!

Rora had forgotten about the other agent. Well, she hadn't forgotten about him exactly, but when she hadn't seen him, she figured he'd either bolted or Bella had got bored of him and killed him. Burke moved further into the room, seeming only to be concerned with aiming at Strike.

"Stand down, Exile," Burke said. "We've got you surrounded."

"If you had me surrounded, you wouldn't be in here alone," Strike said.

Rora tugged some more and found each of her wrists were tied individually to the bannister with the same length of rope. One wrist loosened and her elbow bent, but she kept it there, not revealing that she'd just managed to free one hand. Discreetly, she began to dip her hand in a circle to let the length of rope uncoil and fall from her wrist. When it got long enough, she let the loop fall behind her head to hide it from the room. It had just touched the base of her neck when she ran out of rope to free.

So she had one wrist still fixed to it anchor, a tight circle of rope around the other though it was no longer fixed to the bannister, and a length of rope hidden behind her head. Bella was telling Burke that they were going to be friends, and that he had to be smart because both Exile and Junker were prepared to shoot him if they had to.

But Rora was only half-listening. She watched the confident Burke, his focus on Strike, ready to get his man, or whatever he wanted from the Jewel. Rora didn't care about what he wanted, all she knew was she didn't like this setup one bit.

Burke had discounted her as a threat, so as he crept closer to Strike, he didn't even look at her. She waited, tense, ready for him to move just close enough that she could…

Leaping up, she wrapped both legs around him from behind, catching him off guard, making him fall backward. In a flash, she tipped her own head out of the way and looped her spare length of rope around Burke's neck.

Ignoring the screaming pain in her fixed wrist, she used the other to pull the rope tight around Burke's neck. Using her legs around his waist to pull him down, her own body acted as a weight to choke him.

The gun must have fallen from his hand because he used both to claw at her as she huffed and tugged. Opening her mouth, Rora screamed out the exertion of strength she was using to pull the rope around his throat and in her legs to pull him down.

Strike appeared in front of them. He grabbed Burke by the top of his head while sweeping his legs out from under him. Her victim's weight fell suddenly, jolting her, then Strike laid one punch to Burke's temple and the guy went limp.

It took her a panting second to loosen her own grip from his body. Her legs relaxed, her arm dropped, and as Burke slid onto the floor in an unconscious slump, she too lost the ability to stand upright.

But as she sagged forward, Strike put an arm around her waist to support her. "We gotta untangle this shit," he said and for a second, Rora thought he was talking to her.

But when she looked up, his attention was on Bella who nodded. "Separate them, tie them up!"

Strike nodded once and let her go. It took her a second to tense and hold herself up, but the adrenaline was enough to keep her going.

Bella was holding a weapon now, it had to be one of Strike's. As her love picked Burke from her feet, and carried him up the stairs, Bella enjoyed holding court.

"We have all the time in the world," Bella said. "This is going to be fun, won't this be fun? No one's looking for us out here."

"Wonderland mark two," Rora commented, but didn't think anyone heard her.

"You don't have to restrain me," Junker said, still clinging to his arm. His pallor made her think maybe the wound was worse than she'd first thought. "I want you to have everything you want. I'm not your enemy, Bella. Just give up that maniac, that's all you have to do. He's manipulating you… he's evil."

"I like evil," Bella said.

Junker stumbled forward and caught himself on the couch, which he climbed onto, she guessed to lie down. Rora expected Bella to say something about him staying in view or on his feet. But when she turned, she saw the Black Jewel was admiring her.

"I think we'll give you your own room," Bella said. "The room with the biggest bed."

Rora wanted to spit when Bella winked at her. Strike came running down the stairs and Junker was next to be taken upstairs. He tried to argue and to lunge out with the knife, but Strike took it away from him without much trouble and then forced the man up the stairs.

"My prince tells me he played a little joke on you," Bella said, coming toward her when they were the only two people left in the room. "Did you really think he'd chosen you?" Bella pouted. "We needed to know where Leandra was… You had your chance to answer the question, and you wouldn't play nice with us. But I have to be honest; I don't tire of the chase, do you?" She shivered and grinned. "There's something invigorating about it, isn't there?"

"If you say so."

"Now I don't want you to think I've been naïve," Bella said. "My prince hasn't convinced me yet, but he will… we have a little deal and I do feel it's only fair to warn you since you will be the tool he needs to use."

"What the hell are you talking about?"

Bella touched the barrel of the gun to Rora's breast and traced it down her cleavage and up to the other breast. "I came here prepared to kill you if I had to… now I find you might be willing to play nice… But I will still have to ensure that my prince's mind hasn't been poisoned by you again… Do you love him?"

Rora pulled away as best she could, but her shoulder came up against the side of the stairs. "Go to hell!"

Bella's head fell back when she laughed. "Isn't that where we all plan to meet? In the home of our prince?"

Strike's home wasn't in hell. Rora understood that Bella enjoyed spreading stories about him and what he was capable of, but she failed to see what else Strike could be.

"Junker's going to kill him," Rora said, hoping Bella wouldn't forget the threat, though she made it seem like she was happy about the idea. "He despises Exile for murdering your family."

"He has no idea what they were!"

As crazy as she was? Probably not.

"We'll get the other one from the trunk," Strike's voice sounded behind her and she looked up to see him running down the stairs. "If he suffocates, we lose our bargaining chip."

"Whatever you feel, my prince," Bella said, waving an absent hand and moving away from Rora when Strike came to untie her fixed wrist. But the Jewel came back to peek around him as he reached up. "Tie her flat to the mattress… and strip her too… there are plenty of men for her to entertain."

Strike didn't meet her eyes, but Rora guessed he felt the beat of her hammering heart or the hitch of her shallow breathing. When her arm dropped, her legs almost buckled, but she managed to tug her arm hard, like she was trying to free herself from him. But he yanked her to him and then bent to toss her over his shoulder.

Kicking and shouting, Rora pounded at his back, and ignored the sound of Bella's laughter. He took her into the bedroom she'd slept in last night and tossed her onto the middle of the bed.

Curling her knees up to her chest, Rora wrapped both arms around her legs and rolled herself into a ball. For the first time since she'd got there, she had a moment of safety to try gathering her thoughts. She had so many questions, and so many thoughts, but they only had a few seconds.

She expected Strike to say something, to issue instructions or ask a question. But the first contact they had was when he grabbed her wrist and pulled it hard, dragging her up the bed to begin tying her arm to the bedpost.

"What are you doing?" she asked, trying to pull it away. "Flame?" When one wrist was secure, he walked all the way around the bed and tried to get the other arm. But she wasn't going to hand it over easily. "No. No! No!"

"Shut the fuck up," he hissed and caught her arm.

Her muscles screamed in pain when she tried to resist him extending her arm and tying it to the other bedpost. "What the hell? No!"

When she was secured, he grabbed her chin and hauled her attention to him. "Fighting me will only make it hurt more."

"I know pain," she snarled at him, their eyes as enflamed as each other's. "The physical I can handle."

He shoved her chin and backed a step away from the bed. "Burke could've killed you."

"He could've killed you," she said, spitting her hair from her mouth. "You want to tell me we're still on the same side, or have you screwed me over again?"

"Me? You're the one hanging with the square. Was that part of the plan?"

"He showed up this morning," she said. "What was I supposed to do?"

"Not play house with him." He shook his head. "Doesn't fucking matter. I've gotta get Torres."

"Wait," she called when he started for the door. "Flame?"

He paused and took a second before turning around. "I'll put Torres and Burke in the same room. Torres will get him talking, he'll have his confession, and we'll get away clean."

"How is she going to test you?" she asked, caring less about the NSA than she did about her lover. "She said I was the tool to—"

"You know what she wants me to do. It's just like you said."

She could see how the anger in his eyes became a tortured pain as they trailed down over her. "Will she drug me or do you want me to pretend to fight?"

His attention leaped to her. "Pretend?"

"If fucking me is what she needs to see you do to believe…"

"It won't come to that," he said. "This is going to be over tonight. I'll kill her before I'd think about hurting you… I'm just sorry we won't have the time to make her suffer."

It broke her heart to see how he was tormented by the position Bella had put him in. "It's not rape if I want it. Flame—"

"You don't want it," he said, repulsed. "And I don't want it like that either, not on her terms, with her in the room directing, and you screaming…"

"You like it when I scream," she said and smiled when he looked at her again. "Strike, we talked about this."

"And we're not talking about it again," he said, marching over to the bed.

He propped a knee on the mattress to bow over her and touch his lips to hers.

She managed to draw him into a deeper kiss than he'd intended to give. While she lifted her head and dipped her tongue between his lips, she bent a knee to sneak her leg around him. Looping it around his hips, she swept the other around him and took him by surprise pulling him down on top of her.

"Babe," he chastised her, but she smiled beneath his lips.

"I've needed you so bad this week," she breathed into him and kissed him again.

But he pulled away. "I have to get back downstairs."

"I know," she said, but was in no hurry to relinquish his kiss.

Her need might not have been sexual, well not all sexual, but now that he was here, she felt recharged and ready to face anything. "Did he touch you?"

"No. He told me who he was. I think he wants a relationship with Bella, but doesn't like to see his sister cozying up to you," she said, resisting when he tried to pry her legs from his hips. But she was pleased to feel that he'd had his usual reaction to her, and she pushed up to rub herself against his dick. "I have no problem with you killing him."

"Good, because I plan to," he said and gave up fighting to kiss her more thoroughly. "He asked for you two to be in the same room… I nearly killed him right then."

"Has Torres been any help?"

"This week, yeah, but he refused to sleep with Bella last night and she demanded he be tied up. He's been in the trunk since." She winced, but he brushed his lips across hers. "He'll get what he wants."

"So we get away clean," she said, repeating what he'd said.

"Your ties aren't tight," he said. "You did good downstairs… waiting until the opportune moment."

That was his way of telling her to do the same thing now. "I'll be good."

"Don't try to escape. I'll come for you when it's time to go." He took something from his pocket and held it in front of her face, showing her it was a switchblade. He tucked it down into her cleavage, covering her with the edges of her torn shirt, managing to wrap and conceal the blade at the same time. "If anyone comes in here… use it. Scream, I'll come, and I'll murder anyone I find in here… anyone, Ro."

She nodded and caught his mouth when he tried to get up. When she whimpered and pushed her hips up to his, she tried to let him know she wasn't ready to lose him yet. "Flame…"

"I can't stay up here all night," he said. "How far you want us to go before you'll let me get up?"

That was enough of an invitation to make her smile. "You are supposed to strip me."

"No chance. I'll tell Bella half the fun comes in getting you naked… and that's no lie."

"I love you," she whispered, hating that moisture was gathering in her eyes. "I love you, Flame, so much, I—"

"Hey," he said, stopping her words with a kiss. "We're going to be together, no matter what."

Even if they had to follow each other to hell? Yeah, she understood what he was saying. "I'm scared you'll be out there alone… if Bella talks to Junker…"

"All I gotta do is get my hands on the processor and then we're out of here… I think I know where it is, and I've got one shot."

"If you don't find it and Bella wants you to come up here—"

"I'll kill her," he said. "Fuck the processor, Cupcake. Didn't I say you were more important than tech?"

"But it's sex. We—"

"Don't belong to her and she can't have us… either of us."

He swept his lips over hers and this time when he tried to loosen her legs, she let him part them so he could rise. "Be careful," she said.

Opening the door, he looked at her one last time and then slipped out, leaving her alone.

TWENTY-NINE

RORA HEARD LITTLE else for the rest of the evening. It was getting dark and with every second that passed, she feared what could be going on out there. Torres should have his confession from Burke by now. She trusted that whatever tech Strike had set him up with, the agent would get what he needed to clear his name and although it was heartening to hear that Torres had been supportive, she still classed this as a major favor that she'd expect to be repaid one day when they needed it.

And, if nothing else, she shouldn't have to explain why she had no inclination to roll on her love anymore.

If she knew Strike, he'd have spent the last couple of hours preparing for their escape. No doubt Bella was talking plans for the future, but Rora doubted Strike was thinking much beyond that night.

The next time that door opened, it would either be Strike telling her they were leaving or him coming in with Bella who expected him to violate the prisoner.

His aversion to rape was rooted in what had happened to his mother. She had a feeling that it didn't matter how much she reassured him, her flame would judge himself if he gave into Bella's demands. The hatred he had for his father was entrenched in him, and he'd despise himself if he thought he'd done anything that might make his father proud.

It turned out, she was wrong.

The next time the door opened, she held her breath, waiting to see which version of her man would come in. But it was not him, it was Junker. He had his arm bandaged and was wearing a sling. Someone had treated him, and she couldn't imagine it being Strike.

"So you switched the Point out on me?" he asked.

Wrinkling her nose, she tried to shrug. "I'm sorry."

He sighed. "That's ok. I should've figured it out. Everyone's on edge, no one knows who to trust," he said and showed her a bowl. "I brought some of the soup you made at lunch."

Soup that could be drugged? Was he to have his way with her before Strike got here?

"Thanks," she said. "But it's sort of tough to eat." She was still technically tied to the bed after all, but he came in and set the bowl on the nightstand. "Did you kill him?"

She dreaded the answer, but if Junker had managed to convince Bella he was right, Strike might have been caught unawares. "No," Junker said and started to loosen her bounds. "Bella came to talk to me… I think maybe she likes the idea of having some family around, even if she didn't know I existed. At least, she's not ready to kill me yet."

"That's something," she said, trying not to recoil when he laid across her to untie her other arm. As soon as she was loose, she breathed out and sat up, grateful to rub her aching arms. "Thank you."

He handed her the bowl of soup and she smiled, though she was considering throwing it in his face. There was steam coming from the liquid, but she could hold the bowl without burning herself, so she doubted it was hot enough to cause serious injury.

Rora didn't want to eat and stirred the liquid wondering how she'd fake it; Junker saved her the trouble. He rose from the bed and walked toward the darkened window.

"She's my sister," he said.

Because he wasn't watching her, Rora made the occasional noise with the spoon, but didn't bother to eat. "It must be quite an adjustment for you," she said, because as long as he thought they were friends, she might be able to reason with him. "For both of you."

"Exile isn't as understanding as you are," he said. Junker didn't try to disguise how much he hated Strike. He thought he had reason, but seemed to have forgotten what his father and brothers were doing to Strike when he killed them. "He keeps telling her I can't be trusted. He's using his power over her to turn her against me."

"But you're free," she said, putting the soup on the nightstand and shifting to the edge of the bed. "She must have some trust in you."

Bella had admitted to liking the chase and there was no doubting this whole drama was exciting the Black Jewel. This late, it would be insanity for anyone to go running out into the dark. So, however the night turned out, Bella would be thinking that they were all stuck here and the only person Junker had threatened so far was Exile.

Bella wouldn't be averse to seeing the men fight. She might not want Strike dead, but she did get turned on when anyone got physical with him.

"I need your help, Aurora," he said, and turned to come over and stand in front of her, a grave look on his face. "I need you to help me kill him."

"Junk—"

"Once he's gone, she'll see we're right. We'll be able to convince her…"

And they'd be able to give Bella the Point to complement the processor she'd already stolen. "And Burke?"

She didn't know if Junker knew Torres was there or what he'd said to Bella about the man whose life they'd saved. Anything Junker said might contradict something Strike had told the Black Jewel.

Rora hadn't been around to hear all their conversations over the past few days, so she'd stay quiet on the subject around Bella. But Junker was looking to earn points and discredit Strike, God knew what he'd say.

Sinking down at her side, he caught her face in both hands. "Once we get rid of Exile, the others don't matter," he said. "Please, Rora, help me."

Staring into her, she felt his compulsion, and wondered if it had been his plan all along to ask her to do this for him. Had Junker ever killed? Was he capable? It was one thing to say you wanted someone dead, but following through was something else. She'd caused havoc in her time with Exile, no doubt about that, but even she hadn't killed.

Junker began to pull her closer and she feared he was trying to use seduction to convince her to join his side. But there wasn't going to be a kiss or an alliance. Her fingers began to rise, but she wasn't going to embrace or caress him, her thoughts were wholly on the knife her flame had put in her cleavage.

The time had come; Junker was useless to them and a threat to her love, if she got the chance to finish this now, that's exactly what she was going to do.

A bang came from beyond the room. Short and sharp, there was only one thing it could be.

"A gunshot," she said, surging to her feet in time with Junker who shared her panicked look.

Together, they dashed from the room.

Every other door in the hallway was open. Burke, Torres, and Strike were all crowded around Bella, who was shorter than all of them, so it was tough to see what was going on.

Bella coughed. "Prince," she said and fell against Strike who caught her and guided her down to the floor.

Junker called out and pushed her aside to rush over and pull Strike to his feet. "Get away from her!"

Strike moved away, and Rora felt herself drawn toward him. He didn't face her, but she caught the seam of his tee-shirt and peeked around him at the bleeding woman on the floor.

Junker dropped down to Bella's side, gaping and dismayed by the sight of the blood staining her dress. For a second, he just sat there, looking at the growing stain, then he pressed both his hands to her.

"No," Bella said, mustering her strength to sit up and push him away. "Prince… I need my prince."

Rora released him, expecting him to go, but he shook his head. "There's nothing I can do for you, Bell," Strike said, cold as ice.

Bella coughed, and blood trickled from the corner of her mouth. Junker flew to his feet and grabbed Strike's shirt in both hands, pulling him across to Bella and urging him down to his knees.

"Fix her! Fix her like you fixed him!" Junker demanded and shoved Strike's shoulders.

Rora went closer, moving to Bella's feet, her eyes wide and unblinking. She was watching the life seep out of this woman. There was no way Bella would make it out of this, her eyes were glazed, her skin gray, and the blood saturated her dress. It pooled on the floor, smudging as she rolled toward Strike, and grabbed at his tee-shirt.

He took her wrist and pushed her away, but Bella kept trying to get hold of him. Rora didn't know she'd moved until she kneeled at her love's side. Taking Bella's hand, Rora closed it around Strike's, holding them together. She could feel Strike's disgust and his anger, but he didn't pull away.

Bella's eyes met hers, and a tear slipped from her lashes in time with the one Rora felt streaking her own cheek. "I forgive you," Rora said and bowed to kiss Bella's cheek.

The Jewel's wet eyes were filled with fear and gratitude though they grew heavier before they moved toward Strike.

When Rora looked to her love, she saw nothing but stoic resignation. "Say something, Flame," she whispered encouraging him to offer the dying woman some words of comfort.

"Prince," Bella breathed out the weak word. "You will… come to…"

"No," he said, taking his hand away from Bella's and pushing Rora's away when she tried to touch Bella again.

He folded Bella's hands on her chest and then bent over to whisper in her ear. Rora didn't hear what was said, but when Strike rose enough to look the woman in the eye, she could see his severe expression. In Bella's eyes, there was nothing but horror and heartache.

Strike touched his lips to Bella's and brushed her hair from her forehead. He kept his hand there, his eyes fixed on hers as the life slowly seeped from her.

A last breath seeped from her lips and her body loosened.

There was a moment of peace.

Strike's hand slid down from her forehead, closing her eyes, and then he stood, pulling Rora to her feet too.

Everyone else seemed to be in shock. But Strike picked up her hand and kissed her knuckles. "We're out of here, Kero," he murmured on her skin.

"You!" Junker screamed. "You did this!"

Leaping over his sister, he shoved Strike. Rora took her chance to put herself in front of her love just as Bella had done earlier in the day.

"No!" Torres shouted, drawing everyone's attention. "It was Burke! He shot her! She came in to seduce him, trying to make Exile jealous! She gave him a gun with one bullet, told Burke to shoot me for rejecting her, but he shot her instead!"

"No!" Burke said, but looked guilty as hell. "I didn't!"

Rora didn't know who had pulled the trigger, all she knew was there was a dead woman on the floor and tension crackling in the air. She and Strike were stuck here with everyone else between them and the stairs. It seemed that Junker didn't know who to believe either and was glaring at them all with suspicion.

Strike's hand slid over her hip and up the front of her top. She thought this wasn't exactly the most appropriate moment for getting handsy but didn't move. His fingertips crept into her cleavage from beneath, using the fabric as a cover for retrieving the switch blade he'd put in there earlier.

Rora couldn't have guessed he'd need it after Bella's death, but she was pleased it was there to protect both of them. Junker turned back to them a second after Strike's hand slipped out of her top. Rora stepped forward and coughed, giving her love space, and cover, to open the blade just behind her ass.

"It was him," Torres said. "I have no reason to lie. Kill Exile if you want, I don't care, but this is one murder not on him."

"Shut the fuck up!" Burke hollered. "You fucking—"

"It was you!"

Junker dug a hand in his pocket and pulled out a knife. Lunging forward, he swept it across Burke's throat before he could say another word. The man stuttered and coughed, grabbing for his throat and stumbling forward, forcing Junker out of the way. Just as Burke started to go down next to Bella, Junker shoved him hard, sending him headfirst down the stairs, leaving a trail of fresh blood all the way down.

Rora couldn't see the bottom of the stairs from where she was, but when the gurgling silenced, she guessed that was the end of Burke. So it turned out Junker did have a murderous streak after all.

"But I'm taking no chances," Junker said and set Strike in his sights.

"No!" she called, opening her arms to block Strike when Junker started toward him.

"Cupcake," Strike said, sweeping her aside with a strong arm.

She fought to get in front of him, protecting him was all she could think about. But, Torres appeared behind Junker, holding a heavy bronze candlestick aloft. He brought it down hard on the back of Junker's head, sending him to the floor.

Junker slumped over Bella.

Those still on their feet, stayed suspended in time. Torres held the candlestick, and Strike had a blade, but it wasn't strong enough to take the weight of that candlestick. But if they started to fight…

She looked from Torres to Strike and back, her lips dry, her pulse sprinting. "Take Burke's vehicle, it's less than a half-mile up the road," Strike said. "You have your confession?"

Some of the strength left Torres' arm and he let it sink a little, then a little more. "We're square?" Torres asked.

"Wouldn't go that far," Strike said. "Game resets at sunrise."

Torres actually smiled. "As always, Ex," he said and took a tentative step forward to hold out a hand.

Her eyes widened a little as she waited to see how her flame would handle this offer. Though it was clear he was hesitant, Strike slowly raised his hand and the two men shook.

If she wasn't so shocked, she might have smiled. After the handshake, Torres tipped his imaginary cap at her. He dropped the candlestick and then turned to flee.

Strike folded the blade and stuck it in his pocket. "Least we've got time to pack this time," he said. "Grab your shit."

"What do you mean?"

"I'm not hanging around to bury bodies. This place is compromised, there's no way Leandra can come back here now."

"But, I…" He took his phone from his pocket to wave it once. "Wonderland?" she asked.

"Wonderland."

Jumping into action, she went to gather everything she'd brought and wiped down anything she thought either of them might have touched. It wasn't a thorough job, but it was better than nothing.

Strike was doing his own tasks, which she guessed included making sure there wasn't going to be any evidence of their presence. When he was done, he bundled her into the truck with their things, and put Opal on her lap.

Typing on his phone, he did what had to be done and then handed the device to her to get the car started.

"Wait," Rora said after the car rolled an inch.

"If you've forgotten anything, you're too late."

"I did forget something," she said and put the tech on the dash to lean over the center console.

With a hand on his cheek, she drew his mouth to hers. Ignoring the growing spread of orange coming from the back window, and the encroaching heat, she poured all her love and gratitude into that kiss. Not just because she loved the man, but because she was grateful they'd had the chance to leave that place together.

"Love you, Cupcake."

He didn't say it much, but saying it now told her his thoughts were as potent as hers in that moment. "You walked away from your toy for me," she said. "You chose me."

"I did," he said, but his lips curled. They kept on rising until there was no mistaking his smile. "But my love isn't the only thing I'm packing."

She bumped her nose on his. "You found it?"

"I found it."

"Strike," she sighed, leaning back, her hand cradling his jaw.

"Don't think I need it though," he said, and she tilted her head in question. "I already figured it out."

She didn't follow. "Figured what out?"

"What's the point," he said, and her mouth opened in a silent 'ah' of understanding. Curling his fingers, he brushed them down her jaw and under her chin to tip it up. "This… this is the point."

"You're goddamn right it is," she whispered and welcomed his kiss.

Their life together wasn't going to be conventional. Rora didn't have the first clue what it was going to be. The important thing was that they were going to share it. That was all they needed. Because as long as they were together, they didn't need another soul. They were happy with the one they shared.

Thank you for reading this tale!
If you can, please take the time to review.

~

Ask your local library for more Scarlett Finn novels!

~

For all things Scarlett Finn
check out:

www.scarlettfinn.com

EXILE JOINS THE ADVENTURE IN:

SCARLETT FINN